The Right Word in Cantonese

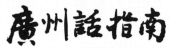

廣州話指南

Gwóng-jàu-wá
jí-nàahm

Kwan Choi Wah

U0132629

増　訂　版
Revised Edition

THE COMMERCIAL PRESS

Painting and Calligraphy on the cover
Zhou Wai Min （周懷民）

廣州話指南（增訂版）
The Right Word in Cantonese (Revised Edition)

Author: Kwan Choi Wah （關彩華）
Executive Editor: K. L. Wong
Published by : The Commercial Press (H.K.) Ltd.
8/F, Eastern Central Plaza, 3 Yiu Hing Road,
Shau Kei Wan, Hong Kong
http://www.commercialpress.com.hk
Distributed by: SUP Publishing Logistics (H.K.) Ltd.
3/F, C&C Building, 36 Ting Lai Road,
Tai Po, New Territories
Printed by: Elegance Printing & Book Binding Co. Ltd.
Block A, 4/F, Hoi Bun Industrial Building,
Hong Kong
Edition: Revised edition Third Printing January 2019
© The Commercial Press (H.K.) Ltd.
ISBN 978 962 07 1898 4
Printed in Hong Kong.
All rights reserved.

This book

is dedicated to all my students of Cantonese over the years, whose determination to learn the language often touched me and made me proud to be a language teacher.

I wish them success.

PREFACE

This book is designed to serve as both a dictionary for students of Cantonese and as a handbook for visitors to Hong Kong. For students of Cantonese, I hope this book will be useful in expanding their vocabulary. For those living in Hong Kong, I hope they will find the vocabulary to be both relevant and practical for use in their daily lives. And I hope that visitors to Hong Kong will be encouraged to make an attempt to communicate with the local people by looking up a word and pronouncing it in Cantonese — or, if this fails, by simply showing the entry, with the corresponding Chinese character, to the people they are trying to communicate with.

There are two parts to the book, with a total of more than 7800 entries. Part one consists of everyday vocabulary, while part two includes glossaries of material that is specific to Hong Kong.

In this revised edition, all informative vocabularies have been updated and new entries have been added, including 270 entries which were added to part one and two new sections: "How do you describe...?" and "Major Festivals People Observe in Hong Kong" in part two.

"Yale Romanization", a system that teaches students how to pronounce Cantonese sounds, is provided for each English entry, followed by the Chinese character(s). So in general, the entries follow this pattern: a) English, b) Cantonese pronunciation, c) Chinese character. In most cases, the English entries are given in alphabetical order. Some of the Chinese characters used in this book are not the traditional characters used in Chinese writing. I call them Cantonese characters and they are used to put Cantonese, one of the spoken dialects of Chinese, into written form. Therefore, it is necessary to note that not every Cantonese sound has a character in written form. (I use the sign " □ " to indicate such cases.) The reason for including characters in the book is the hope that they will make it easier for students or visitors to get help from their Cantonese-speaking friends in pronouncing the sounds more accurately. Most Cantonese speakers do not know much, if anything, about Romanization systems.

Many people have contributed to this book in one way or another. I owe special thanks to Ms. Mary Ann Ganey, Brother Patrick Tierney, Miss Joyce Shiu, Mr. Donald Keesee and the staff of The Commercial Press for their information, criticism, advice, correction, typing and editing. I am particularly grateful to my parents, friends and students for their much-needed encouragement while preparing the first edition of this book. To my son Mateo Agustin Aponte, my good friends Miss Jannet Wong and Miss Joy Turner go special thanks for their ideas and support during the revision of this book.

Any errors or shortcomings of the book should be attributed solely to me. Suggestions for improvement will be deeply appreciated and may be sent to me by email at gwaangwaan@yahoo.com

關彩華

Contents

Introduction to Cantonese Pronunciation

There are several romanization systems used in teaching Cantonese to non-Chinese speakers. The system used in this book is the Yale system.

A syllable in Cantonese is made up of three elements:

| Initial
Sìngmóuh
聲母 | + | Final
Wáhnmóuh
韻母 | + | Tone
Yàmdiuh
音調 | = | Syllable
Yàmjit
音節 |

An initial is the beginning consonant(s) of the syllable. A final is the vowel(s) and consonant(s) that follow the initial in the syllable. A tone is the pitch contour of the syllable. In the Yale system there are 19 initials, 51 finals and 7 tones.

Initials

The 19 initials are: b, ch, d, f, g, gw, h, j, k, kw, l, m, n, ng, p, s, t, w, y. According to the articulation, they can be grouped into aspirated stops, non-aspirated stops, nasals, fricative and continuants, and semi-vowels.

The 19 initials in Cantonese

Articulation	Symbol	IPA	Key Word
Aspirated stops	*p* *t* *k* *ch* *kw*	*p'* *t'* *k'* *ts'* *kw*	pàh 爬 tà 他 kà 卡 chà 叉 kwà 誇
Non-aspirated stops	*b* *d* *g* *j* *gw*	*p* *t* *k* *ts* *kw*	bà 爸 dá 打 gà 家 jà 渣 gwa 掛
Nasals	*m* *n* *ng*	*m* *n* *ŋ*	mà 媽 nàh 拿 ngàh 牙
Fricative and continuants	*f* *l* *h* *s*	*f* *l* *h* *S*	fa 化 lā 啦 hà 蝦 sá 灑
Semi-vowels	*y* *w*	*j* *w*	yáh 也 wàh 華

Finals

In pronouncing the finals in Cantonese, the following points should be noted. First, the vowel length in the finals may be long or short and this affects the pronunciation of the syllable. A long vowel has a weak ending as in "sàam 三", "gàai 街", while a short vowel has a strong ending as in "sàm 心", "gai 計". Second, final endings p, t, k are not aspirated as in "laahp-saap 垃圾", "yāt-yaht 一日", "sihk-jūk 食粥". Third, finals starting with eu, u and yu are pronounced with rounded lips as in "hèu 靴", "gú 鼓", "syù 書"

The 51 finals in Cantonese

Finals starting with	Vowel Length Long	Key Word				Vowel Length Short	Key Word			
		Initial	Final	Tone	in Character		Initial	Final	Tone	in Character
"A"	a aai aau aam aan aang aap aat aak	p d g ch s ch g b j	a aai àau áam àan áang aap aat aahk	M.L. M.L. H.F. H.R. H.F. H.R. M.L. M.L. L.L.	怕 帶 交 慘 山 橙 甲 八 摘	ai au am an ang ap at ak	g t s m d j ch d	ai àu àm ahn áng àp āt ahk	M.L. H.F. H.F. L.L. H.R. H.F. H.L. L.L.	計 偷 心 問 等 執 七 特
"E"	e eng ek	j l s	e eng ehk	M.L. M.L. L.L	借 靚 石	ei	m	éih	L.R	美
"EU"	eu eung euk	h ch g	èu ēung euk	H.F. H.L. M.L.	靴 窗 腳	eui eun eut	g j ch	eui ēun ēut	M.L. H.L. H.L.	句 樽 出
"I"	i iu im in ip it	j y s t g d	ì iu ím ìn ip it	H.F. M.L. H.R. H.F. M.L. M.L.	知 要 閃 天 劫 跌	ing ik	m s	ìhng ihk	L.F. L.L.	明 食
"O"	o oi on ong ot ok	g t ng m h gw	ō ói òn ohng ot ok	H.L. H.R. H.F. L.L. M.L. M.L.	歌 枱 安 望 喝 國	ou	l	óuh	L.R.	老
"U"	u ui un ut	g f w f	ù ùi uhn ut	H.F. H.F. L.L. M.L	姑 灰 換 闊	ung uk	j d	ùng uhk	H.F. L.L.	鐘 讀
"YU"	yu yun yut	j ch s	yù yùn yut	H.F. H.F. M.L.	珠 穿 雪					

Tones

There are 7 tones in Cantonese with three main contours: falling, rising and level, which are distinguished by using diacritics/tone marks on top of the first vowel in the final.

The 7 tones are: high falling as in "gà 家 ", high rising as in "dá 打 ", middle level as in "seun 信 ", high level as in "bāk 北 ", low falling as in "chèuhng 長 ", low rising as in "máh 馬 " and low level as in "faahn 飯 ", when spelling, h is inserted after the vowel(s) of the final to indicate low tones and is not voiced.

Please note that some publications of Cantonese simplified the 7 tones into 6 tones by combining the High Falling and High Level tones. In those cases, only the length of the High Falling sound becomes longer ; the meaning of the word does not change.

Below is a diagram of the tones in Cantonese.

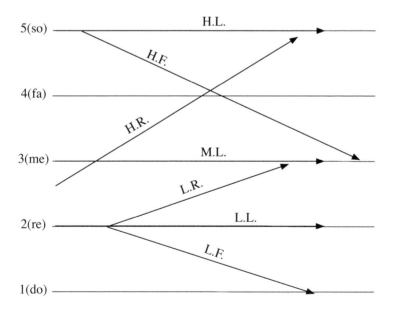

The 7 tones in Cantonese

	Tone	H.F.	H.R.	M.L.	H.L.	L.F.	L.R.	L.L.
Word	in symbol	sì	sí	si	sī	sìh	síh	sih
	in character	施	史	試	詩	時	市	是
	in symbol	mà	má	ma	mā	màh	máh	mah
	in character	媽			嗎	麻	馬	罵
	in symbol	chèung	chéung	cheung	chēung	chèuhng	chéuhng	cheuhng
	in character	槍	搶	唱	窗	詳		
Key	in symbol	sàm	sám	sam	sām	sàhm	sáhm	sahm
	in character	心	審	滲	深	岑		甚
	in symbol	fàn	fán	fan	fān	fàhn	fáhn	fahn
	in character	分	粉	訓	芬	墳	奮	份

Comparative Chart of Four Romanization Systems

INITIALS

YALE	IPA	SIDNEY LAU	MEYER-WEMPE
p	p'	p	p'
b	p	b	p
t	t'	t	t'
d	t	d	t
k	k'	k	k'
g	k	g	k
ch	tʃ'	ch	ch', ts'
j	tʃ	j	ch, ts
kw	k'w	kw	k'w
gw	kw	gw	kw
m	m	m	m

YALE	IPA	SIDNEY LAU	MEYER-WEMPE
n	n	n	n
ng	ŋ	ng	ng
f	f	f	f
l	l	l	l
h	h	h	h
s	ʃ	s	s, sh
y	j	y	i, y
w	w	w	oo, w

FINALS

YALE	IPA	SIDNEY LAU	MEYER-WEMPE
a	aː	a	a
aai	aːɪ	aai	aai
aau	aːu	aau	aau
aam	aːm	aam	aam
aap	aːp	aap	aap
aan	aːn	aan	aan
aat	aːt	aat	aat
aang	aːŋ	aang	aang
aak	aːk	aak	aak
ai	ai	ai	ai
au	au	au	au
am	am	am	am, om
ap	ap	ap	ap, op
an	an	an	an
at	at	at	at
ang	aŋ	ang	ang
ak	ak	ak	ak
e	ɛː	e	e
eng	ɛːŋ	eng	eng
ek	ɛːk	ek	ek
ei	ei	ei	ei
eu	oeː	euh	oeh

eung	oe:ŋ	eung	eung
euk	oe:k	euk	euk
eui	oei	ui	ui
eun	oen	un	un
eut	oet	ut	ut

i	i:	i	i
iu	i:u	iu	iu
im	i:m	im	im
ip	i:p	ip	ip
in	i:n	in	in
it	i:t	it	it
ing	iŋ	ing	ing
ik	ik	ik	ik

o	ɔ:	oh	oh
oi	ɔ:ɪ	oi	oi
on	ɔ:n	on	on
ot	ɔ:t	ot	ot
ong	ɔ:ŋ	ong	ong
ok	ɔ:k	ok	ok
ou	ɔu	o	o

u	u:	oo	oo
ui	u:i	ooi	ooi
un	u:n	oon	oon
ut	u:t	oot	oot
ung	u:ŋ	ung	ung
uk	u:k	uk	uk

yu	y:	ue	ue
yun	y:n	uen	uen
yut	y:t	uet	uet

TONES

YALE		SIDNEY LAU		MEYER-WEMPE	
HIGH FALLING	à	HIGH FALLING 1	a^1	UPPER EVEN	a
HIGH RISING	á	MIDDLE RISING 2	a^2	UPPER RISING	á
MIDDLE LEVEL	at	MIDDLE LEVEL 3	a^3	UPPER GOING MIDDLE ENTERING	à àt
HIGH LEVEL	ā, āt	HIGH LEVEL 1°	$a^{1°}$	UPPER EVEN UPPER ENTERING	a at
LOW FALLING	àh	LOW FALLING 4	a^4	LOW EVEN	ā
LOW RISING	áh	LOW RISING 5	a^5	LOWER RISING	ǎ
LOW LEVEL	ah, aht	LOW LEVEL 6	a^6	LOWER GOING LOWER ENTERING	â ât

Part I

Everyday Vocabulary

A

a dozen	yāt dā	一打
a kind of	yeuhng	樣
a little dizzy	wàhn-wán-déi	暈暈地
a little, a few	yāt dī	一啲
a tiny bit (a small portion)	dī-gam-dēu, dīt-gam-dēu, dīk-gam-dēu, dīk-gam-dō	啲咁多
A.D. (anno domini)	géi-yùhn hauh	紀元後
abacus	syun-pùhn	算盤
abalone	bāau-yùh	鮑魚
abandon	fong-hei	放棄
Aberdeen	Hèung-góng-jái	香港仔
ability	nàhng-lihk, bún-sih	能力，本事
ablaze (with brilliant lights)	dāng-fó-fāi-wòhng	燈火輝煌
able	hó-yíh, nàhng-gau	可以，能夠
able to tell	tái-dāk-chēut	睇得出
abnormal	m̀-jing-sèuhng	唔正常
abortion	doh-tòi	墮胎
about to	jèung-gahn, jèung-gán	將近
about, concerning	gwàan-yù	關於
above a certain number or grade	...yíh-seuhng	……以上
abrasion	syún	損
absolute	jyuht-deui	絕對
abundant, rich	fùng-fu	豐富
academic	hohk-seuht	學術
accent (spoken)	háu-yām	口音
accept	jip-sauh	接受
accident	yi-ngoih, sāt-sih	意外，失事
accidentally	ngáuh-yìhn	偶然
accommodate (for charity)	sàu-yùhng	收容

accommodate	yùhng-naahp	容納
accompany	pùih	陪
accomplish, complete	yùhn-sìhng	完成
according to	jiu, yì-jiu	照，依照
account in a bank	wuh-háu	戶口
accountant	wuih-gai-sī, wuih-gai	會計師，會計
accurate (pronounciation)	jeng	正
accustomed to	gwaan	慣
achievement	sìhng-jauh, sìhng-jīk	成就，成績
act, as an actor	jouh-hei	做戲
action	hàhng-duhng	行動
active, lively	wuht-put	活潑
activities	wuht-duhng	活動
actually	kèih-saht	其實
acupuncture	jàm-gau	針灸
acute disease	gāp-jing	急症
add to, increase	jāng-gā	增加
address	deih-jí	地址
address (with proper title)	chìng-fù	稱呼
adhere	chì	黐
administration	hàhng-jing	行政
administrator	hàhng-jing yàhn-yùhn	行政人員
admire	pui-fuhk, yàn-séung	佩服，欣賞
adult	daaih-yàhn	大人
adult education	sìhng-yàhn gaau-yuhk	成人教育
adversity	waahn-naahn	患難
advertisement	gou-baahk, gwóng-gou	告白，廣告
advertising company	gwóng-gou gùng-sī	廣告公司
advise, persuade	hyun	勸
advocate, suggest	jyú-jèung	主張
aerogram	yàuh-gáan	郵簡
affable, kind	hóu-sèung-yúh, hóu-yàhn-sí	好相與，好人事

3

affairs, matter	sih-chìhng	事情
afraid	gèng	驚
Africa	Fèi- jàu	非洲
after...	...jì-hauh	……之後
after all	gau-gíng, dou-dái	究竟，到底
afternoon	hah-jau	下晝
afternoon nap	ngaan-gaau	晏覺
afternoon tea	hah-ńgh chàh	下午茶
afterwards, later on	hauh-lòih, sāu-mēi	後來，收尾
afterwards, then again	yìhn-hauh	然後
again	yauh	又
again, once more	joi	再
against (in opposition to)	fáan-deui, ...sēung-fáan	反對；……相反
age	nìhn-géi	年紀
agent, be agent	doih-léih	代理
ago	...jì-chìhn	……之前
agree	tùhng-yi, jaan-sìhng	同意，贊成
agriculture	nùhng-yihp	農業
Aids	ngoi-jī-behng	愛滋病
aim at	ji-joih	志在
aim, object, goal	muhk-dīk	目的
air	hùng-hei	空氣
air force	hùng-gwàn	空軍
air hostess	hùng-jùng síu-jé	空中小姐
air-conditioner	láahng-hei-gēi	冷氣機
air-conditioning	láahng-hei	冷氣
air-line company	hòhng-hùng gūng-sī	航空公司
aircraft-carrier	hòhng-hùng móuh-laahm	航空母艦
airmail letter	hòhng-hùng seun	航空信
airplane	fèi-gèi	飛機
airport, airfield	(fèi) gèi-chèuhng	（飛）機場
alas!	séi-lo!	死咯！

all	tùng-tùng, só-yáuh-ge	通通，所有嘅
all around	sei-wàih	四圍
all of a sudden	daht-yìhn-gāan, dahk-yìhn-gāan	突然間
all the time	jàu-sìh	周時
allergic, allergy	máhn-gám	敏感
allocate	buht	撥
allow	jéun, béi	准，俾
Alma Mater	móuh-haauh	母校
almost, hardly	gèi-fùh	幾乎
almost, nearly	chā-bāt-dō, chā-m̀-dō	差不多，差唔多
alphabet	jih-móuh	字母
already	yíh-gìng	已經
also, as well	dōu, yihk-dōu	都，亦都
alter, correct	gói	改
although	sèui-yìhn	雖然
altogether	hahm-baahng-laahng	冚唪呤
altruistic	waih-yàhn	為人
aluminium pot	tāi-bōu	鍚煲
alumni association	haauh-yáuh-wúi	校友會
always	sìh-sìh- dōu	時時都
ambassador	daaih-si	大使
ambition	yéh-sàm, ji-hei	野心，志氣
ambitious	gau-ji-hei	夠志氣
ambulance	gau-sēung-chè	救傷車
ambulance corps	gau-sēung-déui	救傷隊
America	Méih-jàu	美洲
America (U.S.A.)	Méih-gwok	美國
among	kèih-jùng	其中
amusing, enjoyable	hóu-wáan	好玩
anaemia	pàhn-hyut	貧血
anaesthetic	màh-jeui-yeuhk	麻醉藥

anaesthetist	màh-jeui-sī	麻醉師
ancestor	jóu-sìn	祖先
ancestral hall	chìh-tóng	祠堂
ancient times	gú-doih, gú-sìh	古代，古時
and	tùhng	同
and so on, etc.	dáng-dáng	等等
angel	tìn-si	天使
anger	fáhn-nouh	忿怒
angry	nàu	嬲
any	yahm-hòh	任何
animal	duhng-maht	動物
ankle	geuk-ngáahn	腳眼
annual ball	jàu-nìhn móuh-wúi	週年舞會
annual meeting	jàu-nìhn daaih-wúi	週年大會
another	daih-yih	第二
another one	lihng-ngoih yāt-go	另外一個
answer (v)*	daap	答
antiques, curio	gú-dúng, gú-wún	古董，古玩
any time	chèuih-sìh	隨時
anyway, anyhow	wàahng-dihm	橫掂
apartment building	daaih-hah	大廈
apathetic	láahng-daahm	冷淡
apologize	douh-hip	道歉
appear	chēut-yihn	出現
appearance, features	yéung	樣
appendicitis	màahng-chéung-yìhm	盲腸炎
appendix (of a book)	fuh-luhk	附錄
appetite	waih-háu	胃口
applaud	paaksáu	拍手
apple	pìhng-gwó	蘋果
appliances, tools	yuhng-geuih	用具
application form	sànchíng-bíu	申請表
apply	sàn-chíng	申請

apply lipstick	chàh sèuhn-gòu	搽唇膏
apply on, put on	chàh	搽
apply powder	chàh fán	搽粉
appreciate (of a favor)	gám-gīk	感激
apprentice	hohk-tòuh, tòuh-dái	學徒，徒弟
approximately, about	yeuk-mók… , … jó-yáu	約莫，左右
apricot	hahng	杏
April	Sei-yuht	四月
apron	wàih-kwán	圍裙
architect	(waahk) jīk-sì	(畫) 則師
are, be	haih	係
area (location)	deih-kèui	地區
area (measurement for a place)	mihn-jīk	面積
argue	ngaau-géng	拗頸
arm	sáu-bei	手臂
armed forces	gwàn-déui	軍隊
army	luhk-gwàn	陸軍
aroma	hèung-meih	香味
arouse	yáhn-héi	引起
arrange (things in a place)	bou-ji	佈置
arrange, display	báai	擺
arrange, dispose	ngòn-pàaih, chyú-léih	安排，處理
arrest	làai	拉
arrive, reach	dou	到
art	ngaih-seuht	藝術
artificial	yàhn-jouh, gá	人造，假
artist	ngaih-seuht-gā	藝術家
as far as I know	jiu-ngóh-só-ji	照我所知
as if, seems	chih-fùh	似乎
as much (many) as possible	jeuhn-leuhng	盡量
as one pleases, whatever one likes	chèuih...jùng-yi lā, chèuih (bin)...lā	隨……中意啦，隨 (便) ……啦

as soon as possible	jeuhn-faai	盡快
as to, as for	ji-yù	至於
ascend	sìng	升
ash	fùi	灰
ash tray	yīn-fùi-díp	煙灰碟
Asia	Nga-jàu	亞洲
ask	mahn	問
ask after, send regards to	mahn-hauh	問候
ask for a leave	chéng-ga, gou-ga	請假，告假
ask for advice (polite form)	chéng-gaau	請教
ask for directions	mahn-louh	問路
askew, not straight	mé	歪
Aspro	A-sih-bāt-lìhng	亞士畢靈
assistant	joh-sáu, bòng-sáu	助手，幫手
assorted fruit	jaahp-gwó	雜果
astigmatism	sáan-gwòng	散光
astronaut	taai-hùng-yàhn	太空人
astronomer	tìn-màhn	天文
at any time, any moment	chèuih-sìh	隨時
at dark	tìn-hàak	天黑
at daybreak	tìn-gwòng	天光
at present	muhk-chìhn	目前
at that time, at that moment	gó-jahn-sí, dòng-sìh	嗰陣時，當時
atom	yùhn-jí	原子
atomic bomb	yùhn-jí-dáan	原子彈
attitude	taai-douh	態度
attorney	leuht-sī	律師
attractive	leng	靚
audience	ting-jung	聽眾
audience, spectators	gùn-jung	觀眾
auditorium	láih-tòhng	禮堂
August	Baat-yuht	八月
Australia	Ngou-jàu, Ou-jàu	澳洲

author	jok-jé, jok-gā	作者，作家
autobiography	jih-jyún	自傳
automatic	jih-duhng	自動
automobile, car	chè, hei-chè	車，汽車
autumn	chàu-tìn	秋天
avail oneself of an opportunity	je nī-go gèi-wuih	借呢個機會
average	pìhng-gwàn	平均
average grade	pìhng-gwàn-fàn	平均分
aviation	hòhng-hùng	航空
avoid	beih-hòi, beih-míhn	避開，避免
awakened (by noise)	chòuh-séng	嘈醒
awesome	sāi-leih	犀利
axe	fú-táu	斧頭
azalea	douh-gyūn-fā	杜鵑花

B

B. A. or B. S.	hohk-sih	學士
B. C. (before Christ)	géi-yùhn chìhn	紀元前
baby	bìh-bī-jái	BB 仔
back (of the body)	bui-jek	背脊
back door	hauh-mún	後門
back up	tan-hauh	退後
background	bui-gíng	背景
bacon	yīn-yuhk	煙肉
bad	waaih	壞
bag	dói	袋
baggage, luggage	hàhng-léih	行李
bake	guhk	焗
balcony	kèh-láu	騎樓
ball	bō, kàuh	波，球
ball-pen	yùhn-jí-bāt	原子筆

ballet	bā-lèuih-móuh	芭蕾舞
ballroom	tiu-móuh-tèng	跳舞廳
bamboo	jūk	竹
bamboo scaffolding	jūk-pàahng	竹棚
banana	hèung-jìu	香蕉
band	ngohk-déui	樂隊
bandage (n)*	bāng-dáai	繃帶
bandage (v)*	bāau-jaat	包紮
bank	ngàhn-hòhng	銀行
bankrupt	po-cháan	破產
banquet	yin-wuih	宴會
bar, pub	jáu-bā	酒吧
barber shop	fèi-faat-póu	飛髮鋪
bargain	góng-ga	講價
bargirl	bā-néui	吧女
bark (n)*	syuh-pèih	樹皮
bark (v)*	faih	吠
base on (upon)	gàn-geui	根據
baseball	lèuih-kàuh	壘球
basement, cellar	deih-lòuh	地牢
basic, basis	gàn-bún, gèi-chó	根本，基礎
basically	gàn-bún-seuhng	根本上
basin, pot	pùhn	盆
basket	láam	籃
basketball	làahm-kàuh	籃球
bat (use for hitting ball)	kàuh-páahng	球棒
bat (animal)	pìn-fūk	蝙蝠
bath towel	mòuh-gàn	毛巾
bath-robe	yuhk-pòuh	浴袍
bath-tub	yuhk-gōng	浴缸
bathing suit	wihng-yī	泳衣
bathroom, shower	chùng-lèuhng-fóng	沖涼房
batman (in movie)	pìn-fūk-hahp	蝙蝠俠

battery	dihn-sām	電心
battery (for car)	dihn-chìh	電池
bay	hói-wāan	海灣
be (a doctor, teacher, etc.)	jouh	做
be expert, experienced	joih-hòhng, yáuh gìng-yihm	在行，有經驗
be named, be called by	giu, giu-jouh	叫，叫做
be sure to	ji-gán	至緊
be touching	lihng yàhn gám-duhng	令人感動
beach	sā-tāan	沙灘
bean curd	dauh-fuh	豆腐
beans	dáu	豆
bear	hùhng	熊
bear, stand	yán	忍
beard	sōu, wùh-sòu	鬚，鬍鬚
beat, hit	dá	打
beat, win	yèhng	贏
beautiful	leng	靚
because	yàn-waih	因為
because of, due to	yàuh-yù	由於
become, change into	bin-sèhng	變成
become rich	faat-daaht	發達
bed	chòhng	牀
bed room	seuih-fóng	睡房
bed spread	chòhng-kám	牀冚
bee	maht-fùng	蜜蜂
beef	ngàuh-yuhk	牛肉
beef steak	ngàuh-pá	牛扒
beer	bē-jáu	啤酒
before, formerly	yíh-chìhn	以前
beforehand, in advance	sih-sìn, yuh-sìn	事先，預先
beg	kàuh	求
beggar	hāt-yī	乞兒
begin, commence	hòi-chí	開始

behind	hái...hauh-mihn	喺……後面
beige	máih-sīk	米色
believe	sèung-seun, seun	相信，信
believe (in a religion)	seun-gaau	信教
believe it or not	seun bāt seun yàuh néih	信不信由你
bell	jūng	鐘
belly, stomach	tóuh	肚
belong to	suhk-yù	屬於
below a certain number or grade	...yíh-hah	……以下
belt	pèih-dáai	皮帶
bench	chèuhng-dang	長凳
beneficial, conducive	yáuh-yīk, yáuh yīk-chyu	有益，有益處
benefit, interest	leih-yīk	利益
beside, next to	pòhng-bīn	旁邊
besides, moreover	yìh-ché	而且
besides, the other	lihng-ngoih	另外
best	jeui-hóu	最好
best man	buhn-lóng	伴郎
bet	syù-dóu	輸賭
better	hóu-dī	好啲
between..., among...	...jì-gàan	……之間
beware of	dōng-sàm	當心
bib	háu-séui-gìn	口水肩
Bible	Sing-gìng	聖經
bicycle	dāan-chè	單車
big	daaih	大
biology	sāng-maht (hohk)	生物 (學)
bird	jéuk, jeuk-jái	雀，雀仔
birth control	jit-yuhk	節育
birthday	sàang-yaht	生日
birthday card	sàang-yaht kāat	生日咭
birthday gift	sàang-yaht láih-maht	生日禮物

biscuit	béng-gòn	餅乾
bite (v)*	ngáauh	咬
bitter	fú	苦
black	hāak	黑
black-and-white	hāak-baahk	黑白
black coffee	jāai-fē	齋啡
blackboard	hāak-báan	黑板
bladder	pòhng-gwòng	膀胱
blame	gwaai	怪
blanket	jīn, péih	氈，被
bleach	piu-baahk	漂白
bleed	làuh-hyut	流血
bless	bóu-yauh, jūk-fūk	保佑，祝福
blessings	hahng-fūk	幸福
blind	màahng (ngáahn)	盲（眼）
block (in distance)	gaāi-háu	街口
blood	hyut	血
blood brothers	chàn hìng-daih	親兄弟
blood pressure	hyut-ngaat	血壓
blood test	yihm-hyut	驗血
blood transfusion	syù-hyut	輸血
blouse	(néuih-jòng) sēut-sāam	（女裝）恤衫
blow	chèui	吹
blue (color)	làahm-sīk, làahm	藍色，藍
board (wooden)	muhk-báan	木板
boarding card	dāng-gèi-jing	登機證
boarding student	gei-sūk-sāng	寄宿生
boat, ship	syùhn	船
body	sàn-tái	身體
boil (n)*	chōng	瘡
boil (v)*	bōu	煲
boiled water	gwán-séui	滾水
bone	gwāt	骨

book	syù	書
book case	syù-gwaih	書櫃
book shelf	syù-gá	書架
bookstore	syù-póu, syù-dim	書舖，書店
boot	hēu	靴
boring	muhn	悶
born	chēut-sai	出世
borrow	je	借
borscht	lòh-sung-tòng	羅宋湯
boss, proprietor	sih-táu, lóuh-báan	事頭，老闆
both (with nouns)	léuhng go dōu	兩個都
bothersome	fai-sih	費事
both hands	sēung-sáu	雙手
both~and~	m̀-jí ~ yìh-ché ~	唔止～而且～
bottle	jēun	樽
bottom	dái	底
bottom (part of the body)	pei-gú, pēt-pēt	屁股，□□
bow of a vessel	syùhn-tàuh	船頭
bow tie	bōu-tāai	煲呔
bowl	wún	碗
box	háp, sēung	盒，箱
boy	nàahm-jái	男仔
bracelet	ngáak	鈪
brain	nóuh (gàn)	腦（筋）
brake, switch	jai	掣
branch (of a tree)	syuh-jī	樹枝
branch of a bank or firm	fān-hóng, fān-gūng-sì	分行，分公司
brand-name	pàaih (jí)	牌（子）
Brandy	Baahk-lāan-déi	白蘭地
brassiere	hùng-wàih	胸圍
bread	mihn-bāau	麵包
break (v)*	jíng-laahn, dá-laahn	整爛，打爛
brake (v)*	saat-jai	刹掣

breakfast	jóu-chāan	早餐
breast	hùng, sàm-háu	胸，心口
breast-feeding	wai-yàhn-náaih	餵人奶
breathe	táu-hei, fū-kāp	唞氣，呼吸
bribe	kúi-louh	賄賂
bride	sàn-néung	新娘
bride's family	néuih-gā	女家
bridegroom	sàn-lòng, sàn-lòhng-gō	新郎，新郎哥
bridegroom's family	nàahm-gā	男家
bridesmaid	buhn-néung	伴娘
bridge	kìuh	橋
brief case	gùng-sih-bāau	公事包
bright	gwòng (máahng)	光（猛）
bring (accompany person)	daai	帶
bring (carry thing)	nīk, daai	□，帶
broad (in size)	fut	闊
broadcast	gwóng-bo	廣播
broken (into two parts)	tyúhn	斷
broken, rotten	laahn	爛
broker	gìng-géi	經紀
bronchitis	jì-hei-gún-yìhm	支氣管炎
bronze statue	tùhng-jeuhng	銅像
broom	sou-bá	掃把
brothers	hìng-daih	兄弟
brown	ga-fē-sīk	咖啡色
brown sugar	wòhng-tòhng	黃糖
bruise	yú	瘀
brush	sóu, cháat	掃、擦
brush one's teeth	chaat-ngàh	擦牙
bucket, barrel	túng	桶
Buddhist, Buddhism	Faht-gaau	佛教
budget	yuh-syun	預算
buffet	jih-joh-chāan	自助餐

build	héi	起
building	láu	樓
bully, take advantage	hà	蝦
bump into (persons etc.), collide (cars)	johng	撞
burn, put fire to burnt	sìu	燒
burnt (overcook)	jyú-lūng	煮燶
bury	jong	葬
bus	bā-sí	巴士
bus lane	bā-sí jyūn-sin	巴士專線
business administration	gùng-sèung gún-léih	工商管理
business of an organization	yihp-mouh	業務
business trade	sàang-yi	生意
bustling	yiht-naauh	熱鬧
busy (not free)	m̀-dāk-hàahn	唔得閒
but, however	daahn-haih	但係
butter	ngàuh-yàuh	牛油
butterfly	wùh-díp	蝴蝶
button	náu	鈕
button up	kau-náu	扣鈕
buy	máaih	買
buy groceries	máaih-sung	買餸
by (bus, boat)	daap	搭
by all means, be sure	chìn-kèih	千祈
by coincidence	ngāam-ngāam	啱啱
by that time	dou-sìh	到時
by the way	góng-héi-séuhng-làih	講起上嚟

C

| cabin (in a ship) | syùhn-chòng | 船艙 |
| cable car | laahm-chè | 纜車 |

cake	béng	餅
calculate, figure out	gai	計
calendar	yaht-lihk	日曆
call, ask	giu	叫
call, to be called	giu-jouh	叫做
calm, still	pìhng-jihng	平靜
calm, undisturbed	jan-dihng, daahm-dihng	鎮定，啖定
camera	(yíng) séung-gèi	（影）相機
camp (live in tents or huts)	louh-yìhng	露營
can (know how to), be able to	wúih	會
can, may	hó-yíh	可以
can-opener	gun-táu-dōu	罐頭刀
can't help but	yán-m̀-jyuh	忍唔住
Canada	Gā-nàh-daaih	加拿大
canal	wahn-hòh	運河
cancer	ngàahm, kēng-sá	癌；□□
candle	laahp-jūk	蠟燭
candlestick	jūk-tòih	燭台
candy	tóng	糖
canned food, can	gun-táu	罐頭
cannot handle	ying-fuh m̀-làih	應付唔嚟
canteen	faahn-tòhng	飯堂
Cantonese (dialect)	Gwóng-dùng-wá, Gwóng-jàu-wá	廣東話，廣州話
Cantonese opera	daaih-hei, yuht-kehk	大戲，粵劇
cape (garment)	dáu-pùhng	斗蓬
capital (money)	bún-chìhn, jì-gàm	本錢，資金
capital (of a nation)	sáu-dōu	首都
capitalism	jì-bún jyú-yih	資本主義
captain (of a ship)	syùhn-jéung	船長
car	chè	車
car accident	gāau-tùng yi-ngoih	交通意外
car key	chè-sìh	車匙

carboard box	jí-háp	紙盒
card	kāat	咭
care about, concern	gwàan-sàm	關心
career, enterprise	sih-yihp	事業
careful, cautious	síu-sàm	小心
carnation	hōng-náaih-hìng	康乃馨
carpenter	dau-muhk sì-fú	鬥木師傅
carpentry	dau-muhk	鬥木
carpet, rug	deih-jín	地氈
carry (as by vehicle)	joi	載
carry (under one's arm)	gihp	挾
carry between two or more persons	tòih	抬
carry on one's shoulder	dāam	擔
carry out	saht-hàhng	實行
carve, carving	dīu-hāk	雕刻
case	ngon-gín, go-ngon	案件，個案
cash	yihn-chín, yihn-gām	現錢，現金
cashier	sàu-ngán-yùhn	收銀員
casino	dóu-chèuhng, dóu-gún	賭場，賭館
casual acquaintance	póu-tùng pàhng-yáuh	普通朋友
casually	kàuh-kèih	求其
cat	māau	貓
catalogue, list	muhk-luhk	目錄
catch	jūk	捉
catch cold	láahng-chàn	冷親
Catholic, Catholicism	Tìn-jyú-gaau	天主教
catsup	ké-jāp	茄汁
cattle	ngàuh	牛
catty	gàn	斤
cause	lihng	令
cavity	jyu-ngàh	蛀牙
ceiling	tìn-fā-báan	天花板

celebrate	hing-jūk	慶祝
celebrate the new year	gwo-nìhn	過年
cell phone, mobile phone	sáu-gēi	手機
cement	hùhng-mòuh-nàih	紅毛泥
cent	sīn	仙
centre	jùng-sàm	中心
century	sai-géi	世紀
ceremony	yìh-sīk	儀式
certainly, definitely	yāt-dihng, gáng	一定，梗
certainly, really	jàn-haih	真係
certificate, diploma	jing-syù, màhn-pàhng	證書，文憑
certificate of stock	gú-piu	股票
chain	lín	鏈
chair	yí	椅
chairman	jyú-jihk	主席
champagne	hèung-bàn (jáu)	香檳（酒）
champion	gun-gwān	冠軍
chance	gèi-wuih	機會
change, alter	gói-bin	改變
change, exchange	wuhn	換
change, money in small unit	sáan-ngán	散銀
change a date	gói kèih	改期
change address	gói deih-jí	改地址
change another train, bus etc.	jyun-chè	轉車
change clothes	wuhn-sāam	換衫
chaos	wahn-lyuhn	混亂
chapel, church	gaau-tòhng, láih-baai-tòhng	教堂，禮拜堂
chapel, church (used by Catholics)	sing-tóng	聖堂
chapter (of book)	jēung	章
character (of a person)	sing-gaak	性格
characteristics	dahk-dím	特點

charge by the month	on yuht gai	按月計
charity	chìh-sihn	慈善
chart, drawing	tòuh	圖
chart	tòuh-bíu	圖表
chase, pursue	jèui	追
chase away	gón	趕
chat, converse	kìng-gái	傾偈
cheap	pèhng	平
check	chēk, gím-chàh	□，檢查
cheek	mihn	面
cheese	chī-si, jì-sí	芝士
chef	chyùh-sī, daaih-chyú	廚師，大廚
chemistry	fa-hohk	化學
cheque	jì-piu	支票
chest	sàm-háu	心口
chick	gāi-jái	雞仔
chicken	gāi	雞
chief (of a tribe)	yàuh-jéung, juhk-jéung	酋長，族長
child	sai-mān-jái, sai-lóu-gō	細蚊仔，細佬哥
children	sai-mān-jái, síu-tùhng	細蚊仔，小童
chin	hah-pàh	下巴
China	Jùng-gwok	中國
China Mainland	Daaih-luhk	大陸
Chinatown	Tòhng-yàhn-gāai, Tòhng-yàhn-fauh	唐人街，唐人埠
Chinese (language)	Jùng-màhn, Jùng-mán	中文
Chinese brush pen	mòuh-bāt	毛筆
Chinese character	Jùng-gwok-jih	中國字
Chinese medicine doctor	jùng-yī	中醫
Chinese dress	tòhng-jòng	唐裝
Chinese food	tòhng-chāan, jùng-choi	唐餐，中菜
Chinese ink	mahk	墨
Chinese mushroom	dùng-gù	冬菇

Chinese New Year's Eve	Nìhn-sāam-sahp-máahn, Nìhn-sāah-máahn	年三十晚，年卅晚
Chinese style ladies' dress	kèih-póu, chèuhng-sāam	旗袍，長衫
chocolate	jyū-gù-līk	朱古力
cholera	fok-lyuhn	霍亂
choose	gáan, syún-jaahk	揀，選擇
chop, cut	jáam	斬
chop, stamp, seal	tòuh-jēung, yan	圖章，印
chopper	choi-dōu	菜刀
chopping block	jām-báan	砧板
chopsticks	faai-jí	筷子
chorus	hahp-cheung-tyùhn	合唱團
Christ	Gēi-dūk	基督
Christian	Gēi-dūk-tòuh	基督徒
Christmas	Sing-daan jit	聖誕節
Christmas card	Sing-daan kāat	聖誕咭
Christmas carol	Sing-daan gō	聖誕歌
Christmas caroling	bou-gāai-yām	報佳音
Christmas Eve	Sing-daan chìhn-jihk	聖誕前夕
Christmas gift	Sing-daan láih-maht	聖誕禮物
chrysanthemum	gūk-fà	菊花
cicada, broad locust	sìhm	蟬
cigarette	yīn, yīn-jái	煙，煙仔
cigarette ashes	yīn-fūi	煙灰
cigarette butts	yīn-táu	煙頭
cigarette-lighter	dá-fó-gèi	打火機
circle (n)	yùhn-hyūn	圓圈
circle (round space)	yùhn-hyūn	圓圈
circle (same profession)	huūn-jí, ... gaai	圈子，……界
circumstance, condition	chìhng-yìhng	情形
circus	máh-hei	馬戲

citizen	gùng-màhn	公民
city	sìhng-síh	城市
City Hall	Daaih-wuih-tòhng	大會堂
claim	yīu-kàuh, saak-chéui	要求，索取
class (social)	gāai-kāp	階級
class is over	lohk-tòhng	落堂
classic music	gú-dín yàm-ngohk	古典音樂
classmate	tùhng-hohk	同學
classroom	fo-sāt, gaau-sāt, bāan-fóng	課室，教室，班房
clean (n)*	gòn-jehng	乾淨
clean (v)*	dá-sou	打掃
clean and neat	gòn-jehng kéih-léih	乾淨企理
clear, distinct	chìng-chó	清楚
clear the garbage	dóu laahp-saap	倒垃圾
clever, smart	chùng-mìhng	聰明
clever and smart	chùng-mìhng lìhng-leih	聰明伶俐
climb	pàh	爬
clinic	chán-lìuh-só, yī-mouh-só	診所，醫務所
clock, bell	jūng	鐘
close (book, eye, box, etc.)	hahp-màaih	合埋
close (door, window)	sāan	閂
close (in relationship)	maht-chit	密切
closely related	chàn	親
closing time (for business)	sàu-síh	收市
cloth, material	bou	布
clothes, dress	sāam	衫
clothing	yì-fuhk	衣服
cloud	wàhn	雲
club	kēui-lohk-bouh, wuih-só	俱樂部，會所
clumsy, awkward	leuhn-jeuhn	論盡
coach, instructor	gaau-lihn	教練
coal	mùih	煤

coat	lāu	褸
coast	hói-ngohn	海岸
Coca Cola	(hó-háu) hó-lohk	（可口）可樂
cock	gāi-gūng	雞公
cockroach	gaahk-jáat	甲由
cocktail party	gāi-méih jáu-wúi	雞尾酒會
coffee	ga-fē	咖啡
coffin	gùn-chòih	棺材
coincidental	kíu	〔嚙〕
cold	dung	凍
cold (usually for weather)	láahng	冷
cold cream	syut-fā-gōu	雪花膏
cold dish	láahng-pún	冷盤
cold meat	dung-yuhk	凍肉
collar	léhng	領
collar pin	léhng-jām	領針
colleague	tùhng-sìh	同事
collect	sāu, sāu-jaahp	收，收集
colony	jihk-màhn-deih	殖民地
color	ngàahn-sīk	顏色
color picture	chói-sīk-séung	彩色相
color-blindness	sīk-màahng	色盲
colorful, gaudy	ńgh-ngàahn-luhk-sīk	五顏六色
column (part of a newspaper)	jyūn-làahn	專欄
columnist	jyūn-làahn jok-gā	專欄作家
coma	yàu-hāak	休克
comb hair	sò-tàuh	梳頭
comb, to comb	sò	梳
come, came	làih	嚟
come back	fāan-làih	番嚟
come in	yahp-làih	入嚟
come up	séuhng-làih	上嚟
comfortable	syù-fuhk	舒服

comical, funny	waaht-kài	滑稽
comics (book or magazine)	maahn-wá, gùng-jái-syù	漫畫，公仔書
commerce	sèung-yihp	商業
commercial port	sèung-fauh	商埠
commission, brokerage	yúng-gām	佣金
commit suicide	jih-saat	自殺
common	póu-tùng	普通
common saying	juhk-wá, juhk-yúh	俗話，俗語
common sense	sèuhng-sīk	常識
communism	guhng-cháan-jyú-yih	共產主義
communist party	guhng-cháan-dóng	共產黨
company, corporation	gùng-sì	公司
compare	béi-gaau	比較
compassionate	m̀-yán-sàm	唔忍心
compel, supervise	gàam-jyuh	監住
compensate, compensation	pùih-sèuhng	賠償
compete	dau	鬥
competition	béi-choi	比賽
complete	chàih-beih	齊備
completely, 100%, extremely	sahp-fān	十分
complicated	fūk-jaahp	複雜
compose	jok, sé	作，寫
composer	jok-kūk-gā	作曲家
compulsorily	gaap-ngàang	夾硬
computer	dihn-nóuh	電腦
conceivable, deduce	hó-séung-yìh-jì	可想而知
concept	gùn-lihm	觀念
concern	gwàan-sàm, gwa-jyuh	關心，掛住
concert	yàm-ngohk-wúi	音樂會
concubine	chip-sih	妾侍
concur, agree	jaan-sìhng	贊成
condition (of a patient)	behng-chihng	病情

condition	ch̀ihng-fong, chyúh-gíng	情況，處境
condition (of an agreement)	tìuh-gín	條件
conditioner	wuh-faat-sou	護髮素
conductor, to conduct	jí-fāi	指揮
confections, refreshment	dím-sām	點心
conference	wuih-yíh	會議
conflicts	chùng-daht	衝突
Confucianist, Confucianism	Húng-gaau	孔教
Confucius	Húng-jí	孔子
congee, rice gruel	jūk	粥
congenital	tìn-sàang	天生
congratulate, congratulations	gùng-héi	恭喜
connect	lìhn-jip	連接
connect (a telephone etc.)	bok, jip	駁，接
connection, relevance	gwàan-haih	關係
conscience	lèuhng-sàm	良心
conservative	bóu-sáu	保守
consider, think it over	háau-leuih	考慮
consider with dislike	yìhm	嫌
console, comfort	ngòn-wai	安慰
constipation	bihn-bei	便秘
constitution	hin-faat	憲法
construct	gin-jūk, héi	建築，起
construction company	gin-jūk gùng-sì	建築公司
construction work	gùng-chìhng	工程
consul	líhng-sí	領事
consul general	júng-líhng-sí	總領事
consulate	líhng-sí-gún	領事館
consulate general	júng-líhng-sí-gún	總領事館
consult a dictionary	chàh jih-dín	查字典
consult with, discuss	sèung-lèuhng	商量
consultant, advisor	gu-mahn	顧問

contact	jip-jūk	接觸
contact lenses	yán-yìhng ngáahn-géng	隱形眼鏡
contain (have)	hàhm-yáuh	含有
contagious disease	chyùhn-yíhm-behng	傳染病
container (for goods)	fo-gwaih	貨櫃
contemplate, think	nám / lám	諗
contented	jì-jùk, ngòn-lohk	知足，安樂
contents, list	muhk-luhk	目錄
contest, compete, competition	béi-choi	比賽
continuously	gai-juhk	繼續
continent	daaih-luhk	大陸
continue	gai-juhk	繼續
contract	hahp-yeuk, hahp-tùhng	合約，合同
contractor (of a building project)	sìhng-gin-sēung	承建商
contradictory, contradiction	màauh-téuhn	矛盾
contrary to expectations	gēui-yín, gēui-yìhn	居然
contribute, contribution	gung-hin	貢獻
control	hung-jai	控制
convenient	fòng-bihn	方便
convolvulus	hìn-ngàuh-fā	牽牛花
cook (n)*	chyùh-sī, jyú-faahn	廚師，煮飯
cook (v)*	jyú, jyú-faahn	煮，煮飯
cooked rice	faahn	飯
cooked, ripe	suhk	熟
cookies, crackers	kūk-kèih-béng, béng-gōn	曲奇餅，餅乾
cool	lèuhng, lèuhng-sóng	涼、涼爽
cooperate, cooperative	hahp-jok	合作
cooperatively (coll.)	gaap-sáu-gaap-geuk	夾手夾腳
cope with, handle	ying-fuh	應付
copper, bronze	tùhng	銅
copy (v)*	chàau	抄

coral	sàan-wùh	珊瑚
corn	sūk-máih	粟米
corn oil	sūk-máih yàuh	粟米油
corn soup	sūk-máih gāng	粟米羹
corner	gok-lōk-táu	角落頭
corporate business	gú-fán sāang-yi	股份生意
correct (an error)	gói	改
correct, fit	ngāam	啱
corrupt	fuh-baaih	腐敗
corsage	kàm-tàuh-fā	襟頭花
cosmetics	fa-jōng-bán	化妝品
cost of living	sàng-wuht sìu-fai	生活消費
cotton	mìhn-fā	棉花
cough	kāt, kāt-sau	咳，咳嗽
could (request)	hó-yíh	可以
could (indicating possibility)	hó-nàhng	可能
count	gai	計
counter	gwaih-mín	櫃面
countless	sóu-jí-bāt-jeuhn	數之不盡
country	gwok-gā	國家
couple, husband and wife	léuhng fū-chài, léuhng fū-fúh, léuhng gùng-pó	兩夫妻，兩夫婦，兩公婆
courage	yúhng-hei	勇氣
course, curriculum	fo-chìhng	課程
courtesy	láih-maauh	禮貌
cover (v)*	kám	冚
cover, lid	goi	蓋
crab	háaih	蟹
cramp	chàu-gàn	抽筋
crane	hohk, hók	鶴
crash into, hit	pung	碰
crazy	sàhn-gìng, chì-sin	神經，黐線
cream	geih-lìm	忌廉

27

crease (on paper)	jip-hàhn	摺痕
crease (in the skin)	jau-màhn	皺紋
create	chong-jok	創作
credit	seun-yuhng	信用
credit card	seun-yuhng kāat	信用咭
cremate	fó-jong	火葬
cricket	sīk-sēut	蟋蟀
crime	jeuih	罪
crispy	cheui	脆
criticize, criticism	pài-pìhng	批評
crocodile	ngohk-yùh	鱷魚
crop	sāu-sìhng	收成
cross (n)*	sahp-jih-gá	十字架
cross over	gwo	過
cross-harbour tunnel	hói-dái seuih-douh	海底隧道
crowd	yàhn-kwàhn	人群
crow	wū-ngā	烏鴉
crowded	bīk	逼
cruet-stand	ńgh-meih-gá	五味架
crutch	gwáai-jéung	拐杖
cry, weep	haam	喊
cucumber	chèng-gwà	青瓜
cufflinks	jauh-háu-náu	袖口鈕
cultivate, (give care to younger generation)	jòi-pùih	栽培
culture	màhn-fa	文化
cultured, well-behaved	sì-màhn	斯文
cultured pearl	yéuhng-jyū	養珠
cunning	gáau-waaht	狡猾
cup	būi	杯
cupboard in kitchen	chyùh-gwaih, wún-gwaih	櫥櫃，碗櫃
cure (v)*	yī	醫

curiosity	hou-kèih-sàm	好奇心
curious	hou-kèih	好奇
currency	fo-baih	貨幣
current (happening now)	muhk-chìhn, yihn-hàhng	目前，現行
curry	ga-lēi	咖喱
curtain	chēung-lím	窗簾
cushion (n)*	yí-jín	椅墊
cushion (v)*	sip	攝
custom	fùng-juhk	風俗
custom-house	hói-gwàan	海關
cut (with knife)	chit	切
cut (with scissors)	jín	剪
cut apart	chit-hòi	切開
cute	dāk-yi, cheui-ji	得意，趣緻
cypress	paak	柏

D

daddy	bàh-bā	爸爸
daffodil	séuisìn-fā	水仙花
dial the wrong number	daap-cho-sin, dá-cho	搭錯線，打錯
daily	yaht-sèuhng, múih-yaht	日常，每日
daily life	sāng-wuht	生活
daisy	chō-gùk	雛菊
dance	tiu-móuh	跳舞
dancing party	móuh-wúi	舞會
dandelion	pòuh-gùng-yìng	蒲公英
dangerous, danger	ngàih-hím	危險
dare	gám	敢
daring, foolhardy	daaih-dáam	大膽
dark, black	hāak	黑

dark color	sām-sīk	深色
dark green	sām-luhk (sīk)	深綠（色）
data	jì-líu	資料
date	yaht-kèih	日期
date of birth	chēut-sāng yaht-kèih	出生日期
daughter	néui	女
dawn	tìn-mūng-gwòng	天矇光
day, date	yaht	日
day after tomorrow	hauh-yaht	後日
day before yesterday	chìhn-yaht	前日
day of the month	houh	號
daytime	yaht-táu	日頭
dazzled, blurred	ngáahn-fā	眼花
dead	seí-ge	死嘅
deaf	lùhng	聾
deal (agreement)	hip-yíh	協議
dear, loved	chàn-ngoi ge	親愛嘅
death	seí, seí-mòhng	死，死亡
debate	bihn-leuhn	辯論
debt	jaai	債
deceive, cheat	ngāak, tam	呃，諂
December	Sahp-yih-yuht	十二月
decide, decision	kyut-dihng	決定
decimal	síu-sou	小數
decimal system	sahp-jeun-jai	十進制
decorate	jōng-sīk	裝飾
deep, dark (of colors)	sàm	深
deep breath	sàm fū-kàp	深呼吸
deep fry	ja, jaau	炸，□
deer	lúk	鹿
definitely	yāt-dihng	一定
degree (college)	hohk-wái	學位
degree, level	chìhng-douh	程度

delay, postpone	yìhn-chìh	延遲
delegate, representative	doih-bíu	代表
delicious	hóu-sihk, hóu-meih-douh	好食，好味道
delighted, joyful	gòu-hing	高興
deliver	sung	送
deliver (letter)	paai	派
demand	yìu-kàuh	要求
democracy, democratic	màhn-jyú	民主
dense, close	math	密
dentist	ngàh-yì	牙醫
dentistry	ngàh-fō	牙科
deny	fáu-yihng	否認
department (of University)	haih	系
department store	baak-fo gùng-sì	百貨公司
depend upon	yí-kaau, kaau	倚靠，靠
depend on	tái	睇
deposits, savings	chyùhn-fún	存款
describe	yìhng-yùhng	形容
desert (barrenland)	sā-mohk	沙漠
deserted (area)	pīn-pìk	偏僻
design	chit-gai	設計
designer	chit-gai-sì	設計師
desk	syù-tói	書枱
dessert	tìhm-bán	甜品
destine	jíng-dihng	整定
destiny	mihng-wahn	命運
destroy	po-waaih	破壞
detective	jìng-taam	偵探
detergent	sái-git-jīng	洗潔精
determinately	kyut-sām	決心
determination	kyut-sām	決心
determine	kyut-dihng	決定

develop, expand	faat-jín	發展
devil, Satan	mō-gwái	魔鬼
devoted, very patient	hóu-sām-gèi	好心機
diagnose	tái-jing, chán-jing	睇症，診症
diagonally opposite	chèh-deui-mihn	斜對面
dialects	fòng-yìhn	方言
diamond	jyun-sehk	鑽石
diarrhoea	tóuh-ngò, tóuh-se	肚疴，肚瀉
diary	yaht-gei	日記
dictionary	jih-dín	字典
did not expect	gú m̀-dou	估唔到
die, dead	séi	死
died (of sickness)	behng-séi	病死
differ	m̀-tùhng	唔同
difference	fàn-biht	分別
difficult	nàahn	難
difficulty	kwan-nàahn	困難
dig	gwaht	掘
digestion, digest	sìu-fa	消化
dignified, generous	daaih-fōng	大方
dim, dark	ngam	暗
dime	hòuh-jí	毫子
dining room (at home)	faahn-tēng	飯廳
dining table	chāan-tói, faahn-tói	餐枱，飯枱
dinner	máahn-faahn, máahn-chāan	晚飯，晚餐
dinner knife	chāan-dōu	餐刀
dinner party	chāan-wúi	餐會
dip into	dím	點
diplomacy	ngoih-gāau	外交
diplomat	ngoih-gāau-gùn	外交官
direct, directly	jihk jip	直接
director, head of a section	jyú-yahm	主任

dirty	wū-joù	污糟
disappointed	sāt-mohng	失望
disco	dīk-sih-gōu	的士高
discriminate, discrimination	kèih-sih	歧視
discuss (in order to solve a problem)	tóu-leuhn	討論
disease	jaht-behng	疾病
dish of food	sung	餸
dish-washer	sái-wún-gèi	洗碗機
dissimilar, different	m̀-tùhng	唔同
distant (faraway)	hóu-yúhn	好遠
distinguish	fān-dāk-chēut	分得出
distress, suffering	tung-fú	痛苦
disturb, trouble	sòu-yíu	騷擾
divide into	fàn-sèhng	分成
divorce	lèih-fān	離婚
do	jouh	做
do as one wishes	jih-bín	自便
do business	jouh sāang-yi	做生意
do homework	jouh gùng-fo	做功課
do not (imperative)	m̀-hóu	唔好
do one's best	jeuhn-lihk	盡力
dock, park	paak	泊
doctor	yī-sāng	醫生
doctor of surgery, surgeon	ngoih-fō yī-sāng	外科醫生
doctor's fee	chán-gàm	診金
doctor's private office	yī-mouh-só	醫務所
doctrine, -ism	jyú-yih	主義
document	màhn-gín	文件
dog	gáu	狗
doll	gùng-jái, yèuhng-wā-wā	公仔，洋娃娃
dollar	mān, ngàhn-chín	蚊，銀錢
don't	m̀, m̀-hóu	唔，唔好

donate	gyùn	捐
donate money	gyùn-chín	捐錢
donation	gyùn-fún	捐款
door, entrance	mùhn-háu	門口
door, gate	mùhn	門
door bell	mùhn-jùng	門鐘
door keeper	hōn-gāang	看更
door key	mùhn-sìh	門匙
dormitory	sūk-se, sūk-séh	宿舍
double	gā-púih	加倍
double registered	sèung gwa-houh	雙掛號
double room	sèung-yàhn fóng	雙人房
doubt (v)*	wàaih-yìh	懷疑
down cast	móuh-sām-gèi	冇心機
downstairs, the ground floor	làuh-hah	樓下
drag	tō	拖
dragon	lùhng	龍
drain (for clean water)	séui-kèuih	水渠
draw (as blood)	chàu	抽
draw, paint	waahk	畫
dream	muhng	夢
dream of	muhng-gin	夢見
dress (n)*	kwàhn	裙
dress (v)*	jeuk	着
dress, adorn	dá-baan	打扮
drink	yám	飲
drinking-fountain	yám-yuhng pan-chyùhn	飲用噴泉
drinking straw	yám-túng	飲筒
drive (a car)	jā-chè	揸車
driver	sī-gèi	司機
driving licence, licence plate	chè-pàaih	車牌
drop off, fall off	lāt-jó	甩咗
drug store	yeuhk-fòhng	藥房

drugs	duhk-bán	毒品
drum	gú	鼓
drunk, tipsy	yám-jeui	飲醉
dry	gōn	乾
dry-cleaning	gōn-sái	乾洗
duck	ngaap	鴨
due to, because of	yàn-waih ... ge gwàan-haih	因為……嘅關係
dull, bored	muhn	悶
durable, (lasting)	kàm-sái, kàm	捱使，捱
during	hái...kèih-gāan, hái...gó-jahn-sí	喺……期間，喺……嗰陣時
dust (n)*	chàhn	塵
dynasty	chìuh, chìuh-doih	朝，朝代

E

each	múih yāt go	每一個
each day	múih yaht	每日
each other	béi-chí, béi-chí-gàan	彼此，彼此間
eager	hóu-séung	好想
eagle	yìng	鷹
ear	yíh, yíh-jái	耳，耳仔
ear-nose-throat department	yih-beih-hàuh fō	耳鼻喉科
ear-rings	yíh-wáan	耳環
early	jóu	早
earn	jaahn	賺
earnest	yihng-jàn	認真
earth, globe	deih-kàuh	地球
ease	syū-sīk	舒適
ease of mind	sām-chìhng-syū-cheung	心情舒暢
east	dùng	東
easter	fuhk-wuht-jit	復活節

easy	yih, yùhng-yih	易，容易
eat	sihk	食
eat at teahouse, drink tea	yám chàh	飲茶
eclipse (of the moon)	yuht-sihk	月蝕
eclipse (of the sun)	yaht-sihk	日蝕
economy, economics	gìng-jai	經濟
edge (of a knife)	dōu-fūng	刀鋒
edge (of a table)	tói-bīn	枱邊
edit, editor	pīn-chāp	編輯
editor-in-chief	júng-pīn-chāp	總編輯
editorial	séh-leuhn	社論
educate, education	gaau-yuhk	教育
eel	síhn	鱔
effect, outcome	haauh-gwó	效果
effect (of medicine)	lìuh-haauh	療效
efficient	yáuh haauh-léut	有效率
effort	nóuh-lihk	努力
egg	dáan	蛋
egg-beater	dá-dáan-gēi	打蛋機
egg white	dáan-baahk	蛋白
egg yolk	dáan-wóng	蛋黃
eight	baat	八
elbow	sáu-jāang, jáau	手踭，肘
elder brother	a-gō	阿哥
elder sister	gā-jē	家姊
elect	syún	選
election, elect	syún-géui	選舉
electric fan	fùng-sin	風扇
electric iron	dihn tong-dáu	電熨斗
electric light	dihn dāng	電燈
electric plug	chap-sōu	插蘇
electric rice cooker	dihn faahn-bōu	電飯煲
electric stove	dihn lòuh	電爐

electrical appliance	dihn-hei	電器
electricity	dihn	電
electricity bill	dihn-fai-dāan	電費單
elegant	gòu-gwai, sì-màhn	高貴，斯文
elephant	(daaih-bahn) jeuhng	（大笨）象
elevator, lift	sìng-gong-gēi, līp	升降機，軺
eliminate	sìu-miht	消滅
email	dihn-yàuh	電郵
embarrassed, ashamed to	m̀hóu-yi-si	唔好意思
embassy	daaih-si-gún	大使館
embrace, hug	láam-jyuh	攬住
embroidered, embroidering	sau-fā	繡花
emergency	gán-gāp sih-gín	緊急事件
emergency room in hospital	gāp-jing-sāt	急症室
emperor	wòhng-dai	皇帝
emphasize	jyu-juhng, kèuhng-diuh	注重，強調
employer	sih-táu	事頭
empty	hùng ge	空嘅
encourage	gú-laih	鼓勵
encourage by means of reward	jéung-laih	獎勵
encyclopedia	baak-fō chyùhn-syù	百科全書
end (v)*	git-chūk	結束
end of street	gāai-háu, gāai-méih	街口，街尾
end of the month	yuht-dái, yuht-méih	月底，月尾
end of the year	nìhn-dái, nìhn-méih	年底，年尾
endure, suffer	ngàaih	捱
enemy	dihk-yàhn	敵人
energy	jīng-lihk	精力
engagement (promise to marry)	dihng-fān	訂婚
engine	gēi-hei	機器
engineer	gùng-chìhng-sī	工程師
England	Yìng-gwok	英國

English (language)	yìng-màhn, yìng-mán	英文
enjoy, appreciate	yàn-séung	欣賞
enjoy, enjoyment	héung-sauh	享受
enlarge	fong-daaih	放大
enough	gau	夠
enter	yahp	入
entertain	jìu-doih	招待
enthusiastic	lohk-lihk, yiht-sām	落力，熱心
entirely, completely	yùhn-chyùhn	完全
entrance	yahp-háu	入口
entrust, request	tok, baai-tok	託，拜託
envelope	seun-fùng	信封
environment	wàahn-gíng	環境
envy (v)*	sihn-mouh, douh-geih	羨慕，妒忌
epidemic disease	làuh-hàhng-jing	流行症
equal to	dáng-yù	等於
equality, equal	pìhng-dáng	平等
equipment	chit-beih	設備
eraser (rubber)	chaat-jí-gàau	擦紙膠
error, mistake	cho	錯
escalator	dihn-tài	電梯
escort, see off	sung	送
especially	yàuh-kèih-sih	尤其是
establish, set up	gin-lahp	建立
established by government or community	gùng-lahp	公立
Europe	Ngāu-jàu	歐洲
even	lìhn...dōu	連……都
even, even to the extent of	sahm-ji	甚至
even if...	jīk-sí...dōu	即使……都
even number	sēung-sou	雙數
evening, night-time	yeh-máahn, yeh-máahn-hāak	夜晚，夜晚黑

evening dress	máahn láih-fuhk	晚禮服
evening party	máahn-wúi	晚會
event	daaih-sih, sih-gín	大事，事件
ever since	jih-chùhng	自從
every	múih	每
everywhere	dou-syu, syu-syu	到處，處處
evidence	jing-geui	證據
evil	jeuih-ngok	罪惡
exact	jéun-kok	準確
exaggerate	kwà-jèung	誇張
examination paper	síh-gyún	試卷
examine	gím-chàh	檢查
examine, take an examination	háau-síh	考試
examining room	chán-jing-sāt	診症室
example	laih, laih-jí	例，例子
example, model	bóng-yeuhng	榜樣
exceedingly, very	gwái-gam	鬼咁
excellent	hóu-dou-gihk	好到極
except	chèuih-jó	除咗
exchange, interchange	gàau-wuhn	交換
exchange rate	wuih-léut	匯率
excited, tense	gán-jèung	緊張
exercise	lihn-jaahp	練習
exercise book	lihn-jaahp-bóu	練習簿
exert one's strength	chēut-lihk	出力
exhausting	sok-hei	索氣
exhibit, display	jín-láahm	展覽
exhibition	jín-láahm-wúi	展覽會
exit	chēut-háu	出口
expand	kwong-chùng	擴充
expand, swell	pàahng-jeung	膨脹
expect, expectation	kèih-mohng	期望
expected date of delivery	yuh-cháan-kèih	預產期

expenses	fai-yuhng	費用
expensive	gwai	貴
experience (n)*	gìng-yihm	經驗
experience (v)*	tái-yihm, gám-sauh	體驗，感受
experiment	saht-yihm	實驗
expert	jyūn-gā	專家
explain, interpret	gáai-sīk, gáai	解釋，解
explode	baau	爆
export	(wahn) chēut-háu	（運）出口
export commodity	chēut-háu fo	出口貨
express, signify	bíu-sih	表示
expression (of emotion)	bíu-chìhng	表情
exquisite	gwāt-jí	骨子
extension (telephone)	noih-sin	內線
extra	ngaahk-ngoih	額外
extra large	gā-daaih-máh	加大碼
extraordinarily, exceptionally	fèi-sèuhng	非常
extravagant	chè-chí	奢侈
extremely	m̀-jì-géi, bāt-jì-géi	唔知幾，不知幾
eye	ngáahn	眼
eye drops	ngáahn yeuhk-séui	眼藥水
eye shadow	ngáahn-koi gōu	眼蓋膏
eyebrow	ngáahn-mèih	眼眉
eyebrow pencil	meih-bāt	眉筆
eyelashes	ngáahn-jiht-mòuh	眼睫毛

F

fable	yuh-yìhn	寓言
face	mihn	面
face, confront	mihn-deui	面對
face, look on	heung	向

face to face	dòng-mín	當面
facilitate	leih-bihn	利便
facilities, fixture	chit-beih	設備
fact	sih-saht	事實
factory	gùng-chóng, chóng	工廠，廠
fail, failure	sāt-baaih	失敗
faint, dizzy	wàhn, tàuh-wàhn	暈，頭暈
fair, just	gùng-pìhng	公平
fairly, rather	géi	幾
fairy	sáhn-sìn	神仙
faith	seun-sàm	信心
fall	dit	跌
fall, autumn	chāu-tìn	秋天
fall down	daat-dài	噠低
fall down on...	dit-lohk...	跌落……
false teeth	gá ngàh	假牙
false, untrue	gá	假
familiar with	suhk	熟
family	gà-tìhng	家庭
family clan	gà-juhk	家族
family members	gā-yàhn	家人
famous, well-known	chēut-méng	出名
fan (n)*	sin	扇
fan (v)*	put	撥
far	yúhn	遠
Far East	yúhn-dùng	遠東
farewell party	fùn-sung-wúi	歡送會
farm	nùhng-chèuhng	農場
farmer	nùhng-fù	農夫
farsighted, hyperopia	yúhn-sih	遠視
fashionable	sìh-mōu	時髦
fashions	sìh-jòng	時裝
fast, quick	faai, faai-cheui	快，快趣

fat & short	fèih-fèih-ngái-ngái	肥肥矮矮
fat, obese	fèih	肥
fate	mihng-wahn	命運
father	bàh-bā	爸爸
father (not used in direct address)	fuh-chàn	父親
father (slang)	lóuh-dauh	老豆
Father's Day	fuh-chàn-jit	父親節
fatherland	jóu-gwok	祖國
favor, favour	jīchìh, jaan-sìhng	支持，贊成
fear, be afraid of	pa	怕
fearful	hó-pa	可怕
February	Yih-yuht	二月
fee	fai	費
feed	wai	餵
feel, sense	gok-dāk	覺得
feel in pocket or bag	ngàhm	唸
feel with one's hand	mó, mō	摸
feelings, mood	sàm-chìhng	心情
feet, foot	geuk	腳
ferryboat	gwo-hói-syùhn	過海船
festival	jit, jit-yaht	節，節日
fetch, get	ló	攞
few, little	síu	少
fiancé	meih-fān-fù	未婚夫
fiancée	meih-fān-chài	未婚妻
fiction, novel	síu-syut	小説
field, farmland	tìhn	田
fig	mòuh-fā-gwó	無花果
fight	dá-gàau	打交
fight for	jàang	爭
fight the fire	gau-fó	救火
figure, number	sou-jih	數字

figure (body shape)	sān-chòih	身材
figure up a bill (usually used in a restaurant)	màaih-dāan	埋單
filial	haau-seuhn	孝順
fill, stuff	sāk	塞
fill in a form	tìhn-bíu	填表
film	fēi-lám	菲林
final	jeui-hauh	最後
finally	jēut-jì	卒之
find	wán	搵
find out, discover	faat-yihn	發現
fine (money paid as punishment)	faht-fún	罰款
fine (of weather)	chìhng-lóhng	晴朗
fine, minute	yau-sai	幼細
finger	sáu-jí	手指
finger-nail	jí-gaap	指甲
finger-print	jí-mòuh, jí-màhn	指模，指紋
finish	yùhn	完
fire	fó	火
fire-cracker	paau-jéung	炮仗
fire-engine	siu-fòhng-chè, fó-jūk-chè	消防車，火燭車
fire-escapes	wàhn-tài	雲梯
fire-place	bīk-lòuh	壁爐
firewood	chàaih	柴
fireworks	yīn-fā	煙花
firm, safe	wán-jahn	穩陣
first	daihyāt	第一
first class	tàuh-dáng	頭等
first prize	tàuh-jéung	頭獎
fish	yú	魚
fish, fishing	diu-yú	釣魚

fit, suitable	sīk-hahp	適合
five	ńgh	五
fix, arrange	gáau-dihm	搞掂
fixed deposit	dihng-kèih chyùhn-fún	定期存款
flashlight	dihn-túng	電筒
flashlight (of the camera)	sím-gwòng-dàng	閃光燈
flat, level	pìhng	平
flat tyre	baau-tāai	爆呔
flatter	gùng-wàih	恭維
flavor, taste	meih-douh	味道
flea	sāt	虱
flee, escape	jáu-naahn	走難
flimsy, feeble	fa-hohk	化學
float	fàuh	浮
floating restaurant	hói-sīn-fóng	海鮮舫
floor	deih-há, deih-báan	地下，地板
floors (in a building)	chàhng	層
flour	mihn-fán	麵粉
flourishing, prosperous	wohng	旺
flow	làuh	流
flower	fā	花
flower garden	fā-yún	花園
flower market	fā-síh	花市
flower-pot	fā-pùhn	花盆
fly (n)*	wū-yīng	烏蠅
fly (v)*	fèi	飛
fly-over, over-pass	tìn-kìuh	天橋
flying time	fèi-hàhng sìh-gaan	飛行時間
fog, mist	mouh	霧
folding umbrella	sūk-gwàt-jē	縮骨遮
folk song	màhn-gō	民歌
follow	gàn (jyuh)	跟（住）
food	sihk-maht	食物

fool (n)*	chéun-chòih	蠢材
foolish, stupid	sòh	傻
foot (measure)	chek	尺
foot (part of the body)	geuk	腳
foot brake	geuk-jai	腳掣
foot-bridge	hàahng-yàhn tìn-kìuh	行人天橋
for, for the sake of	waih	為
for example	laih-yùh, pei-yùh	例如，譬如
for instance, if supposing	pei-yùh, pei-yùh-wah	譬如，譬如話
for rent, to let	chēut-jòu	出租
force, compel	bīk	迫
force, supervise	gāam (jyuh)	監（住）
forceps	kím	鉗
forehead	ngaahk-tàuh	額頭
foreign country	ngoih-gwok	外國
foreigner	(fàan) gwái-lóu, ngoih-gwok yàhn	（番）鬼佬，外國人
forest	sàm-làhm	森林
forget	m̀-gei-dāk	唔記得
forgive, excuse	yùhn-leuhng	原諒
fork	chā	叉
form (for information)	bíu	表
formal, official	jing-sīk	正式
formal dinner, banquet	jáu-jihk, yin-wuih	酒席，宴會
formal dress	láih-fuhk	禮服
formal visit	baai-fóng	拜訪
formerly, previously	yíh-chìhn, gauh-sìh	以前，舊時
fortunate, lucky	hóu-chói	好彩
forward (a letter)	jyún	轉
found	gin-lahp, chit-lahp	建立，設立
foundation	gèi-chó	基礎
foundation-fund	gèi-gàm	基金
fountain	pan-séui-chìh, pan-chyùhn	噴水池，噴泉

fountain pen	mahk-séui-bāt	墨水筆
four	sei	四
fox	wùh-léi	狐狸
fragrant	hèung	香
France	Faat-gwok	法國
frank, frankly	táan-baahk	坦白
frank, outspoken	sēut-jihk	率直
free (not busy)	dāk-hàahn	得閒
free of charge	míhn-fai	免費
freedom, free	jih-yàuh	自由
freezer	bīng-gaak	冰格
freighter	fo-syùhn	貨船
French (language)	Faat-màhn	法文
fresh	sān-sìn	新鮮
fresh water	táahm-séui	淡水
Friday	láih-baai-ńgh	禮拜五
fried noodles	cháau-mihn	炒麵
fried rice	cháau-faahn	炒飯
friend	pàhng-yáuh	朋友
friendly	yáuh-sihn	友善
friendship	yáuh-yìh, yáuh-ngoi	友誼，友愛
frighten	haak	嚇
frightened	haak-chàn	嚇親
frog	chìng-wà	青蛙
from	hái	喺
from afar	lèih-yúhn	離遠
from now on	chùhng-gām-yíh-hauh	從今以後
from time to time	gáu-m̀-gáu, noih-bāt-nói	久唔久，耐不耐
front	chìhn-bihn	前便
front door	chìhn-mún	前門
frown	jau-mèih-tàuh	皺眉頭
frozen food	gāp-dung sihk-maht	急凍食物
fruit	sāang-gwó	生果

46

fruit juice	gwó-jāp	果汁
fry	jīn	煎
fry (stir)	cháau	炒
frying-pan	pìhng-dái-wohk	平底鑊
fulfill one's duty	jeuhn jaak-yahm	盡責任
full (stomach)	báau	飽
full, filled	múhn	滿
full house	múhn-joh	滿座
full name	sing-mìhng	姓名
full of life, active	sāang-máahng	生猛
fun, pleasure	hōi-sām	開心
fund	gìng-fai	經費
funeral	sōng-láih	喪禮
funeral home	ban-yìh-gún	殯儀館
funny, ridiculous	hóu-siu	好笑
fur	pèih-chóu	皮草
furlough	yàu-ga	休假
furniture	gā-sì	傢俬
furthermore, moreover	yìh-ché	而且
future	jèung-lòih	將來
future prospect	chìhn-tòuh	前途

G

gab	ngāp	噏
gall stone	dáam-sehk	膽石
gamble	dóu-chín	賭錢
gambler	laahn-dóu-gwái, dóu-tòuh	爛賭鬼，賭徒
game, recreation	yàuh-hei	遊戲
garbage	laahp-saap	垃圾
garbage can	laahp-saap-túng	垃圾桶

garden	fā-yún	花園
gardener	fā-wòhng	花王
gas	hei-tái	氣體
gasoline	dihn-yàuh	電油
gasoline station	yàuh-jaahm	油站
gather up (things)	jāp-màaih	執埋
general, common	póu-pin, póu-tùng	普遍，普通
general condition of ...	daaih-ji ge chìhng-yìhng	大致嘅情形
general idea	daaih-ji ge yi-si	大致嘅意思
general manager	júng-gìng-léih	總經理
generator	faat-dihn-gēi	發電機
generous	fut-lóu, hóng-koi	闊佬，慷慨
gentle	wān-yàuh, chìh-chèuhng	溫柔，慈祥
gentleman	sān-sí	紳士
geography	deih-léih	地理
German (language)	Dāk-màhn	德文
Germany	Dāk-gwok	德國
get, fetch	ló	攞
get, receive	sàu-dóu, dāk-dou	收到，得到
get along	sèung-chyú	相處
get off (a train, bus, etc.)	lohk chè	落車
get on (a train or bus, etc.)	séuhng chè	上車
get on a boat	séuhng syùhn	上船
get on a plane	séuhng fēi-gèi, séuhng gèi	上飛機，上機
get out	chēut-heui	出去
get up	héi-sàn	起身
ghost, devil	gwái	鬼
gift, present	láih-maht	禮物
ginger	gēung	薑
girl	néuih-jái	女仔
give	béi	俾
give (a present)	sung	送

give (disease to someone else)	chyùhn-yihm	傳染
give a name	héi-méng, gói-méng	起名，改名
give a party	chéng-haak	請客
give a speech	yín-góng	演講
give an example	géui-laih	舉例
give birth	sāang	生
give New Year's greetings	baai-nìhn	拜年
glad to, a pleasure to	lohk-yi	樂意
glass	bō-lēi	玻璃
glass for drinks	bō-lèi-būi, séui-būi	玻璃杯，水杯
glasses (optical)	ngáahn-géng	眼鏡
gleam, flash	sím	閃
globe	deih-kàuh-yìh	地球儀
gloves	sáu-maht, sáu-tou	手襪，手套
glue	gàau-séui	膠水
glue on, stick on	nìhm, tip	黏，貼
glutinous rice	noh-máih	糯米
go	heui	去
go away	ché, jáu	扯，走
go for a honeymoon	douh maht-yuht	度蜜月
go off from work, get out of work	fong-gùng	放工
go out	chēut-gāai, chēut-heui	出街，出去
go to bed	fan-gaau	瞓覺
go to class	séuhng tòhng	上堂
go to school	fàan-hohk	番學
go to work	fàan-gùng	番工
go up	séuhng	上
go upstairs	séuhng láu	上樓
goal, objective	muhk-bīu	目標
God	Seuhng-dai, Tìn-jyú	上帝，天主
god, gods	sàhn	神
going down-hill	lohk che-lóu	落斜路

gold	gām	金
gold chain	gām-lín	金鍊
gold color	gām-sīk	金色
goldfish	gām-yú	金魚
golf	gō-yih-fū-kàuh	哥爾夫球
gong	lòh	鑼
good (obedient)	gwàai	乖
good night	jóu-táu	早唞
good, well, all right	hóu	好
good-looking	hóu-yéung, leng	好樣，靚
goods	fo, fo-maht	貨，貨物
gorgeous	ga-sai	架勢
gossip (n)*	sih-fēi	是非
gossip (v)*	góng sih-fēi	講是非
got wet by rain	dahp-sāp	揞濕
got, attained	dāk-dóu	得到
govern	túng-jih, gún-jih	統治，管治
government	jing-fú	政府
Governor of Hong Kong	Góng-dūk	港督
grab, snatch	chéung	搶
grade, mark	fān (sou)	分（數）
gradually (development)	jihm-jím, juhk-jím	漸漸，逐漸
graduate	bāt-yihp	畢業
graduate school	yìhn-gau-yún	研究院
grammar	màhn-faat	文法
grand, magnificent	wàhng-wáih	宏偉
grant, endow	chi	賜
granulated sugar	sā-tòhng	沙糖
grap, hold of	jūk-jyuh	捉住
grape	pòuh-tàih-jí, tàih-jí	菩提子，提子
grasp, assurance	bá-ngāak	把握
grass	chóu	草
grasshopper	ja-máang	蚱蜢

grateful	gám-gīk	感激
gravy	jāp	汁
gray (color)	fūi-sīk	灰色
greasy	yàuh-leih	油膩
great (of people)	wáih-daaih	偉大
great, big	daaih	大
greedy	tàam-sàm	貪心
green (color)	luhk-sīk, luhk	綠色，綠
green wrasse	chèng-yì	青衣
grilled pork	chā-sìu	叉燒
grind	mòh	磨
groceries	jaahp-fo	雜貨
grocery store	jaahp-fo-póu	雜貨舖
ground	deih-há	地下
ground floor	deih-há, làuh-hah	地下，樓下
ground pepper	wùh-jìu-fán	胡椒粉
group, organization	tyùhn-tái	團體
grow, plant	jung	種
grow a beard	làuh sōu	留鬚
grow up	jéung-daaih	長大
grumble	ngàhm-ngàhm-chàhm-chàhm	吟吟沉沉
Guangzhou	Gwóng-jàu	廣州
guarantee	dāam-bóu	擔保
guarantor	dāam-bóu-yàhn	擔保人
guess, think	gú	估
guest	yàhn-haak	人客
guest (polite form)	lòih-bān	來賓
guide (n)*	douh-yàuh	導遊
guide (v)*	líhng-douh	領導
guitar	git-tā	結他
gum	ngàh-yuhk	牙肉
gun, rifle, pistol	chēung	槍

gutter (for dirty water)	hāang-kèuih	坑渠
gymnasium	tái-yuhk gún	體育館

H

habit, custom	jaahp-gwaan	習慣
hair (fine)	mòuh	毛
hair (on the head)	tàuh-faat	頭髮
hair style	faat-yìhng	髮型
hair stylist	faat-yìhng-sī	髮型師
haircut (for lady)	jín tàuh-faat	剪頭髮
haircut (for man)	fēi-faat	飛髮
hairdresser, barber	léih-faat-sī, fēi-faat-lóu	理髮師，飛髮佬
hairpin	faat-gíp, déng-gíp	髮夾，頂夾
half	yāt-bun	一半
hallway, corridor	jáu-lòhng, jáu-lóng	走廊
ham	fó-téui	火腿
hammer (n)*	chéui, chèuih-jái	鎚，鎚仔
hammer (v)*	dahp	揼
hand	sáu	手
hand bag	sáu-dói	手袋
hand brake	sáu-jai	手掣
hand over to	gàau-béi	交俾
hand to, pass	daih	遞
handicraft	sáu-gùng-ngaih	手工藝
handkerchief	sáu-gān-jái	手巾仔
handle (a tough problem or person)	deui-fuh	對付
handsome	yìng-jeun	英俊
handwork	sáu-gùng	手工
hang	gwa	掛

hang to dry	lohng	晾
hang up	gwa-héi	掛起
hanger (for clothes)	yī-gá	衣架
happen, occur	faat-sāng	發生
happy	hòi-sàm, fùn-héi	開心，歡喜
happy, happiness	faai-lohk	快樂
happy birthday	sàang-yaht faai-lohk	生日快樂
happy New Year	sàn-nìhn faai-lohk	新年快樂
hard (quality)	ngaahng	硬
hard, tough	ngàhn	韌
hard-working	kàhn-lihk	勤力
hardship, difficulty	gāan-nàahn	艱難
harm (n)*	hoih-chyu	害處
harm, injure	sèung-hoih	傷害
harmonica	háu-kàhm	口琴
harmony	wòh-hàaih	和諧
harp	syu-kàhm	豎琴
has a happy look	hóu-siu-yuhng	好笑容
hat	móu	帽
hate, desire	hahn	恨
have, has	yáuh	有
have a cold	sèung-fùng	傷風
have a dream	faat-mùhng	發夢
have a fever	faat-sìu	發燒
have a fire	fó-jūk	火燭
have a holiday	fong-ga	放假
have a law suit	dá gùn-sì	打官司
have a meeting	hòi-wúi	開會
have a re-union	tyùhn-jeuih	團聚
have a sad look	sàuh-yuhng-múhn-mihn	愁容滿面
have a shock (mentally)	sauh chi-gīk	受刺激
have a stool	daaih-bihn	大便

have good memory	hóu gei-sing	好記性
have indigestion	sihk-jaih-jó, m̀-siu-fa	食滯咗，唔消化
have not	móuh	冇
have the tooth filled	bóu-ngàh	補牙
have to, must	yiu	要
he, she, him, her	kéuih	佢
head	tàuh	頭
head of a team	deuih-jéung	隊長
head of the family	gā-jéung	家長
headache	tàuh-tung	頭痛
headline	bīu-tàih	標題
headmaster	haauh-jéung	校長
headphones	tèng-túng	聽筒
health	sàn-tái, gihn-hōng	身體，健康
hear, heard	téng	聽
hearing	ting-gok	聽覺
heat	yiht	熱
heart disease, heart attack	sàm-johng-behng	心臟病
heart, mind	sàm	心
heart-broken	sèung-sàm	傷心
heartbeat	sàm-tiu	心跳
heater (for heating water)	yiht-séui-lòuh	熱水爐
heaven	tìn-tòhng	天堂
heavy	chúhng	重
heel	geuk-jāang	腳踭
hell	deih-yuhk	地獄
hello! (on the phone)	Wái!	喂
help	bòng, bòng-joh	幫，幫助
help out	gwàan-jiu	關照
Help! Help!	Gau-mehng a!	救命呀
hemorrhoids	jih-chōng	痔瘡
hen	gāi-ná	雞乸
hepatitis	gōn-yìhm	肝炎

here	nī-douh	呢喥
hereafter, thereafter	yíh-hauh	以後
hero	yìng-hùhng	英雄
hero (of a play)	jyú-gok	主角
heroin	hói-lok-yīng	海洛英
heroine	néuih-jyú-gok	女主角
hiccup, hiccough	dá-sī-īk	打思噎
hide	nēi, nēi-màaih	匿，匿埋
high, tall	gòu	高
high heel shoes	gòu-jàang hàaih	高踭鞋
highway	gùng-louh	公路
hill, mountain	sāan	山
hill-side	sāan-bīn	山邊
hinder, stop	jó-jí	阻止
hire (a person)	chéng	請
his, her	kéuih ge	佢嘅
history	lihk-sí	歷史
hit	dá	打
hit the bull's eye	dá-jung	打中
hobby	si-hou	嗜好
hold	jā	揸
hold (in one's arm)	póuh	抱
hold (in one's hand)	nīng-jyuh	拎住
hold (meeting, etc.)	géui-hàhng	舉行
hole	lūng	窿
holiday	ga-kèih	假期
home	ngūk-kéi	屋企
home for aged people	lóuh-yàhn-yún	老人院
homeless	mòuh-gā-hó-gwài	無家可歸
homework	gùng-fo	功課
honest	lóuh-saht	老實
honey	math-tòhng, fùng-maht	蜜糖，蜂蜜
Hong Kong	Hèung-góng	香港

Hong Kong dollar	Góng-jí, Góng-ngán, Góng-baih	港紙，港銀，港幣
Honolulu	Tàahn-hēung-sāan	檀香山
honor (n)*	wìhng-yuh	榮譽
honor (v)* with one's presence	séung-mín	賞面
hope, expect	hèi-mohng	希望
horse	máh	馬
horse race	choi-máh	賽馬
hospital	yī-yún	醫院
hospital fee	jyuh-yún-fai	住院費
host, master	jyú-yán, jyú-yàhn	主人
hostess	néuih jyú-yán	女主人
hot	yiht	熱
hot, high temperature	yiht	熱
hot, spicy	laaht	辣
hot sauce	laaht (jiu)-jeung	辣（椒）醬
hot spring	wān-chyùhn	溫泉
hot tempered	ngok	惡
hot water	yiht-séui	熱水
hotel	jáu-dim	酒店
hour	jùng-tàuh	鐘頭
house	ngūk	屋
housemate	tùhng-ngūk	同屋
how?	dím, dím-yéung	點，點樣
how long? (time)	géi-nói	幾耐
how many, how much	géi-dō	幾多
however...	bāt-gwo...	不過……
huge	geuih-daaih	巨大
human being	yàhn-leuih	人類
human nature	yàhn-sing	人性
humble	hìm-hèui	謙虛
humorous	yāu-mahk	幽默
hundred	baak	百

hungry	tóuh-ngoh	肚餓
hunt	dá-lihp	打獵
hunter	lihp-yàhn	獵人
hurry up!	faai-dī lā!	快啲啦！
hurt, ache	tung	痛
hurt, injure	sauh-sēung	受傷
husband	jeuhng-fū	丈夫
husband (colloq.)	lóuh-gùng	老公
hustling and bustling	yiht-naauh	熱鬧
hut	muhk-ngūk	木屋
hydrofoil	séui-yihk-syùhn	水翼船
hymn, doxology	jaan-méih-sī, sing-sī	讚美詩，聖詩
hypnotize	chèui-mìhn	催眠

I

I, me	ngóh	我
ice	bīng	冰
ice water	bīng-séui	冰水
ice-cream	syut-gōu	雪糕
ice-cream cone	tìhm-túng	甜筒
idea	jyú-yi	主意
ideal	léih-séung	理想
idiom	sìhng-yúh	成語
idle, lazy	láahn-sáan	懶散
if, in case	yùh-gwó	如果
if only	jí-yiu	只要
ignore	fāt-sih	忽視
ill	behng, m̀-syù-fuhk	病，唔舒服
illiterate	màhn-màahng	文盲
illness	behng	病
imagination	sàm-léih jok-yuhng	心理作用

imagination (creative power)	séung-jeuhng-lihk	想像力
imagine	séung-jeuhng	想像
imitate, imitation	mòuh-fóng	模仿
immediately, at once	jīk-hāak	即刻
immigrant	yìh-màhn	移民
immoral	móuh douh-dāk	冇道德
impatient, be anxious	sàm-gàp	心急
imperialism	dai-gwok-jyú-yih	帝國主義
import	wahn yahp-háu	運入口
import and export	chēut-yahp-háu	出入口
import commodity	yahp-háu-fo	入口貨
importance	juhng-yiu-sing	重要性
important	juhng-yiu	重要
impossible	móuh-hó-nàhng, m̀-hó-nàhng	冇可能，唔可能
impression	yan-jeuhng	印象
improper	m̀-sàam-m̀-sei-ge	唔三唔四嘅
improved	yáuh jeun-bouh	有進步
in	hái...	喺……
in vain	baahk-baahk	白白
in a hurry	chùng-mòhng	匆忙
in a low voice	sai-sēng	細聲
in a moment	yāt-jahn-gāan	一陣間
in a short time	dyún-kèih	短期
in a word	júng-jì	總之
in back of	hauh-bihn	後便
in case	maahn-yāt	萬一
in detail	chèuhng-sai	詳細
in detail, carefully	jí-sai	仔細
in disorder	lyuhn	亂
in fact	sih-saht-seuhng	事實上
in front of	chìhn-bihn	前便
in general	daaih-ji-seuhng	大致上

in good spirits	hóu jìng-sàhn	好精神
in order to	waih-jó	為咗
in other words	wuhn-yìhn-jì	換言之
in style	hìng	興
in style, stylish	sìh-mōu	時髦
in summary	júng-jì	總之
in that case	gám	噉
in the middle	jùng-gàan	中間
in the past	gwo-heui	過去
in the process, carry out	jeun-hàhng	進行
in the same boat	tùhng-behng-sèung-lìhn	同病相憐
in the world	sai-gaai-seuhng	世界上
incense stick	hēung	香
inch	chyun	吋
incinerator	fàhn-fa-lòuh	焚化爐
include	bāau-kwut, bāau-màaih	包括，包埋
income	sàu-yahp, yahp-sīk	收入，入息
increase	jāng-gà	增加
indecisive	sàm-daaih-sàm-sai	心大心細
India	Yan-douh	印度
indicate	jí-sih, hín-sih	指示，顯示
indigestible	nàahn-sìu-fa	難消化
indirect, indirectly	gaan-jip	間接
individual	go-yàhn	個人
industrious, diligent	kàhn-lihk	勤力
industry	gùng-yihp	工業
inexpensive	pèhng	平
inflammation	faat-yìhm	發炎
influence, affect	yíng-héung	影響
influenza	làuh-hàhng-sing gám-mouh	流行性感冒
inform, notify	tùng-jì	通知

informal	fèi jing-sĩk	非正式
information desk	sēun-mahn-chyu	詢問處
influenced by	sauh...yíng-héung	受⋯⋯影響
infuriated	fó-gwán	火滾
inhale	kāp	吸
initiate, launch (a campaign)	faat-héi	發起
injection	dá-jām	打針
ink	mahk-séui	墨水
innate, be born with	tìn-sàang	天生
inquire	dá-ting	打聽
insect	kwān-chùhng	昆蟲
inside	léuih-bihn, yahp-bihn	裏便，入便
inside story	noih-mohk	內幕
insist	haih-yiu	係要
insistently	yāt-méi	一味
insomnia	sāt-mìhn	失眠
inspect, check, examine	gím-chàh	檢查
install	jòng, gaau	裝，較
instant	jĩk-hāak	即刻
instant coffee	jĩk-yùhng ga-fē	即溶咖啡
instant noodle	jĩk-sihk-mihn	即食麵
instruct, direct	jí-sih	指示
instruct, tell	gàau-daai	交帶
instruction, order	fàn-fu	吩咐
instrument (musical)	ngohk-hei	樂器
insult	móuh-yuhk	侮辱
insurance	yin-sō, bóu-hím	燕梳，保險
intention	yuhng-yi	用意
intentionally	dahk-dāng, gu-yi	特登，故意
interest	hing-cheui	興趣
interest (on capital)	leih-sĩk	利息
interested in	deui...yáuh hing-cheui	對⋯⋯有興趣
interesting	yáuh-cheui	有趣

interesting, cute	dāk-yi	得意
interfere, intrude	gòn-sip	干涉
interior design	sāt-noih chit-gai	室內設計
intern doctor	saht-jaahp yī-sāng	實習醫生
international	gwok-jai	國際
international airport	gwok-jai gèi-chèuhng	國際機場
interpreter, translator	chyùhn-yihk-yùhn, fàan-yihk-yùhn	傳譯員，翻譯員
intersection	sahp-jih louh-háu	十字路口
interview	fóng-mahn	訪問
interview (for a job)	mihn-síh	面試
intestine	chéung	腸
introduce	gaai-siuh	介紹
invade, invasion	chàm-faahn	侵犯
invent, invention	faat-mìhng	發明
investigate	chàh, diuh-chàh	查，調查
invitation card	chéng-típ, chéng-tip	請帖
invite	chéng	請
involve	hìn-sip	牽涉
involve others (into trouble)	tòh-leuih	拖累
iron	tit	鐵
iron gate	tit-jaahp	鐵閘
ironing	tong-sāam	熨衫
ironing board	tong-sāam báan	熨衫板
is, are	haih	係
island	dóu	島
issue, publish	chēut	出
it all depends...	tái...làih-chau lā!	睇……嚟湊啦！
it doesn't matter	móuh-māt-só-waih	冇乜所謂
it is a long story	yāt-yìhn-nàahn-jeuhn	一言難盡
it is right	móuh cho	冇錯
it is someone's time to take his turn	lèuhn-dou...	輪到……
it's a deal	yāt-yìhn-wàih-dihng	一言為定

Italy	Yi-daaih-leih	意大利
itchy	hàhn	痕
itinerary	hàhng-chìhng (bíu)	行程（表）
ivory	jeuhng-ngàh	象牙
ivy	chèuhng-chēun-tàhng	長春籐

J

jacket	ngoih-tou	外套
jade	yúk	玉
jail	chóh-gāam	坐監
jam	gwó-jeung	果醬
January	Yāt-yuht	一月
Japan	Yaht-bún	日本
jaw	ngàh-gaau	牙較
jazz music	jeuk-sih yàm-ngohk	爵士音樂
jealous	douh-geih	妒忌
jeans	ngàuh-jái-fu	牛仔褲
jerky, trembling	jan	震
Jesus	Yèh-sōu	耶穌
jet plane	pan-seh-gēi	噴射機
jetfoil	fèi-chèuhng-syùhn	飛翔船
jewel, jewelry	sáu-sīk	首飾
jewelry box	sáu-sīk-sēung	首飾箱
job, work	gùng-jok	工作
Jockey Club	Máh-wúi	馬會
jockey	kèh-sì	騎師
jog	páau-bouh	跑步
join, take part in	gā-yahp	加入
joint	gwāan-jit	關節
joke	siu-wá	笑話
joke (banter)	góng-síu	講笑

jolt	chok	刜
journey	léuih-hàhng	旅行
joy	fùn-héi, faai-lohk	歡喜，快樂
judge (n)* (in a contest)	pìhng-pun	評判
judge (n)* (in a court)	faat-gùn	法官
judge (v)*	pun-dyun	判斷
juice, sauce	jāp	汁
July	Chāt-yuht	七月
jump	tiu	跳
June	Luhk-yuht	六月
junk (ship)	fàahn-syùhn	帆船
jury (in a court)	pùih-sám-tyùhn	陪審團
just a moment, please	chéng dáng-yāt-dáng	請等一等
just a moment ago	jing-wah, jeng-wah	正話
just a while ago	tàuh-sìn	頭先
just about to	jing-joih-yiu	正在要
just at the moment of	jing-joih...gó-jahn-sí	正在……嗰陣時
just, fair	gùng-pìhng	公平
just, only	jí-haih	只係
justice	gùng-jing	公正

K

keep one's eye on	hāu-jyuh	吼住
keep, save	làuh-fàan	留番
kerosene	fó-séui	火水
kettle	chàh-bōu	茶煲
key	só-sìh	鎖匙
kick	tek	踢
kid	sai-mān-jái	細蚊仔
kidnap	bóng-ga	綁架

63

kidney	sáhn, yìu	腎，腰
kill	saat	殺
kilogram	chìn-hàk	千克
kilometre	gùng-léih	公里
kind, good hearted	hóu-sàm	好心
kind, merciful	wòh-ngói, yàhn-chìh	和藹，仁慈
kind, sort	júng	種
king	gwok-wòhng	國王
kiss (v)*	sek	錫
kitchen	chyùh-fóng, chèuih-fóng	廚房
kite	jí-yíu	紙鳶
kleenex	jí-gàn	紙巾
knee	sāt (tàuh)	膝（頭）
kneel	gwaih	跪
knife	dōu	刀
knit	jīk	織
knock	hāau	敲
knock on a door	paak-mùhn, hāau-mùhn	拍門，敲門
know, become acquainted with	sīk	識
know, know about	jì, jì-dou	知，知道
know how to	sīk	識
know something well	suhk-sīk	熟識
knowledge	jì-sìk	知識
Korea	Hòhn-'gwok	韓國
Kowloon	Gáu-lùhng	九龍
Kowloon Tong	Gáu-lùhng-tòhng	九龍塘

L

laboratory	fa-yihm-sāt	化驗室
laboratory technician	fa-yihm-sī	化驗師

laboratory fee	fa-yihm-fai	化驗費
lack of, short of	kyut-faht	缺乏
ladder	tāi	梯
lady	néuih-sih	女士
lake	wùh	湖
lamb	yèuhng	羊
lamb chop	yèuhng-pá	羊扒
lamp, light	dāng	燈
lampshade	dāng-jaau	燈罩
land	deih	地
land (as an airplance)	gong-lohk	降落
landlord (owner of house)	ngūk-jyú	屋主
landlord (owner of land)	deih-jyú	地主
landscape, scenery	fùng-gíng	風景
language	yúh-yìhn	語言
lantern	dāng-lùhng	燈籠
large size	daaih-máh	大碼
large, big, older	daaih	大
last (in time or order)	jeui-hauh	最後
last night	kàhm-máahn	噚晚
last time	seuhng-chi	上次
last week	seuhng go láih-baai	上個禮拜
last year	gauh-nín, gauh-nìhn	舊年
late, later	chìh	遲
late at night	yeh	夜
Latin	Lāai-dīng-màhn	拉丁文
laugh, laugh at	siu	笑
launch	yàuh-téhng-hó	遊艇河
laundry	sái-yī-póu	洗衣舖
lavatory	chi-só	廁所
law	faat-leuht	法律
lawn-mower	jín-chóu-gèi	剪草機
lawyer	leuht-sī	律師

lay, put	fong	放
lay down	fan-dāi	瞓低
lazy	láahn	懶
lead (metal)	yùhn	鉛
leader	líhng-jauh	領袖
leaf	syuh-yihp	樹葉
leafy vegetable	choi	菜
lean (meat)	sau	瘦
lean against	ngàai	挨
lean to one side, be tilted askew	jāk	側
learn, study	hohk	學
learning	hohk-mahn	學問
lease	jòu-yeuk	租約
least	jeui-síu	最少
leather	pèih	皮
leave, depart	lèih-hòi	離開
leave (v)*	jáu	走
leave, vacation	ga-kèih	假期
leave a message	làuh háu-seun	留口訊
leave a note	làuh jih-tìuh	留字條
leave hospital	chēut-yún	出院
leave work at lunch time	fong ngaan-jau	放晏晝
left	jó	左
leg	geuk	腳
legal	hahp-faat	合法
legal right	kyùhn-leih	權利
legend	chyùhn-syut	傳説
lemon	nìhng-mūng	檸檬
lend to	je...béi	借……俾
length	chèuhng-douh	長度
less	síu-dī	少啲
less and less	yuht-làih-yuht-síu	越嚟越少

lessen, reduce	gáam-síu	減少
lest	míhn-dāk	免得
let, allow	dáng	等
let loose, put	fong	放
letter	seun	信
letter paper	seun-jí	信紙
lettuce	sāang-choi	生菜
level, even, flat	pìhng	平
liberate, liberation	gáai-fong	解放
library	tòuh-syù-gún	圖書館
library card	je-syù-jing	借書證
licence (commercial)	pàaih-jiu, jāp-jiu	牌照，執照
lie	góng daaih-wah	講大話
lid, cover	goi	蓋
lie down	fan-dài	瞓低
life	sāng-mihng	生命
lift	tòih-héi, géui-héi	抬起，舉起
life insurance	yàhn-sauh yin-sō, yàhn-sauh bóu-hím	人壽燕梳，人壽保險
life-guard	gau-sāng-yùhn	救生員
life-jacket	gau-sāng-yī	救生衣
light	gwòng-sin, dāng-gwòng	光線，燈光
light (not heavy)	hēng	輕
light bulb	dāng-dáam	燈膽
light color	chín-sīk	淺色
light music	hìng yàm-ngohk	輕音樂
light switch	dāng-jai	燈掣
light up	dím	點
lighten (burden, responsibility)	gáam-hēng	減輕
lighter	dá-fó-gèi	打火機
lighthouse	dāng-taap	燈塔
lightly (gently)	hehng-hēng	輕輕

lightning	sím-dihn	閃電
lightning-rod	beih-lèuih-jām	避雷針
like, be fond of	jùng-yi	鍾意
like, similar to	chíh	似
lily	baak-hahp (fā)	百合（花）
limited	yáuh-haahn	有限
limitless	mòuh-haahn	無限
line	hòhng	行
linguist	yúh-yìhn-hohk-gā	語言學家
linguistics	yúh-yìhn-hohk	語言學
link	lìhn-jip	連接
lion	sì-jí	獅子
lip	(háu) sèuhn	（口）唇
lipstick	seuhn-gōu	唇膏
liquid	yihk-tái	液體
list (of items)	chīng-dāan	清單
list, bill	dāan	單
listen to	tèng	聽
litter-bin	fai-maht-sēung	廢物箱
little, few	síu	少
live in a school dormitory	gei-sūk	寄宿
live, stay	jyuh	住
liver	gōn	肝
live, stay in	jyuh-hái	住喺
living room	haak-tēng	客廳
living standard	sàng-wuht séui-jéun	生活水準
lizard	yìhm-sé	鹽蛇
loan (money)	je-fún	借款
loath to, be reluctant to	m̀-sé-dāk	唔捨得
local	bún-deih	本地
located at, in or on	hái	喺
location	deih-dím	地點
lock	só	鎖

68

locomotive	fó-chè-tàuh	火車頭
logical, right	yáuh douh-léih	有道理
London	Lèuhn-dēun	倫敦
lone	gū-duhk	孤獨
long	chèuhng	長
long (time)	noih	耐
long-distance call	chèuhng-tòuh dihn-wá	長途電話
long-sleeved	chèuhng-jauh	長袖
look, read	tái	睇
look afar	mohng	望
look after, take care of	jiu-liuh, jiu-gu	照料，照顧
look downward	dāp-dài (go)-tàuh	嗒低（個）頭
look for, call on	wán	搵
look for a job	wán-gùng	搵工
look like	chíh, hóu-chíh	似，好似
look upward	dāam-gòu go tàuh	擔高（個）頭
looks familiar	mihn-sihn	面善
loose	sùng	鬆
loose, scattered	sáan	散
Lord's prayer	kèih-tóu-màhn	祈禱文
Los Angeles	Lòh-sáang	羅省
lose	m̀-gin-jó	唔見咗
lose (as a game)	syù	輸
lose (in business)	siht-bún	蝕本
lose (in gambling)	syù-chín	輸錢
lose face	dìu-gá	丟架
loss, lose	syún-sāt	損失
lost	sāt-jó, móuh-jó	失咗，無咗
lots of	hóu-dō	好多
lost one's way	dohng-sāt-louh	蕩失路
lotus	hòh-fā	荷花
loud, loudly	daaih-sēng	大聲
lovable	hó-oi	可愛

love	ngoi, ngoi-sàm	愛，愛心
love (between lovers)	ngoi-chìhng, nyún-ngoi	愛情，戀愛
love-letter	chìhng-seun	情信
love story	ngoi-chìhng gu-sih	愛情故事
lover	ngoi-yàhn, chìhng-yàhn	愛人，情人
low	dài	低
low, short	ngái	矮
loyal	jùng-sàm	忠心
luck	wahn-hei	運氣
lucky	hóu-chói	好彩
lucky, happy	hahng-wahn, yáuh fūk-hei	幸運，有福氣
lucky money (in a red envelope)	laih-sih	利是
lunar calendar	gauh-lihk, yàm-lihk, nùhng-lihk	舊曆，陰曆，農曆
lunch	ngaan-jau	晏晝
lung	fai	肺

M

M. A. or M. S.	sehk-sih	碩士
M. C. (master of ceremony)	sì-yìh	司儀
Macau	Ngou-mún, Ou-mún	澳門
macaroni	tùng-sàm-fán	通心粉
machine	gèi-hei	機器
machine-gun	gēi-gwàan-chēung	機關槍
magazine	jaahp-ji	雜誌
maid servant	néuih gùng-yàhn	女工人
mail, send	gei	寄
mailbox (for mailing letter)	yàuh-túng	郵筒
mailbox (for receiving mail)	seun-sēung, yàuh-sēung	信箱，郵箱

mailman, postman	yàuh-chāai	郵差
main	jeui jyú-yiu	最主要
maintain, support	wàih-chìh	維持
major	juhng-yiu	重要
majority	dò-sou, daaih-dò-sou	多數，大多數
make (something)	jouh	做
make, cause	lihng	令
make a date or appointment	yeuk	約
make a draft	héi-góu	起稿
make a fortune	faat-chòih	發財
make a knot	dá-lit	打結
make a living	wán-sihk	搵食
make a noise	héung	響
make a phone call	dá dihn-wá	打電話
make a reservation	dehng	訂
make a turn	jyun-wāan	轉彎
make change	jáau-juhk	找贖
make coffee	chùng ga-fē	沖咖啡
make decision	hah kyut-sàm	下決心
make ends meet	jàu-jyún	周轉
make into	jouh-sìhng	做成
make out a list	hōi-dāan	開單
make profit	jaahn	賺
make public, open	gùng-hòi	公開
make tea	chùng chàh	沖茶
make up (in studying)	bóu-jaahp	補習
make use of	leih-yuhng	利用
make war	dá-jeung	打仗
male	nàahm	男
malodorous, ill smelling	chau	臭
man	nàahm-yán	男人
man-made	yàhn-jouh	人造
manageable	gàau-dāk-dihm	攪得掂

management, manage	gún-léih	管理
manager	gìng-léih	經理
Mandarin	Póu-tùng-wá	普通話
Mandarin duck	yūn-yēung	鴛鴦
Mandarin orange	gām	柑
mantis	tòhng-lòhng	螳螂
manufacture	jai-jouh	製造
manuscript	góu	稿
many	hóu-dò	好多
map	deih-tòuh	地圖
marijuana	daaih-màh	大麻
March	Sàam-yuht	三月
mark, stain	wū-jīk	污漬
mark, sign	gei-houh	記號
market	gāai-síh	街市
marry, get married	git-fān	結婚
mask	mihn-geuih	面具
mask (for doctors or nurses)	háu-jaau	口罩
mass (in Catholic Church)	nèih-saat	彌撒
Mass Transit Railway	deih-tit	地鐵
master (opp. of apprentice)	sī-fú	師傅
master, employer	jyú-yán, sih-táu	主人，事頭
mat	jehk	蓆
match (can be compared with)	paak-dāk-jyuh	拍得住
match (fire stick)	fó-cháai, fó-chàaih	火柴
match, competition	béi-choi	比賽
match-maker	mùih-yán	媒人
material	chòih-líu	材料
mathematics	sou-hohk	數學
matriculation	daaih-hohk yuh-fō	大學預料
matter, affair	sih	事
May	Ńgh-yuht	五月
may, might	waahk-jé	或者

may not, not necessarily	meih-bīt	未必
me, I	ngóh	我
meal	faahn	飯
mean, stingy	gū-hòhn	孤寒
meaning, idea	yi-si, yi-sī	意思
meaningful	yáuh yi-sī	有意思
measles	màh-chán	麻疹
measure	dohk	度
meat	yuhk	肉
medical check-up	gím-chàh sàn-tái	檢查身體
medical fee	yì-yeuhk- fai	醫藥費
medical insurance	yì- lìuh-bóu-hím	醫療保險
medical prescription	yeuhk-fōng	藥方
medicine	yeuhk	藥
medicine charge	yeuhk-fai	藥費
medium size	jùng-máh	中碼
meet, encounter	yuh-dóu	遇到
meet, pick up	jip	接
meet, see	gin	見
meeting, conference	wúi, wuih-yíh	會，會議
melody	syùhn-léut	旋律
melon, gourd	gwā	瓜
melt	yùhng	溶
member	wúi-yùhn	會員
member of a church	gaau-tòuh, gaau-yáuh	教徒，教友
member of a team	deuih-yùhn	隊員
members of one's family	chàn-yàhn	親人
memory (power of the mind)	gei-sing	記性
memory (things, events that is remembered)	wùih-yīk	回憶
men	nàahm-yán	男人
menses, menstruation	yuht-gìng, gìng-kèih	月經，經期
mental hospital	sàhn-gìng behng-yún	神經病院

mention	góng-kahp, tàih-kahp	講及，提及
menu (Chinese food)	choi-páai	菜牌
menu (Western food)	chāan-páai	餐牌
merits, good points	yāu-dím	優點
Merry Christmas	sing-daan faai-lohk	聖誕快樂
messenger	seun-chāai	信差
metal	gām-suhk	金屬
metre	gùng-chek	公尺
meter (in a taxi)	māi-bīu	咪錶
method, way	faat-jí, baahn-faat	法子，辦法
Mexico	Mahk-sāi-gō	墨西哥
microphone	māi	咪
microwave – oven	mèih-bō (guhk)lòuh	微波（焗）爐
middle	jūng-gāan	中間
middle school, high school	jùng-hohk	中學
midnight	bun-yé	半夜
midnight snack	sìu-yé	宵夜
midwife	joh-cháan-sih	助產士
might, may	hó-nàhng	可能
might as well	m̀-ngāam	唔啱
mile	māi, léih	咪，哩
military	gwān-sih	軍事
military officer	gwān-gùn	軍官
milk	ngàuh-náaih	牛奶
milk bottle	náaih-jēun	奶樽
milkshake	náaih-sīk	奶昔
million	baak-maahn	百萬
millionaire	baak-maahn fu-yūng	百萬富翁
mind, feel objection to	gaai-yi	介意
mind, intention	sàm-yi	心意
mind, pay attention	léih	理
mine	ngóh ge	我嘅
minister, pastor	muhk-sī	牧師

mink fur	dìu-péi	貂皮
minority	síu-sou	少數
minute	fàn, fàn-jùng	分，分鐘
miracle	kèih-jīk, sàhn-jīk	奇蹟，神蹟
miraculous, incredible	bāt-hó-sì-yíh ge	不可思議嘅
mirror	geng	鏡
miscarry, abort	síu-cháan	小產
miscellaneous	sāp-sāp-seui-seui	濕濕碎碎
mischievous, naughty	baak-yim, fáan-dáu	百厭，反斗
miserable, sorrowful	cháam	慘
misjudge	gwaai-cho	怪錯
miss, unmarried woman	síu-jé	小姐
missionary, evangelist	chyùhn-douh-yàhn, chyùhn-gaau-sih	傳道人，傳教士
misunderstand, misunderstanding	ngh-wuih	誤會
mix	kàu	溝
mixer	gáau-buhn-gēi	攪拌機
model	mòuh-dahk-yìh	模特兒
model, fine example	mòuh-faahn	模範
modern	yihn-doih, mō-dāng	現代，摩登
modernize, modernization	yihn-doih-fa	現代化
moment	sìh-hāak	時刻
Monday	láih-baai-yāt	禮拜一
money	chín	錢
money in small denomination	sáan-jí, sáan-ngán	散紙，散銀
monk (Buddist)	wòh-séung	和尚
monkey	máh-lāu	馬騮
monopoly	jyùn-leih-kyùh	專利權
month	yuht	月
monthly ticket	yuht-piu,yuht-fēi	月票，月飛
mood, atmosphere	hei-fān	氣氛
moon, moonlight	yuht-gwòng	月光

mooncake	yuht-béng	月餅
moral	douh-dāk	道德
more	dō-dī	多啲
more or less	dō-síu	多少
morning	jìu-tàuh-jóu, jìu-jóu	朝頭早，朝早
morning (forenoon)	seuhng-jau	上晝
Muslim, Islamic	Wùih-gaau	回教
mosquito	mān	蚊
most	jeui	最
most recently	jeui gahn	最近
mother	màh-mā, a-mā	媽媽，阿媽
Mother's Day	móuh-chàn-jit	母親節
motor	mō-dá	摩打
motorcycle	dihn-dāan-chē	電單車
mountain	sāan	山
mouth	háu, jéui	口，嘴
mouthful, puff (of smoke breath, etc.)	daahm	啖
move, arouse	gám-duhng	感動
move, change position	yūk	郁
move (things)	bùn	搬
move house	būn-ngūk	搬屋
movement, campaign	wahn-duhng	運動
movie	dihn-yíng, hei	電影，戲
Mr., gentleman, teacher, husband (polite)	sìn-sàang	先生
Mrs., madam, wife (polite), lady (married)	taai-táai	太太
much, many	dò	多
mud	nàih	泥
muddled, foolish	wùh-tòuh	糊塗
multiply	sìhng	乘
muscle	gēi-yuhk	肌肉

muscle cramp	chàu-gàn	抽筋
museum	bok-maht-gún, bok-maht-yún	博物館，博物院
music	yàm-ngohk	音樂
musician	yàm-ngohk gā	音樂家
mussel	daahm-choi	淡菜
must	yāt-dihng-yiu	一定要
must be, certainly	gáng-haih...lā	梗係⋯⋯啦
mustard paste	gaai-laaht	芥辣
mute	ngá	啞
mutton	yèuhng-yuhk	羊肉
mutually	wuh-sēung	互相
my, mine	ngóh ge	我嘅
myself	ngóh jih-géi	我自己
mysterious	sàhn-bei	神秘

N

nag	lō-sò	囉嗦
nail (n, v) *	dēng	釘
nail-clippers	jí-gaap-kím	指甲鉗
nail-varnish	jí-gaap-yàuh	指甲油
name	méng	名
name card	kāat-pín	卡片
named brand, well known brand	mìhng-pàaih	名牌
napkin	chāan-gān	餐巾
narcissus	séui-sīn (fā)	水仙（花）
narrow	jaak	窄
nasal discharge	beih-tai	鼻涕
nation	gwok-gā, gwok-màhn	國家，國民
nationality	gwok-jihk	國籍
natural	jih-yìhn	自然

natural science	jih-yìhn fō-hohk	自然科學
naturalize (as a citizen)	yahp-jihk	入籍
naturally	jih-yìhn	自然
nature	daaih jih-yìhn	大自然
naughty	yáih, baak-yim	曳，百厭
navy	hói-gwàn	海軍
near	káhn	近
near, close to	gahn-jyuh	近住
neat	kéih-léih	企理
neat & tidy	jíng-chàih	整齊
necessary	bīt-sēui ge	必須嘅
neck	géng	頸
necklace	géng-lín	頸鍊
necktie	léhng-tāai	領呔
necktie clip	tāai-gíp	呔夾
necktie pin	tāai-jām	呔針
need, in need of	sèui-yiu	需要
needle	jām	針
negative (attitude)	sìu-gihk	消極
negative (film)	séung-dái	相底
negro	hāak-yàhn	黑人
neighbour	lèuhn-se	鄰舍
neon sign	gwòng-gún jìu-pàaih, ngàih-hùhng dāng	光管招牌，霓虹燈
nephew	ját	姪
nervous	gán-jèung	緊張
nervous breakdown	sàhn-gìng-sèui-yeuhk	神經衰弱
never before	chùhng-lòih-meih	從來未
new	sàn	新
new style	sàn-sìk	新式
New Territories	Sàn-gaai	新界
New Testament	Sàn-yeuk	新約
New Year's Eve	Chèuih-jihk	除夕

New Year's Eve (Chinese New Year)	Nìhn-sā'ah-máahn, Daaih-chèuih-jihk	年卅晚，大除夕
New York	Náu-yeuk	紐約
newly	sàn-gahn	新近
news	sàn-mán, sàn-màhn	新聞
news agency	tùng-seun-séh	通訊社
news report	sàn-màhn bou-gou	新聞報告
news script	sàn-màhn góu	新聞稿
news, information	sìu-sìk	消息
newspaper	bou-jí	報紙
newsstand	bou-tāan, bou-jí dong	報攤，報紙檔
next (in position)	gaak-lèih	隔籬
next time	hah-chi	下次
next year	chēut-nín, chēut-nìhn	出年
nice	hóu	好
nickname	fā-méng	花名
night	yeh-máahn	夜晚
night club	yeh-júng-wúi	夜總會
night-time	máahn-hāak, máahn-tàuh-hāak	晚黑，晚頭黑
nightmare	ngok-muhng	惡夢
nine	gáu	九
no comment	mòuh-hó-fuhng-gou	無可奉告
no harm to	bāt-fòhng	不妨
no matter..., whether... or	mòuh-leuhn	無論……
no trouble at all	móuh mahn-tàih gé	冇問題嘅
no wonder	m̀-gwaai-dāk	唔怪得
no, not	m̀h	唔
no, not any	móuh	冇
nod one's head	ngahp-táu	揞頭
noise	sēng	聲
noisy	chòuh	嘈
noon	ngaan-jau, jūng-ngh	晏晝，中午

noontime	ngaan-jau	晏晝
normal	jing-sèuhng	正常
north	bāk	北
North America	Bāk-méih-jàu	北美洲
northeast	dūng-bāk	東北
northwest	sāi-bāk	西北
nose	beih (gō)	鼻（哥）
not bad	m̀-cho	唔錯
not feeling well	m̀-haih géi jìng-sàhn	唔係幾精神
not interested in	deui...móuh hing-cheui	對……冇興趣
not necessarily	meih-bīt	未必
not only	m̀-jí	唔止
not until, before	sìn-ji	先至
note	bāt-gei	筆記
note-book	bóu, bāt-gei-bóu	簿，筆記簿
nothing	móuh-yéh	冇嘢
notice (n)*	tùng-gou	通告
notice (v)*	jyu-yi	注意
notice board	bou-gou-báan	佈告板
noun	mìhnng-chìh	名詞
novel	síu-syut	小說
November	Sahp-yāt-yuht	十一月
now, at present, at this time	yìh-gā	而家
number	houh-máh, houh-sou	號碼，號數
numeral	sou-jih	數字
nun (Buddist)	sī-gù	師姑
nun (Catholic)	sāu-néui	修女
nurse	wuh-sih, hōn-wuh	護士，看護
nursery	tok-yìh-só	托兒所
nut	gwó-yàhn	果仁
nutrition, nourishment	yìhng-yéuhng	營養
nylon stocking	sī-maht	絲襪

O dear me! Gosh!	Baih-gā-fó la !	弊傢伙嘞！
o'clock, hour	dím, dím-jùng	點，點鐘
oatmeal	mahk-pín, mahk-pèih	麥片，麥皮
obedient	tèng-wah	聽話
obey	fuhk-chùhng	服從
object, protest	fáan-deui, kong-yíh	反對，抗議
obligation	yih-mouh	義務
observatory	tìn-màhn-tòih	天文台
observe, observation	gùn-chaat	觀察
obstruct, hold up, hinder	jó	阻
obviously	mìhng-mìhng	明明
obviously know	mìhng-ji	明知
occasion (formal)	chèuhng-hahp	場合
occasionally	sìh-bāt-sìh	時不時
occupy	jim	佔
occur, happen	faat-sàng	發生
ocean	hói-yèuhng	海洋
October	Sahp-yuht	十月
odd number	dāan-sou	單數
of course	gáng-haih, dòng-yìhn	梗係，當然
offend	dāk-jeuih, chùng-johng	得罪，衝撞
offer	tàih-gùng	提供
offer money, invest money	chēut-chín	出錢
office	baahn-gūng-sāt, sé-jih-làuh	辦公室，寫字樓
officially, formal	jing-sīk	正式
officiate at a marriage	jing-fān	證婚
officiator at a marriage	jing-fān yàhn	證婚人
often, frequently	sìh-sìh	時時
oh!	ngo! o!	啊！

oil	yàuh	油
oil pitcher	yàuh-jēun	油樽
oil-painting	yàuh-wá	油畫
ointment	yeuhk-gōu	藥膏
okay!	hóu-lā!	好喇！
old (aged)	lóuh	老
old (not new)	gauh	舊
old fashioned	gú-lóuh	古老
old man	baak-yē-gūng	伯爺公
old person (polite form)	lóuh-yàhn-gā	老人家
old style	gú-lóuh, gauh-sīk	古老，舊式
Old Testament	Gauh-yeuk	舊約
old woman	baak-yē-pó	伯爺婆
on (big) sale	daaih gáam-ga	大減價
on behalf of	doih-tai	代替
on day duty	jihk-yaht	值日
on every occasion	múih-fùhng	每逢
on night duty	jihk-yé	值夜
on probation	si-yuhng	試用
once, one time	yāt-chi	一次
one	yāt	一
one of...	...jí-yāt	……之一
one of the best	sóu-yāt-sóu-yih	數一數二
one way	dāan-chìhng	單程
onion	yèuhng-chùng	洋葱
only, no more than	jí-haih, ...jē	只係，……啫
only have	jí-yáuh	只有
open	dá-hòi	打開
open (a book)	kín-hòi	揭開
open, unwrap	chaak-hòi	拆開
open an account in a bank	hòi wuh-háu	開戶口
open fire	hòi-chèung	開槍

open for business (for the first day)	hòi-mohk	開幕
operate	wahn-jok	運作
operation room	sáu-seuht-sāt	手術室
opinion	yi-gin	意見
opium	baahk-fán, ngā-pin	白粉，鴉片
opportunity	gèi-wuih	機會
oppose, object	fáan-deui	反對
opposite (facing)	deui-mihn	對面
optimistic	lohk-gùn	樂觀
or	waahk-jé	或者
or (as a question)	yīk-waahk	抑或
oral examination	háu-síh	口試
orange	cháang	橙
orange (color)	cháang-sīk	橙色
orange juice	cháang-jāp	橙汁
orchestra	gún-yìhn ngohk-déui	管弦樂隊
orchid	làahn-fā	蘭花
order, command	mihng-lihng	命令
order dishes	giu-sung	叫餸
order merchandise	baahn fo	辦貨
ordinarily	pìhng-sìh	平時
ordinary	pìhng-sèuhng	平常
ordinary mail	pìhng-yàuh, pìhng-seun	平郵，平信
ordinary meal	bihn-faahn	便飯
organ	hei-gùn	器官
organ (musical instrument)	fūng-kàhm	風琴
organization	gēi-gwāan, gēi-kàuh	機關，機構
organize	jóu-jīk	組織
origin	héi-yùhn	起源
original	bún-lòih ge	本來嘅
originally	bún-lòih	本來
orphan	gù-yìh	孤兒

orphanage	gù-yìh-yún	孤兒院
other	kèih-tà	其他
other people	yàhn-deih	人哋
otherwise	yùh-gwó-m̀haih	如果唔係
ought to, should	yìng-gòi	應該
ounce	ōn-sí	安士
our	ngóh-deih ge	我哋嘅
out of order (things)	waaih	壞
outer space	taai-hùng	太空
outline	daaih-gòng	大綱
outside	chēut-bihn, ngoih-bihn, chēut-mihn	出便，外便，出面
outspoken	jihk-chèuhng-jihk-tóuh	直腸直肚
oven	guhk-lòuh	焗爐
overcoat	daaih-làu	大褸
overcome	hāak-fuhk	克服
overcrowded, congested	bīk	迫
overdo	gwo-fahn	過分
overseas Chinese	wàh-kìuh	華僑
overslept	fan gwo-lùhng	瞓過龍
overweight	gwo-chúhng	過重
owe	him	欠
owl	māau-tàuh-yìng	貓頭鷹
owner	jyú-yán	主人
oxygen	yéuhng-hei	氧氣
oyster	hòuh	蠔

P

pack	jōng	裝
pack luggage	jāp hàhng-léih	執行李
package, parcel	bāau-gwó	包裹

pedestrian subway	hàahng-yàhn seuih-douh	行人隧道
page	báan, yihp	版，頁
pagoda	taap	塔
painful, sore	tung	痛
paint, put on (paint or color)	yàuh	油
painter	wá-gā	畫家
pair, couple	deui	對
pajamas, pyjamas	seuih-yī	睡衣
palm	sáu-jéung	手掌
panties	sàam-gok-fu	三角褲
pants	chèuhng-fu	長褲
pantyhose	math-fu	襪褲
paper	jí	紙
paper bag	jí-dói	紙袋
paper clip	maahn-jih-gíp	萬字夾
paradise	tìn-tòhng	天堂
paragraph	dyuhn	段
paralysis	màh-bei, táan	麻痺，癱
pardon, excuse	yùhn-leuhng	原諒
parents	fuh-móuh, gā-jéung	父母，家長
Paris	Bā-làih	巴黎
park (n)*	gùng-yún	公園
park a car	paak-chè	泊車
parking lot	tìhng-chè-chèuhng	停車場
parking space	chè-wái	車位
part, a part of	bouh-fahn	部份
participate, join	chāam-gā	參加
particular (of good taste or choice)	góng-gau	講究
partner	pāat-nàh, hahp-fó-yàhn	拍拿，合夥人
pass, cross	gwo	過
pass a set time	gwo-jūng	過鐘

pass by	gìng-gwo	經過
pass flatus	fong-pei	放屁
pass through to	tùng-heui	通去
passable, tolerable	gwo-dāk-heui, màh-má-déi	過得去，麻麻地
passed away, died	gwo-sàn	過身
passed out, unconscious	bāt-síng-yàhn-sih	不省人事
passenger	daap-haak	搭客
passport	wuh-jiu	護照
past	gwo-heui ge	過去嘅
paste, thick sauce	jeung	醬
pastime, amusement	sìu-hín	消遣
pastry	sāi-béng	西餅
pat	paak	拍
patience	noih-sing, yán-noih-lihk	耐性，忍耐力
patient	behng-yàhn	病人
patient (adj)*	yán-noih	忍耐
patient's history sheet	behng-lihk-bíu	病歷表
patriotic	ngoi-gwok	愛國
patronize	bòng-chan	幫趁
pattern	tòuh-ngon	圖案
pay	béi chín	俾錢
pay (the fee)	gàau	交
pay attention to (person)	chói	睬
pay attention to, take notice of	jyu-yi, làuh-sàm	注意，留心
pay by installment	fàn-kèih fuh-fún	分期付款
pay electricity bill	gàau dihn-fai	交電費
pay the rent	gàau jòu	交租
pay the tuition	gàau hohk-fai	交學費
pay water bill	gàau séui-fai	交水費
peace	wòh-pìhng	和平
peaceful, quiet	ngòn-jihng	安靜
peacock	húng-jéuk	孔雀

peak (of hill)	sàan-déng	山頂
peanut	fā-sāng	花生
pear	léi	梨
pearl	jàn-jyù	珍珠
Pearl River	Jyū-gōng	珠江
peas	chèng-dáu	青豆
pediatrics (medical term)	síu-yìh-fō	小兒科
pedicab	sàam-lèuhn-chè	三輪車
peep	jòng	裝
Peking, Beijing	Bāk-gìng	北京
pen	bāt	筆
pencil	yùhn-bāt	鉛筆
pencil sharpener	yùhn-bāt-páau	鉛筆刨
peninsula	bun-dóu	半島
pension	yéuhng-lóuh-gàm	養老金
peony	máuh-dāan	牡丹
people	yàhn-màhn, yàhn	人民，人
peppery, hot	laaht	辣
Pepsi Cola	Baak-sih-hó-lohk	百事可樂
perfect	sahp-chyùhn-sahp-méih	十全十美
perform, performance	bíu-yín	表演
performer, actor	yín-yùhn	演員
perfume	hēung-séui	香水
perhaps	waahk-jé	或者
period	sìh-kèih	時期
perm	dihn-faat	電髮
permit, grant	pài-jéun, jéun	批准，准
persistently, insist on	ngáang-haih	硬係
person	yàhn	人
personally, in person	chàn-jih, chàn-sàn	親自，親身
perspire, sweat	chēut-hohn	出汗
pessimistic	bēi-gùn	悲觀

ph.D.	bok-sih	博士
pharmaceutical company	yeuhk-chóng	藥廠
pharmacist	yeuhk-jāi-sì	藥劑師
Philippines	Fēi-leuht-bān	菲律賓
philosopher	jit-hohk-gā	哲學家
philosophy	jit-hohk	哲學
philosophy of life	yàhn-sāng-gùn	人生觀
phoenix	fuhng-wòhng,fúng	鳳凰，鳳
phone call	dihn-wá	電話
phonograph record	cheung-díp, cheung-pín	唱碟，唱片
photograph (n)*	séung	相
photograph (v) *	yíng-séung	影相
physician, doctor	yī-sàng	醫生
physician trained in Chinese medicine	jūng-yì	中醫
physician trained in Western medicine	sāi-yì	西醫
physics	maht-léih	物理
piano	gong-kàhm	鋼琴
pick (fruit or flower)	jaahk	摘
pick up	jāp-fàan, jāp-héi	執番，執起
pick-pocket	pàh-sáu	扒手
picnic	yéh-chāan	野餐
picture, painting	tòuh-wá, wá	圖畫，畫
pier, dock, wharf	máh-tàuh	碼頭
pig	jyū	豬
pile up, pile of	daahp	沓
pill, tablet	yeuhk-yún	藥丸
pillow	jám-tàuh	枕頭
pillowcase	jám-tàuh-dói	枕頭袋
pilot (of a plane)	gēi-jéung	機長
pimple	am-chōng	暗瘡
pine	chùhng	松

pink	fán-hùhng-sīk	粉紅色
pipe	yīn-dáu	煙斗
piping hot	yiht-laaht-laaht	熱辣辣
pistol	sáu-chēung	手槍
pitch dark	hāak-mā-mā	黑麻麻
pitiful, have pity on	hó-lìhn	可憐
place, location	deih-fōng	地方
plain, clear	chīng-sīk	清晰
plain, flat land	pìhng-yùhn	平原
plan, plan to	gai-waahk, dá-syun	計劃，打算
plant, cultivate	jung	種
plants	jihk-maht	植物
plastic	sou-gāau, gāau	塑膠，膠
plastic bag	gāau-dói	膠袋
plate	dihp, díp	碟
play	wáan	玩
play a prank	nán-fa	撚化
play chess or checker	jūk-kéi	捉棋
play hide and seek	jūk-nēi-nēi	捉匿匿
play mahjong	dá màh-jeuk	打麻雀
play piano	tàahn kàhm	彈琴
please	m̀-gòi	唔該
pleated skirt	baak-jip-kwàhn	百褶裙
plenty of	daaih-bá	大把
pliers (n)*	kím	鉗
plum	mùih	梅
ply (v) *(use pliers)	kìhm	鉗
pneumonia	fai-yìhm	肺炎
pocket	dói	袋
poem, poetry	sī	詩
poet	sī-yàhn	詩人
point at	jí	指
point, dot	dím	點

poisoned	jung-duhk	中毒
police	gíng-chaat, chāai-yàhn	警察，差人
police car	gíng-chè	警車
police inspector	bòng-báan	幫辦
police officer	gíng-sì	警司
police station	chāai-gún, gíng-chaat-gúk	差館，警察局
policewoman	néuih-gíng, chāai-pòh	女警，差婆
policy, administrative policy	jing-chaak	政策
political party	jing-dóng	政黨
political, politics	jing-jih	政治
politician	jing-jih-gā	政治家
pollution	wū-yíhm	污染
pomelo, Chinese grape-fruit	lūk-yáu, sā-tìhn-yáu	椽柚，沙田柚
poor	kùhng, kùhng-fú	窮，窮苦
poor (in quality)	yáih	曳
poor people	kùhng-yàhn	窮人
pop singer	làuh-hàhng gō-sáu	流行歌手
pop song	làuh-hàhng kūk	流行曲
population	yàhn-háu	人口
pork	jyū-yuhk	豬肉
pork chop	jyū-pá	豬扒
pork ribs	pàaih-gwāt	排骨
pornographic	sīk-chìhng, hàahm-sāp	色情，鹹濕
pose	jí-sai	姿勢
position, location	waih-ji	位置
position, status	deih-waih	地位
positive (attitude)	jīk-gihk	積極
possible , possibly, possibility	hó-nàhng	可能
post	jīk-waih	職位
post office	yàuh-jing-gúk, yàuh-gúk	郵政局，郵局
post-secondary college	daaih-jyūn	大專

postage	yàuh-fai	郵費
postcard	mìhng-seun-pín	明信片
poster	hói-bou	海報
pot	wú, wùh	壺
pot (for cooking)	bōu	煲
potato	syùh-jái	薯仔
pound	bohng	磅
pound, ram down	jùng	椿
pour (through a spout)	jàm	斟
pour, pour out	dóu	倒
powder cleaner	heui-wū-fán	去污粉
powdered soap	gáan-fán	梘粉
power, authority	kyùhn-lihk	權力
power, influence	sai-lihk	勢力
powerful	gau-lihk	夠力
practice (in order to learn)	lihn-jaahp	練習
praise	jaan, jaan-méih	讚，讚美
pray (to God), prayer	kèih-tóu, tóu-gou	祈禱，禱告
preach	chyùhn-douh, góng-douh	傳道，講道
precious	bóu-gwai	寶貴
precious stones	bóu-sehk	寶石
preface (of a book)	chìhn-yìhn, jeuih	前言，序
pregnant	yáuh sàn-géi	有身紀
premier	júng-léih	總理
prepare	jéun-beih, yuh-beih	準備，預備
president (of a republic)	júng-túng	總統
present, gift	láih-maht	禮物
press	gahm	撳
press office	bou-gún	報館
press on	gahm	撳
pretend	ja-dai	詐諦
pretty, handsome	leng	靚
preventive inoculation	yuh-fòhng-jām	預防針

price	ga-chìhn	價錢
price of ticket	piu-ga	票價
priest (Catholic)	sàhn-fuh	神父
primary school, grade school	síu-hohk	小學
principal, headmaster	haauh-jéung	校長
print	yan	印
printed matter	yan-chaat-bán	印刷品
printing factory	yan-chaat-chóng	印刷廠
prison	gāam-yuhk	監獄
private (owned by oneself)	sī-yàhn, sī-gā	私人，私家
privately established	sī-lahp, sī-laahp	私立
privileged	wìhng-hahng	榮幸
prize	jéung	獎
probable	yáuh hó-nàhng	有可能
probably	daaih-kói	大概
problem	nàahn-tàih, mahn-tàih	難題，問題
procedure, formality	sáu-juhk	手續
porcelain, chinaware	chìh-hei	瓷器
process	bouh-jaauh, gwo-chìhng	步驟，過程
produce	chēut	出
produce, product	chēut-cháan	出產
product	cháan-bán	產品
profession, job	jīk-yihp	職業
professor	gaau-sauh	教授
profit	leih-yeuhn	利潤
profitable, make profit	jaahn-chín	賺錢
program	jit-muhk	節目
progress, improvement	jeun-bouh	進步
project (n)*	gai-waahk	計劃
projector	fong-yíng-gèi	放映機
promise (n)*	lok-yìhn	諾言
promise (v)*	yīng-sìhng	應承

pronunciation	faat-yām	發音
proof, evidence	jing-geui	證據
proof-reader	gaau-deui-yùhn	校對員
proper	sīk-dong, hāp-dong	適當，恰當
property	chòih-cháan	財產
prosperous	fàahn-wìhng	繁榮
protect, protection	bóu-wuh	保護
Protestant, Protestantism	Gēi-dūk-gaau	基督教
proud	giu-ngouh	驕傲
prove	jing-mìhng	證明
provide	tàih-gūng, gūng-ying	提供，供應
province	sáang	省
public holiday	gùng-jung ga-kèih	公眾假期
public library	gùng-guhng tòuh-syù-gún	公共圖書館
public light bus, minibus	síu-bā	小巴
public opinion	yùh-leuhn	輿論
public relations	gùng-guhng gwàan-haih	公共關係
publish	chēut-báan	出版
publisher	chēut-báan-yàhn	出版人
pull	māng, lāai	搣，拉
pull open (drawers)	tong-hòi	趟開
punish, fine	faht	罰
purge	chìng-syun	清算
purple	jí-sīk	紫色
purse	ngàhn-bāau	銀包
pursue, seek, beg	kàuh	求
push, shove	ngúng, tèui	㩒，推
push aside	buht	撥
put, place	jài, fong	擠，放
put aside	sàu-màaih	收埋
put down	fong-dài, jài-dài	放低，擠低
put down in record	gei-luhk, géi-luhk	紀錄

put on (a hat, watch etc.)	daai	戴
put on (clothes)	jeuk	着
put out (fire or light)	sīk	熄
pyramid	gàm-jih-taap	金字塔

Q

quack	wòhng-luhk yī-sāng	黃綠醫生
quail	ngām-chēun	鵪鶉
qualification	jī-gaak	資格
qualified	gau jī-gaak	夠資格
quality	jāt-déi	質地
quantity	sou-leuhng	數量
quarrel	ngaai-gāau	嗌交
queen	wòhng-hauh	皇后
quench thirsty	jí-hot, gáai-hot	止渴，解渴
question, problem	mahn-tàih	問題
queue, line up	pàaih-déui	排隊
quick	faai	快
quiet	jihng	靜
quietly, softly	jihng-jíng (déi)	靜靜地
quite long (time)	géi-noih	幾耐
quite, fairly	géi	幾
quiz, test	chāak-yihm	測驗

R

rabbit	tou (jái)	兔（仔）
race (between A & B)	béi-choi	比賽
race (a group of people)	júng-juhk	種族
race dragon-boats	pàh-lùhng-syùhn	扒龍船

radicals of Chinese characters	bou-sáu	部首
radio	sāu-yām-gēi, mònh-sin-dihn	收音機，無線電
radio station	dihn-tòih	電台
rail	gwái-douh, louh-gwái	軌道，路軌
railroad	tit-louh	鐵路
railroad station	fó-chè jaahm	火車站
rain (n)*	yúh	雨
rain (v)*	lohk yúh	落雨
rainbow	chói-hùhng	彩虹
raincoat	yúh-lāu	雨褸
raise, elevate	tàih-gòu	提高
raise, keep	yéuhng	養
raise one's hand	géui-sáu	舉手
ransom	suhk-gām	贖金
rash	chán	疹
rat, mouse	lóuh-syú	老鼠
rather, prefer	chìhng-yún, nìhng-yún	情願，寧願
rattan	tàhng	藤
rattan basket	tàhng-láam	藤籃
reach, attain	daaht-dou	達到
read (books)	tái-syù	睇書
read aloud	duhk	讀
reader	duhk-jé	讀者
ready	yuh-beih-hóu	預備好
real, really	jàn ge	真嘅
realize, achieve	saht-yihn	實現
reason	léih-yàuh	理由
reason, cause	yùhn-yān, yùhn-gu	緣因，緣故
reasonable	hahp-léih	合理
receipt	sāu-geui, sāu-tìuh	收據，收條
receive, get	jip-dóu, sàu-dóu	接到，收到
receive baptism	sauh-sái, líhng-sái	受洗，領洗

receive education	sauh gaau-yuhk	受教育
receiver	tèng-túng	聽筒
recently, lately	gahn-lòih	近來
reception at a hotel	jip-doih-chyu	接待處
reception room	wuih-haak-sāt	會客室
receptionist	jip-doih-yùhn	接待員
recognize	yihng-dāk-chēut, yihng-dāk	認得出，認得
recognize, admit	sìhng-yihng	承認
recommend	tèui-jin	推薦
record	gei-luhk	記錄
record player	cheung-gēi	唱機
record, make tape	luhk-yām	錄音
recover (from sickness)	hóu-fàan	好番
recreation	yùh-lohk	娛樂
recruit	jìng-ping	徵聘
recuperate	yàu-yéuhng	休養
red (color)	hùhng-sīk, hùhng	紅色，紅
reduce	gáam	減
refined, gentlemanlike	sì-màhn	斯文
reflection in water	dóu-yíng	倒影
reform, reformation	gói-gaak	改革
refrigerator	syut-gwaih	雪櫃
refugee	naahn-màhn	難民
refuse	kéuih-jyuht	拒絕
regarding..., as to...	ji-yù	至於
register, registry	dāng-gei	登記
registered letter	gwa-houh seun	掛號信
regret	hauh-fui	後悔
regulation, rule	kwài-géui, kwài-laih, kwài-jāk	規矩，規例，規則
relation, relationship	gwàan-haih	關係
relative	chàn-chìk	親戚

relax	fong-sùng	放鬆
relax	fong-sùng	放鬆
reliable, dependable	kaau-dāk-jyuh	靠得住
relief, relieve	gau-jai	救濟
relieve, stop (as pain, etc.)	jí	止
religion	jùng-gaau, gaau	宗教，教
religious belief	seun-yéuhng	信仰
reluctant	míhn-kéuhng	勉強
rely upon	jí-yi	指意
remember	gei-dāk	記得
remind	tàih-séng	提醒
remittance	wuih-fún	匯款
remodel	gói-jòng	改裝
render service to...	waih...fuhk-mouh	為……服務
rent (n)*	ngūk-jòu, jòu-gàm	屋租，租金
rent (v)	jòu	租
rent paid in advance	seuhng-kèih jòu	上期租
repair, fix	jíng	整
repay, requite	bou-daap	報答
repeat	chùhng-fūk	重複
reply (by email or letter)	wùih seun	回信
report, make a report	bou-gou	報告
reporter, correspondent	gei-jé	記者
represent, representative	doih-bíu	代表
reprove, rebuke	jaak-faht	責罰
reputation	mìhng-yuh	名譽
request	chíng-kàuh	請求
request, beg	kàuh	求
require	yīu-kàuh, sēui-yiu	要求，需要
research	yìhn-gau	研究
resemble, look like	hóu-chíh	好似
reserve, book	dehng	訂
reserve, keep	bóu-làuh	保留
resident	gēui-màhn	居民

residential area	jyuh-jaahk-kēui	住宅區
respect	jyūn-juhng, jyun-ging	尊重，尊敬
respond, answer	ying	應
responsibility	jaak-yahm	責任
responsible, in charge	fuh-jaak	負責
rest, relax	táu, yāu-sīk	唞，休息
restaurant	jáu-gā, jáu-làuh	酒家，酒樓
restaurant (Western food)	chāan-sāt	餐室
result, as a result	git-gwó	結果
results, achievement	sìhng-jìk	成績
retail	lìhng-sauh	零售
retire	teui-yāu	退休
return ticket	lòih-wùih-fèi	來回飛
return, pay back	wàahn	還
reveal (a secret)	sit-lauh	洩漏
revenge	bou-sàuh	報仇
reviewer	pìhng-leuhn-yùhn	評論員
revolution	gaak-mihng	革命
rhythm	jit-jau	節奏
rib	lahk-gwāt	肋骨
rice (cooked)	faahn	飯
rice (uncooked)	máih	米
rice ladle	faahn-hok	飯殼
rice noodle	fán	粉
rice-field	tìhn	田
rich, wealthy	yáuh chín	有錢
rickshaw	chè-jái, yàhn-lihk-chè	車仔，人力車
ride a bicycle	yáai dāan-chè, cháai dāan-chè	踹單車，踩單車
ride, to go by	chóh	坐
ridiculous	fòng-mauh	荒謬
right (direction)	yauh	右
right, correct	ngāam	啱

ring	gaai-jí	戒指
riot	bouh-duhng	暴動
rise	seuhng-sīng	上升
risk (n)*	fùng-hím	風險
risk (v)*	mouh-hím	冒險
river	hòh	河
road	louh	路
roast	sìu	燒
roast pork	sìu-yuhk	燒肉
rock	sehk	石
rock & roll music	yìuh-gwán-ngohk	搖滾樂
rocking-chair	ngòn-lohk-yí, yìuh-yí	安樂椅，搖椅
roll-call	dím méng	點名
roller-skates	syut-kehk, làuh-bīng-hàaih	雪屐，溜冰鞋
romanization	lòh-máh ping-yām	羅馬拼音
Rome	Lòh-máh	羅馬
roof	ngūk-déng, tìn-páang	屋頂，天棚
room	fóng	房
room or ward in a hospital	behng-fóng	病房
roommate	tùhng-fóng	同房
root (of plant)	gān	根
rope	síng	繩
rose	mùih-gwai	玫瑰
rouge	yīn-jì	胭脂
rough, coarse	chòu	粗
round, spherical	yùhn	圓
row, line	hòhng	行
row a boat	pàh téhng	扒艇
rub	chaat, chàh	擦，搽
ruby	hùhng-bóu-sehk	紅寶石
rude	chòu-lóuh	粗魯
rule	kwāi-jāk, kwāi-géui	規則，規矩

ruler (measure)	gaan-chék	間尺
ruling queen	néuih-wòhng	女皇
run, go fast	jáu	走
run a newspaper	baahn bou-gún	辦報館
run into trouble	johng-báan	撞板
Russia	Ngòh-lòh-sī	俄羅斯
rust (n)*	sau	銹
rust (v)*	sāang-sau	生銹

S

sacrifice	hēi-sāng	犧牲
sad and lonely	chài-lèuhng	淒涼
safe, safety	ngōn-chyùhn	安全
safety-pin	kau-jām	扣針
sail boat	fàahn-syùhn	帆船
salad	sā-léut	沙律
salary	sān-séui	薪水
salmon	sāam-màhn-yú	三文魚
salon	léih-faat dim, méih-yùhng dim	理髮店，美容店
salt	yìhm	鹽
salty	hàahm	鹹
same, alike	yāt-yeuhng	一樣
San Francisco	Gauh-gām-sāan, Sàam-fàahn-síh	舊金山，三藩市
sand	sā	沙
sandals	lèuhng-hàaih	涼鞋
sandwich	sàam-màhn-jih	三文治
sanitary	hahp waih-sāng	合衞生
Santa Claus	Sing-daan lóuh-yàhn	聖誕老人
sapphire	làahm-bóu-sehk	藍寶石

sardine	sā-dīn-yú	沙甸魚
satisfy, satisfied	múhn-yi	滿意
Saturday	láih-baai-luhk	禮拜六
save, not spend	hāan	慳
save, rescue	gau	救
savings	jīk-chūk	積蓄
saw (n,v)*	geui	鋸
say, talk, speak, tell	góng	講
scald	luhk-chàn	淥親
scales	bóng	磅
scallion	chūng	葱
scalp	tàuh-pèih	頭皮
scandal	cháu-màhn	醜聞
scar	nā, bā-hàhn	疤，疤痕
scare	haak	嚇
scare to death	haak-séi	嚇死
scared	gēng	驚
scarf	géng-gān	頸巾
scenery	fùng-gíng	風景
schedule, time table	sìh-gaan-biu	時間表
scholar	hohk-jé	學者
scholarship	jéung-hohk-gām	獎學金
school	hohk-haauh	學校
school bus	haauh-chè	校車
school of engineering	gùng-hohk-yún, gùng-fò	工學院，工科
school of law	faat-hohk-yún, faat-fò	法學院，法科
school of liberal arts	màhn-hohk-yún, màhn-fō	文學院，文科
school of natural science	léih-hohk-yún, léih-fō	理學院，理科
school physician	haauh-yī	校醫
school uniform	haauh-fuhk	校服
schoolmate, classmate	tùhng-hohk	同學

science	fō-hohk	科學
scissors	gaau-jín	較剪
scold	naauh	鬧
scope, sphere	faahn-wàih	範圍
score	fān-sou	分數
scratch (from a competition)	teui-chēut	退出
scratch to relieve itching	ngàau-hàhn	揹痕
scream, yell	ngaai	嗌
screw	lòh-sī (dēng)	螺絲釘
screwdriver	lòh-sī-pāi	螺絲批
sea	hói	海
sea gull	hói-ngāu	海鷗
sea shell	hín-hok	蜆殼
sea water	hàahm-séui, hói-séui	鹹水，海水
sea-horse	hói-máh	海馬
sea-sick	wàhn-lohng	暈浪
seafood (dried)	hói-méi	海味
seafood (fresh)	hói-sīn	海鮮
seal, chop	tòuh-jēung	圖章
sealed letter	màaih-háu seun	埋口信
search	wán, cháau	搵，抄
seashore	hói-bīn	海邊
season	gwai-jit	季節
seat	wái	位
secluded, quiet	yàu-jihng	幽靜
second	daih-yih	第二
second class	yih-dáng	二等
second handed	yih-sáu	二手
secret, secretly	bei-maht	秘密
secretary	bei-syù	秘書
see a movie	tái-hei	睇戲
see someone off	sung-hàhng	送行
see, perceive	tái-gin	睇見

seed	júng-jí	種子
seem	chíh-fùh	似乎
seesaw	yìuh-yìuh-báan	搖搖板
select	gáan	揀
self support	jih-lahp	自立
self, alone	jih-géi, jih-gēi	自己
self-contradictory	jih-sēung-màauh-téuhn	自相矛盾
selfish	jih-sī	自私
sell	maaih	賣
semester	hohk-kèih	學期
send, dispatch	paai	派
send, post	gei	寄
send a telegram	dá dihn-bou	打電報
senses	jì-gok	知覺
sentence	geui	句
separate	fàn-hòi	分開
separate, part	fàn-sáu	分手
September	Gáu-yuht	九月
serious, important	gán-yiu	緊要
serious, grave	yìhm-juhng	嚴重
seriously	yihng-jàn	認真
servant, worker	gùng-yàhn	工人
serve	fuhk-mouh	服務
serve, wait on	fuhk-sih	服侍
service charge	síu-jeung, (fuhk-mouh-fai)	小賬（服務費）
set, inlay with	sèung	鑲
set up, establish	gin-lahp	建立
settle (in a place)	dihng-gēui	定居
seven	chāt	七
Seven up	Chāt-héi	七喜
several	géi go	幾個
sew button on	dēng-náu	釘鈕

sew by machine	chè	車
sew with needle and thread	lyùhn	聯
sewing machine	yī-chè	衣車
sex	sing-biht	性別
shade (v)*	jē-jyuh	遮住
shadow	yíng	影
shake hands	ngāak-sáu, āak-sáu	握手
shall, will, may	wúih	會
shallow, light	chín	淺
shampoo (n)*	sái-tàuh-séui	洗頭水
shampoo (v)*	sái-tàuh	洗頭
Shanghai	Seuhng-hói	上海
shape, form	yìhng-johng	形狀
share (n)*	fahn	份
share (v)*	fàn	分
share a table (in a restaurant)	daap-tói	搭枱
shareholder	gú-dùng	股東
shark	sā-yùh, sā-yú	鯊魚
sharp	leih	利
sharpener (for pencil)	yùhn-bāt-páau	鉛筆刨
Shatin	Sā-tìhn	沙田
shave	tai	剃
shave beard	tai-sōu	剃鬚
she, her	kéuih	佢
sheep	yèuhng	羊
sheet (for a bed)	chòhng-dāan	牀單
ship, boat	syùhn	船
shirt	sēut-sāam	恤衫
shiver	dá láahng-jan	打冷震
shoe lace	hàaih-dáai	鞋帶
shoe polish	hàaih-yáu	鞋油
shoes	hàaih	鞋
shop	pou-táu	舖頭

short (in length)	dyún	短
short (not tall)	ngái	矮
shoulder	bok-tàuh	膊頭
shout	ngaai	哎
shout at	hot	喝
show, performance	bíu-yín	表演
shower, bathe	chùng-lèuhng	沖涼
shower-head	fā-sá	花灑
shrewd	jēng	精
shrewd (with money)	wúih dá syun-pùhn	會打算盤
shrimp	hā	蝦
shrink (of cloth)	sūk-séui	縮水
shut	sāan-màaih	閂埋
shut up!	máih-chòuh	咪嘈
shy	pa-cháu	怕醜
sickness, be sick	behng	病
side	bīn, bihn	邊
sidewalk, pavement	hàahng-yàhn-louh	行人路
sigh	taan-hei	歎氣
sight	sih-lihk	視力
sign, signature	chìm-méng	簽名
signboard	jīu-pàaih	招牌
significance	yi-yih	意義
silent	jihng	靜
silk	sī	絲
silver	ngàhn, ngán	銀
silver color	ngàhn-sīk	銀色
silverware	dōu-chā, ngàhn-hei	刀叉，銀器
similar	sēung-chíh	相似
simple	gáan-dāan	簡單
simplified character	gáan-bāt-jih, gáan-tái-jih	簡筆字，簡體字
since, because	gei-yìhn	既然

since childhood	jih-sai	自細
sing	cheung	唱
sing (a song)	cheung-gō	唱歌
singer	gō-sáu, gō-sīng	歌手，歌星
single, one only	yāt-go	一個
single, not married	dāan-sān	單身
single room	dāan-yàhn fóng	單人房
sisters	jí-muih	姊妹
sit, drop in	chóh	坐
sit down	chóh-dài	坐低
sit up	chóh-héi-sàn	坐起身
six	luhk	六
size	chek-máh	尺碼
skating-rink	làuh-bīng-chèuhng	溜冰場
skeleton	fū-lòuh-gwāt	骷髏骨
skill, trade	sáu-ngaih	手藝
skin	pèih	皮
skirt	kwàhn, bun-jiht-kwàhn	裙，半截裙
sky, heaven	tìn	天
slave	nòuh-daih	奴隸
sleep, go to bed	fan-gaau, fan	瞓覺，瞓
sleeping pill	ōn-mìhn-yeuhk	安眠藥
sleepy	ngáahn-fan	眼瞓
sleeve	jauh	袖
slide (n)*	waahn-dāng-pín	幻燈片
slightly	sáau-wàih	稍為
slipper	tō-háai	拖鞋
slippery, smooth	waaht	滑
sloping, slanting	che	斜
sloppy	séui-pèih	水皮
slow	maahn	慢
slowly, gradually	maahn-máan	慢慢
small, little	sai	細

small amount, little bit	sē-síu	些少
small boat	téhng	艇
small size	sai-máh	細碼
smallpox	tìn-fà	天花
smart	lēk	叻
smell (n)*	meih-gok	味覺
smell (v)*	màhn	聞
smile	siu	笑
smog	yīn-mouh	煙霧
smoke (n)*	yīn	煙
smoke (v)*	sihk yīn	食煙
smoothly, successfully	seuhn-leih	順利
smuggle, smuggling	jáu-sī	走私
snack	síu-sihk, háu-lahp-sāp	小食，口立濕
snail	wò-ngàuh	蝸牛
snake	sèh	蛇
sneak away	sùng-yàhn	鬆人
sneeze	dá hāt-chī	打乞嗤
snore (n)*	beih-hòhn-sēng	鼻鼾聲
snore (v)*	ché beih-hòhn	扯鼻鼾
snow (n)*	syut	雪
snow (v)*	lohk syut	落雪
so called	só-waih	所謂
so forth, etc.	dáng-dáng	等等
so so, not bad	syun-haih-gám lā	算係咁啦
so, such	gam	咁
soap	fàan-gáan	番梘
soccer	jūk-kàuh	足球
social engagement	ying-chàuh	應酬
social security	séh-wúih bóu-jeung	社會保障
social worker	séh-gùng, séh-wúih-gùng-jok-jé	社工，社會工作者
society, community	séh-wúi	社會

sociologist	séh-wúih-hohk-gā	社會學家
sociology	séh-wúih-hohk	社會學
soda	hei-séui	汽水
sofa	sō-fá	梳化
soft	yúhn	軟
soft-hearted	sàm-chèuhng-yúhn	心腸軟
soldier	gwàn-yàhn	軍人
solicitor, lawyer	leuht-sī	律師
solicitor's office	leuht-sī-làuh	律師樓
solo	duhk-cheung	獨唱
solution	gáai-kyut, daap-ngon	解決，答案
solve, settle	gáai-kyut	解決
some, somewhat	yáuh-dī	有啲
sometimes	yáuh-sìh	有時
son	jái	仔
song	gō	歌
soon, immediately	jauh-làih	就嚟
sooner or later, eventually	chìh-jóu	遲早
soprano	néuih gōu-yām	女高音
sorrowful, melancholy	chài-cháam	淒慘
sorry	deui-m̀-jyuh	對唔住
sound, voice	sìng-yàm	聲音
soup (thick)	gāng	羹
soup (thin)	tòng	湯
soup ladle	tòng-hok	湯殼
soupspoon	tòng-gàng	湯羹
sour	syùn	酸
south	nàahm	南
South America	Nàahm-méih-jàu	南美洲
southeast	dùng-nàahm	東南
Southeastern Asia	Nàahm-yéung, Dùng-nàahm-nga	南洋，東南亞
southwest	sài-nàahm	西南

souvenir	géi-nihm-bán	紀念品
soy sauce	sih-yàuh, chāu-yáu	豉油，抽油
space-ship	taai-hùng-syùhn	太空船
space-shuttle	taai-hùng-chyūn-sō-gēi	太空穿梭機
Spain	Sāi-bāan-ngàh	西班牙
spatula	wohk-cháan	鑊鏟
speak	góng	講
special, unusual	dahk-biht	特別
specialized, exclusively	jyūn-mún, jyūn-mùhn	專門
specially, particularly	jyūn-dāng, dahk-dāng	專登，特登
speculative	tàuh-gèi	投機
speech	yín-góng	演講
speed	chūk-douh	速度
speed boat	faai-téhng	快艇
speedily, in a hurry	gón-jyuh	趕住
speeding	hòi-faai-chè, chìu-chùk	開快車，超速
spend (money)	sái	洗
spider	jī-jyū	蜘蛛
spinal cord	jek-séuih	脊髓
spirit, cheerful	jìng-sàhn	精神
spit	tou-tàahm	吐痰
spoken language or dialect	wá	話
sponge-cake	daahn-gōu	蛋糕
spoon	chìh-gāng	匙羹
sport shoes	bō hàaih, wahn-duhng hàaih	波鞋，運動鞋
spring	chēun-tìn	春天
spring (water source)	pan-chyùhn, chyùhn	噴泉，泉
spring-board	tiu-báan	跳板
spring-water	chyùhn-séui	泉水
square	fōng, sei-fōng	方，四方
square (an open area)	gwóng-chèuhng	廣場
square kilometer	fōng-gùng-léih	方公里

squirrel	chùhng-syú	松鼠
St. Valentine's Day	chìhng-yàhn-jit	情人節
stab, pierce	gāt	剌
stadium	wahn-duhng-chèuhng	運動場
staff member	jīk-yùhn	職員
stainless steel	bāt-sau-gong	不銹鋼
stairs	làuh-tài	樓梯
stall	dong-háu	檔口
stamp	yàuh-piu, sih-dāam	郵票，士擔
stand, stood	kéih	企
stand in a long line	pàaih chèuhng-lùhng	排長龍
stand in line	pàaih déui	排隊
stand up	kéih-héi-sàn	企起身
standard, level	séui-jéun	水準
standard, model	bīu-jéun	標準
star	sīng, sīng-kàuh	星，星球
stare at	mohng-jyuh	望住
start, begin	héi-sáu, hòi-chí	起首，開始
start a journey	hèi-chìhng	起程
state (of the United States)	jāu	州
state of mind	sàm-léih	心理
statement on income tax	seui-dāan	稅單
status, rank	deih-waih	地位
stay	jyuh, dauh-làuh	住，逗留
stay in hospital	làuh-yì	留醫
stay overnight	gwo-yeh, gwo-yé	過夜
steak	ngàuh-pá	牛扒
steal	tàu	偷
steam (n)*	jìng-hei	蒸氣
steam (v)*	jìng	蒸
steel	gong	鋼
steel bar	gong-gān	鋼筋
steering wheel	táaih	舦

step by step	yāt-bouh-yāt-bouh	一步一步
step	geuk-bouh	腳步
sterilize	sìu-duhk	消毒
Sterling pound	Yìng-bóng, Yìng-bohng	英鎊
stewed	mān	炆
still	yìhng-yìhn	仍然
stir fry, saute	cháau	炒
stock market	gú-síh	股市
stocking, sock	maht	襪
stomach	waih	胃
stomach upset	fáan-waih	反胃
stomachache	tóuh-tung, waih-tung	肚痛，胃痛
stone, rock	sehk, sehk-tàuh	石，石頭
stoop down and squat	màu-dài, màu	踎低，踎
stop, halt	tìhng-jí, tìhng	停止，停
stop, station	jaahm	站
stop (someone to do something)	jó-jí	阻止
stop or relieve pain	jí-tung	止痛
store, shop	pou-táu	舖頭
store room	chyúh-maht-sāt, sih-dō-fóng	儲物室，士多房
storm	daaih-fùng-yúh	大風雨
story	gú-jái	古仔
stove, furnace	fó-lòuh	火爐
stove (electric)	dihn-lòuh	電爐
stove (gas)	mùih-hei-lòuh	煤氣爐
stove (L.P. gas)	sehk-yàuh-hei-lòuh	石油氣爐
straight	jihk	直
straight ahead	yāt-jihk	一直
straight forward, open-hearted	sóng-jihk	爽直
strainer (for drying)	sāau-gēi	笊箕
strainer (for frying)	jaau-lēi	炸籬

strainer (tea)	chàh-gaak	茶隔
strange, puzzling	chēut-kèih	出奇
strange, special	dahk-biht, dāk-yi	特別，得意
stranger	sāang-bóu-yàhn	生保人
stream	kāi	溪
street	gāai	街
stretch out, stick out	sàn	伸
strict	yìhm	嚴
strike	bah-gùng	罷工
string	síng	繩
strokes of characters	bāt-waahk	筆劃
stroll	saan-bouh	散步
strong (of will)	gīn-keùhng	堅強
strong (of thing)	gīn-gu	堅固
structure	kau-jouh	構造
stubborn	wàahn-gu	頑固
student	hohk-sāang	學生
student studying abroad	làuh-hohk-sāang	留學生
study (books)	duhk-syù	讀書
study abroad	làuh-hohk	留學
study room	syù-fóng	書房
stuffy	ngai-guhk	翳焗
stupid	chéun, bahn	蠢，笨
style, pattern	fún, fún-sīk	款，款式
stylish	sìh-hìng, sìh-fún	時興，時款
subject, field	fō-muhk	科目
subscribe	dehng, dihng	訂，定
subtract, reduce	gáam	減
success, successful	sìhng-gùng	成功
successively	lìhn-hei, yāt-lìhn	連氣，一連
such as...and the like	hóu-chíh...jì-léui	好似……之類
suddenly	fāt-yìhn, fāt-yìhn-gāan	忽然，忽然間
suffer	sauh-fú	受苦

suffer injury, be wounded	sauh-sēung	受傷
suffer loss, be cheated	siht-dái	蝕底
sufficient	chùng-jūk	充足
sugar	tòhng	糖
sugar cane	je	蔗
suggest, propose	tàih-yíh	提議
suit (for man)	sāi-jōng	西裝
suit (for woman)	tou-jōng	套裝
suitable, fit	hahp-sīk, sīk-hahp	合適，適合
suitcase	pèih-gīp	皮喼
suite	tou-fóng	套房
summer	hah-tìn, yiht-tìn	夏天，熱天
summer vacation	syú-ga	暑假
summit	sāan-déng	山頂
sun (n)*	yaht-táu, taai-yèuhng	日頭，太陽
sun (v)*	saai	曬
sun glasses	taai-yèuhng ngáahn-géng	太陽眼鏡
sun-bathing	saai taai-yèuhng	曬太陽
Sunday	láih-baaih-yaht, láih-baai	禮拜日，禮拜
Sunday school	Jyú-yaht-hohk	主日學
sunflower	heung-yaht-kwàih	向日葵
sunshine	yaht-táu	日頭
superficially	bíu-mihn-seuhng	表面上
superfluous	dò-yùh	多餘
supermarket	chìu-kāp-síh-chèuhng	超級市場
supervise, supervisor	gāam-dūk	監督
supply	gūng-ying	供應
support	jì-chìh	支持
support (with hand or hands)	fùh	扶
suppose, think	yíh-wàih	以為
sure	yāt-dihng	一定

surely will, definitely	yāt-yù	一於
surface	bíu-mihn	表面
surgical operation	sáu-seuht	手術
surgical department	ngoih-fō	外科
surname	sing	姓
surprise	gìng-kèih	驚奇
surround	wàih-jyuh	圍住
suspect, presume	sì-yìh	思疑
suspend	tìhng-deuhn	停頓
suspicious	hó-yìh	可疑
swallow (n)*	yin (jí)	燕（子）
swallow (v)*	tàn	吞
swear (an oath)	saih-yuhn	誓願
sweat, perspire	chēut-hohn	出汗
sweater	lāang-sāam	冷衫
sweep	sou	掃
sweep floor	sou-deih	掃地
sweet	tìhm	甜
sweet potato, yam	fàan-syú	番薯
swell, swelling	júng	腫
swift	faai-jit	快捷
swim	yàuh-séui	游水
swimmers' raft	fàuh-tòih	浮台
swimming cap	wihng-móu	泳帽
swimming pool	wihng-chìh	泳池
swimming suit	(yàuh) wihng-yī	（游）泳衣
swing (for kids)	chāu-chìn	鞦韆
switch (electrical)	dihn-jai	電掣
switch off	sīk, sāan	熄，閂
switch on	hòi	開
symbol	bìu- ji, fùh-hóu	標誌，符號
sympathize	tùhng-chìhng	同情
sympathy	tùhng-chìhng-sàm	同情心

| symphony | gāau-héung-ngohk | 交響樂 |
| system | jai-douh | 制度 |

T

T-shirt	Tī-sēut	T 恤
table, desk	tói	枱
table cloth	tói-bou	枱布
tail	méih	尾
tailor	chòih-fúng	裁縫
Taiwan	Tòih-wāan	台灣
take, bring	daai	帶
take, carry (by hand)	nīk, nīng	搦，拎
take...for example	hóu-chíh...gám	好似……咁
take a chance	bok	搏
take a rest	táu-háh	唞吓
take a shower or bath	chùng-lèuhng	沖涼
take a walk	saan-bouh	散步
take afternoon nap	fan-ngaan-gaau	瞓晏覺
take care, bring up, (baby, kid)	chau	湊
take care of, manage	dá-léih	打理
take good care	bóu-juhng	保重
take in, receive	sàu	收
take it easy	m̀-sái gam gán-jèung	唔駛咁緊張
take lead, lead	líhng-douh	領導
take off	chèuih	除
take off (as an airplane)	héi-fèi	起飛
take one's time	maahn-máan	慢慢
take order (in business)	jip sāang-yi	接生意
take photograph	yíng-séung	影相
take temperature	taam-yiht	探熱
take turns	lèuhn-láu	輪流

take X-ray	jiu X-gwòng	照 X 光
talcum powder	sóng-sàn-fán	爽身粉
talent	tìn-chòih	天才
talented persons	yàhn-chòih	人才
talk	góng syut-wah	講説話
talk back, answer back	bok	駁
talkative (negative meaning)	dò-jéui	多嘴
talkative (positive meaning)	gihn-tàahm	健談
tall, high	gòu	高
tangerine	gāt	桔
Taoist, Taoism	Douh-gaau	道教
tap, faucet	séui-hàuh	水喉
taste (v)	si meih-douh	試味道
tasty, delicious	hóu-meih (douh)	好味（道）
taxi	dīk-sī	的士
taxing, fatiguing	sàn-fú	辛苦
tea	chàh	茶
tea kettle	chàh-bōu	茶煲
tea leaf	chàh-yihp	茶葉
tea party	chàh-wúi	茶會
tea-table, coffee table	chàh-gēi	茶几
teach	gaau	教
teach (at school)	gaau-syù	教書
teacher	lóuh-sī, gaau-yùhn	老師，教員
teakwood	yáu-muhk	柚木
teapot	chàh-wú	茶壺
tear (n)*	ngáahn-leuih	眼淚
tear (v)*	sì-laahn	撕爛
tear down	chaak	拆
tear, rip, open	chaak	拆
teaspoon	chàh-gāng	茶羹
technology	geih-seuht	技術
tedious	mòuh-lìuh	無聊

teeth, tooth	ngàh	牙
telegram	dihn-bou	電報
telegraph office	dihn-bou-gúk	電報局
telephone	dihn-wá	電話
telephone booth	dihn-wá-tìhng	電話亭
telephone directory	dihn-wá-bóu	電話簿
telephone extension	fān-gēi, noih-sin	分機，內線
telephone operator	jip-sin-sāng	接線生
telephone outside line	gāai-sin	街線
telescope	mohng-yúhn-geng	望遠鏡
television	dihn-sih-gēi	電視機
tell	góng	講
tell, order	giu	叫
tell a lie	góng daaih-wah	講大話
temper, disposition	sing-chìhng, pèih-hei	性情，脾氣
temperature (Fahrenheit, centigrade)	wān-douh, (wah-sih, sip-sih)	溫度，(華氏，攝氏)
temple	jí, míu	寺，廟
temporarily	jaahm-sìh	暫時
ten	sahp	十
ten percent	yāt-sìhng	一成
ten thousand	yāt-maahn	一萬
tenant	jyuh-haak, jòu-haak	住客，租客
tennis	móhng-kàuh	網球
tenor	nàahm gòu-yàm	男高音
term (of school year)	hohk-kèih	學期
term, period of time	kèih-haahn	期限
terminus	júng-jaahm	總站
terrifying, frightening	dāk-yàhn-gèng	得人驚
test, quiz	chāak-yihm	測驗
text book	gaau-fō-syù	教科書
textile factory	jīk-jouh-chóng	織造廠
Thailand	Taai-gwok	泰國

thank you	dò-jeh	多謝
Thanksgiving day	Gám-yàn-jit	感恩節
that	gó go	嗰個
The Americas (North and South)	Méih-jàu	美洲
the East	Dùng-fòng	東方
the first time	chò-chi	初次
the Gospel	fūk-yam	福音
The Great Wall	(Maahn-léih-) chèuhng-sìhng	（萬里）長城
the other, the rest	kèih-tà ge, kèih-yùh ge	其他嘅，其餘嘅
the same day	jīk-yaht	即日
the Savior	Gau-sai-jyú	救世主
the West	sāi-fòng	西方
the whole world	chyùhn sai-gaai	全世界
The yellow pages (classified index in the telephone directory)	wòhng-yihp	黃頁
theatre	hei-yún	戲院
their	kéuih-deih ge	佢哋嘅
them	kéuih-deih	佢哋
then, in such a way	gám-yéung	咁樣
then, thereupon	yù-sih	於是
there	gó-syu, gó-douh	嗰處，嗰度
therefore	só-yíh, yàn-chí	所以，因此
thermometer (measuring temperature)	hòhn-syú-bíu	寒暑表
thermometer (taking temperature)	taam-yiht-jām	探熱針
thermos bottle	nyúhn-séui-wú	暖水壺
these	nī dī	呢啲
thesis, essay	leuhn-màhn, leuhn-mán	論文
they, them	kéuih-deih	佢哋

thick	háuh	厚
thick (of high density)	giht	杰
thief, bandit	chaahk, cháak	賊
thigh	daaih-béi	大髀
thin (not fat)	sau	瘦
thin (not thick)	bohk	薄
thin (of low density)	hèi	稀
thing	yéh	嘢
think	nám/lám	諗
think of, think about	séung	想
thirst, thirsty	háu-hot, géng-hot	口渴，頸渴
third	daih sāam	第三
thirty	sàam-sahp	三十
this (here)	nī	呢
this morning	gàm-jiu-jóu, gàm-jìu	今朝早，今朝
this year	gàm-nín, gàm-nìhn	今年
thorough, careful	jàu-dou	周到
those	gó dī	嗰的
those days	gó páai	嗰排
though	sēui-yìhn	雖然
thought, thinking, ideology	si-séung	思想
thoughtful, considerate	yáuh-sàm, sai-sàm	有心，細心
thousand	chìn	千
through	gīng-gwo	經過
thrash board	fàuh-báan	浮板
thread, wire, cord, string	sin	線
three	sàam	三
throat	hàuh-lùhng	喉嚨
throw light on	jiu	照
throw, discard	dám	抌
thumb	sáu-jí-gùng, móuh-jí	手指公，姆指
thumb through (a book)	kín	掀
thundering and lightening	hàahng-lèuih sím-dihn	行雷閃電

Thursday	láih-baai-sei	禮拜四
ticket	piu, fèi	票，飛
tickle	jīt	嘅
tidy up (things)	jāp-sahp	執拾
tidy up a bedroom	jāp-fóng	執房
tie	bóng	綁
tie up (things)	bóng-jyuh, jaat-jyuh	綁住，紮住
tiger	lóuh-fú	老虎
tight	gán	緊
tiles	gāai-jyūn	階磚
time (duration)	sìh-gaan	時間
time (occasion)	chi	次
timid	m̀-gau dáam, sai-dáam	唔夠膽，細膽
tin (metal)	sek	錫
tiny	hóu sai	好細
tip, gratuity	tīp-sí	貼士
tire, tyre	chē-tāai	車呔
tired	guih	癐
tired, bored	yim	厭
tissue	jí-gàn	紙巾
to be	haih	係
toast (n)*	hong mihn-bāau, dō-sí	炕麵包，多士
toast (v)*	hong	炕
toaster	dō-sí-lòuh	多士爐
tobacco	yīn-chóu	煙草
today	gàm-yaht	今日
toe	geuk-jí	腳趾
together	yāt-chái, yāt-chàih	一齊
together with	tùhng, tùhng-màaih	同，同埋
toilet	sái-sáu-gāan, chi-só	洗手間，廁所
toilet cleaner (liquid)	git-chi-yihk	潔廁液
toilet cleaner (powder)	git-chi-fán	潔廁粉
toilet tissue	chi-jí	廁紙

tolerate	(yùhng) yán	(容) 忍
tomato	fàan-ké	番茄
tomato juice	fàan-ké-jāp	番茄汁
tomorrow	tìng-yaht	聽日
tomorrow morning	tìng-jiu-jóu, tìng-jiu	聽朝早，聽朝
tomorrow night	tìng-máahn	聽晚
tones	sìng-diuh	聲調
tongue	leih	脷
tonight	gàm-máahn	今晚
tonsillitis	bín-tòuh-sin faat-yìhm	扁桃腺發炎
tonsils	hàuh-wát, bín-tòuh-sin	喉核，扁桃腺
too, also	dōu, yihk-dōu	都，亦都
too, excessively	taai	太
too bad! what a mess!	baih-la!	弊嘞！
too much trouble	fai-sih	費事
tool	gūng-geuih	工具
tooth	ngàh	牙
tooth paste	ngàh-gòu	牙膏
tooth picks	ngàh-chìm	牙籤
toothache	ngàh-tung	牙痛
toothbrush	ngàh-cháat	牙刷
toothpick-holder	ngàh-chìm-túng	牙籤桶
top	déng	頂
top, above, on	seuhng-bihn	上便
total, altogether	yāt-guhng	一共
totally	júng-guhng	總共
touch (v)*	mó, mō	摸
touched	sauh gám-duhng, gám-gīk	受感動，感激
touching	lihng yàn gám-duhng	令人感動
tour (v)*	yàuh-láahm, yàuh	遊覽，遊
tour around the world	wàahn-yàuh sai-gaai	環遊世界
tour group	léuih-hàhng-tyùhn	旅行團

tourism	léuih-yàuh sih-yihp	旅遊事業
tourist	yàuh-haak	旅客
tourist coach	léuih-yàuh bā-sí	旅遊巴士
tow	tō	拖
toward (the direction of), face	heung	向
towel	sáu-gān, mòuh-gān	手巾，毛巾
town	síh-jan	市鎮
traction engine	tō-chè	拖車
tractor	tō-lāai-gēi	拖拉機
trade	mauh-yihk	貿易
tradition, traditional	chyùhn-túng	傳統
traffic	gāau-tùng	交通
traffic jam	sāk-chè	塞車
traffic sign	gāau-tùng bīu-ji	交通標誌
tragic, pitiable	cháam	慘
train	fó-chè	火車
train, training	fan-lihn	訓練
tram-car	dihn-chè	電車
transform into	bin-sèhng, bin-sìhng	變成
transformation	bin-fa	變化
translate	yihk, fàan-yihk	譯，翻譯
translate into (other language)	yihk-sìhng	譯成
translation	fàan-yihk	翻譯
transport	wahn	運
transportation system	gāau-tùng	交通
travel, trip	léuih-hàhng	旅行
travel agency	léuih-hàhng-séh	旅行社
traveler's check	léuih-hàhng jì-piu	旅行支票
traveling expenses	léuih-fai, séui-geuk	旅費，水腳
tray	tok-pún	托盤
treat (act toward)	deui	對
tree	syuh	樹
tree leaf	syuh-yihp	樹葉

triangle	sāam-gok-yìhng	三角形
tribe, race	júng-juhk	種族
tribulation	fú-naahn	苦難
tricycle	sàam-lèuhn-chè	三輪車
trip	léuih-hàhng	旅行
trouble	màh-fàahn	麻煩
trousers	fu	褲
truck	fo-chè	貨車
true, real	jàn	真
true, reliable	kok-saht	確實
trumpet	la-bā	喇叭
trust	seun-yahm	信任
trustworthy	seun-dāk-gwo	信得過
try	sèuhng-si, si	嘗試，試
try, taste	si	試
tube	si-gún	試管
tuberculosis	fai-behng	肺病
Tuesday	Láih-baai-yih	禮拜二
tuition	hohk-fai	學費
tumor	láu	瘤
tunnel	seuih-douh	隧道
tunnel bus	seuih-douh bā-sí	隧道巴士
tunnel fee	seuih-douh fai	隧道費
turkey	fó-gāi	火雞
turn on	hòi	開
turn one's head	nihng-jyun-tàuh	擰轉頭
turn, make a turn	jyun	轉
turnoff	sīk, sàan	熄，閂
turtle neck	jēun-léhng	樽領
TV movie	dihn-sih-kehk	電視劇
TV set	dihn-sih-gēi	電視機
TV station	dihn-sih-tòih	電視台
twenty	yih-sahp	二十

twin	mā	孖
twin boys	mā-jái	孖仔
twin girls	mā-néui	孖女
twist	náu	扭
two	yih	二
type (v)*	dá-jih	打字
type, kind	leuih-yìhng, júng-leuih	類型，種類
typewriter	dá-jih-gēi	打字機
typhoon	dá-fùng	打風
typhoon shelter	beih-fùng-tòhng	避風塘
typhoon signal	fùng-kàuh	風球
typist	dá-jih-yùhn	打字員

U

U.S. dollar	Méih-gàm	美金
ugly	cháu-yéung	醜樣
ulcer	waih-kwúi-yèuhng	胃潰瘍
umbrella	jē	遮
unbutton	gáai-náu	解鈕
unceasingly	bāt-dyuhn	不斷
unconsciously, unknowingly	bāt-jì-bāt-gok	不知不覺
under, underneath	hah-bihn	下便
under...	hái...hah-bihn	喺⋯⋯下便
under nourished	yìhng-yéuhng bāt-lèuhng	營養不良
underpants	dái-fu	底褲
undershirt	dái-sāam	底衫
underskirt, slip	dái-kwàhn	底裙
understand	mìhng-baahk, líuh-gáai	明白，了解
underwear	noih-yī-fu, dái-sāam-fu	內衣褲，底衫褲
undress, take off	chèuih	除

unforeseen loss	yi-ngoih-syún-sāt	意外損失
unified	tyùhn-git	團結
uniform	jai-fuhk	制服
uniformly (for all)	yāt-leuht	一律
unify	túng-yāt	統一
unintentionally	m̀-gok-yi	唔覺意
unit	dāan-wái	單位
United Nations	Lyùhn-hahp-gwok	聯合國
until	jihk-ji...wàih-jí	直至⋯⋯為止
university, college	daaih-hohk	大學
unless, only if	chèuih-fèi	除非
unmanageable	gáau-m̀-dihm	搞唔掂
unreasonable	móuh douh-léih	冇道理
unsealed letter	hòi-háu seun	開口信
untie	gáai	解
up to now, until now	yāt-heung, yāt-heung- dōu	一向，一向都
upright, straight	jeng	正
upset, irritated	sàm-fàahn	心煩
upstairs	làuh-seuhng	樓上
urban district	síh-kēui	市區
urge, rush	chèui	催
urgent	gán-gāp	緊急
urine	liuh, siu-bihn	尿，小便
us	ngóh-deih	我哋
usage	yuhng-tòuh	用途
use	yuhng	用
used up	yuhng-saai	用曬
useful, helpful	yáuh-yuhng	有用
useless	móuh-yuhng	冇用
usher, greet	jīu-fù	招呼
usual	pìhng-sèuhng	平常
usually	tūng-sèuhng	通常

| utensil | yuhng-geuih | 用具 |
| utter, say (something) | chēut-sēng | 出聲 |

V

vacation	fong-ga	放假
vacation house, villa	biht-seuih	別墅
vaccum cleaner	kāp-chàhn-gēi	吸塵機
valley	sāan-gūk	山谷
valuable	jihk-chín	值錢
value	ga-jihk	價值
various	gok-sīk-gok-yeuhng	各式各樣
vase	fā-jēun	花樽
vaseline	fàahn-sih-làhm	凡士林
vault, safe	gaap-maahn	夾萬
vegetables	choi	菜
vein	jihng-mahk	靜脈
venereal disease	sing-behng	性病
verb	duhng-chìh	動詞
very	hóu	好
very fond of	hóu-jùng-yi	好鍾意
vicinity, near-by	jó-gán, fuh-gahn	左近，附近
victim	sauh-hoih-yàhn	受害人
Victoria Peak	Ché-kèih-sāan-déng	扯旗山頂
victory	sing-leih	勝利
view, scenery	fùng-gíng	風景
village	chyūn, hēung-chyūn	村，鄉村
vinegar	chou, jit-chou	醋，浙醋
violet	ji-lòh-làahn	紫羅蘭
violin	síu-tàih-kàhm	小提琴
virtue, moral	douh-dāk	道德
visa	chìm-jing	簽證

viscid, thick	giht	湽
vision	sih-gok	視覺
visit (a person)	taam	探
visit (a place)	chàam-gùn	參觀
visit a patient	taam-behng	探病
visitor, guest	yàhn-haak	人客
visual acuity	ngáahn-lihk	眼力
vocabulary	chìh-wuih	詞彙
voice, sound	sēng	聲
volley ball	pàaih-kàuh	排球
volunteer (v)*	jih-yuhn	自願
volunteer(n)*	yih-gùng	義工
vomit	ngáu, áu	嘔

W

wage	yàhn-gùng	人工
waist	yīu	腰
wait, wait for	dáng	等
wait a moment	dáng yāt-jahn	等一陣
wait on (upon)	fuhk-sih	服侍
waiter	fó-gei	伙記
waiting room	wuih-haak-sāt	會客室
waiting room (in a doctor's office)	hauh-chán-sāt	候診室
waiting room (in an airport)	hauh-gēi-sāt	候機室
wake (others) up	giu-séng	叫醒
wake up	séng	醒
wake up from dream	faat-séng-muhng	發醒夢
walk, work (of watches, cars, etc.)	hàahng	行
walk by	hàahng-gwo	行過

wall	chèuhng	牆
wall, fence	wàih-chèuhng	圍牆
wallet, purse	ngàhn-bāau	銀包
want	yiu	要
war	jin-jāng	戰爭
wardrobe	yī-gwaih	衣櫃
warm	nyúhn	暖
warship	jin-laahm	戰艦
wash	sái	洗
wash basin	mihn-pún	面盤
wash-room, toilet	chi-só, sái-sáu-gāan	廁所，洗手間
washing machine	sái-yī-gèi	洗衣機
waste	sāai	嘥
waste-paper basket	jih-jí-lō	字紙簍
watch (n)*	bīu	錶
watch (v)*	tái	睇
watch out	gu-jyuh	顧住
water (n)*	séui	水
water (v)*	làhm	淋
water bill	séui-fai	水費
water tank	séui-sēung	水箱
water-color	séui-chói	水彩
water-ski	waaht-séui	滑水
waterfall	buhk-bou	瀑布
watermelon	sāi-gwà	西瓜
waterproof	fòhng-séui ge	防水嘅
watery, thin	hèi	稀
wave (n)*	lohng	浪
wax (n)*	laahp	臘
wax (v)*	dá-laahp	打臘
way, method	fōng-faat, faat-jí	方法，法子
way, route	louh	路
we, us	ngóh-deih	我哋

weak	yeuhk	弱
weakness	hèui-yeuhk, yúhn-yeuhk	虛弱，軟弱
wear (glasses, hat etc.)	daai	戴
wear, dress	jeuk	着
wear a necktie	dá tāai	打呔
wear a scarf	laahm géng-gàn	攬頸巾
wearing a long face	báan-héi faai mihn	板起塊面
weather	tìn-hei	天氣
weave	jīk	織
wedding cake	láih-béng	禮餅
wedding ceremony	fàn-láih	婚禮
wedding gown	git-fàn láih-fuhk	結婚禮服
Wednesday	láih-baai-sāam	禮拜三
week	láih-baai, sìng-kèih	禮拜，星期
week by week	juhk go láih-baai	逐個禮拜
weep	haam	喊
weigh	bohng	磅
weigh (by Chinese scale)	ching	稱
welcome	fùn-yìhng	歡迎
welfare	fūk-leih	福利
well (n)*	jéng	井
well informed	sìu-sìk lìhng-tùng	消息靈通
well known	chēut-méng	出名
well off, rich	yáuh-chín	有錢
west	sāi	西
western calendar	sāi-lihk	西曆
western food	sāi-chāan	西餐
western style	sāi-sìk	西式
western suit	sāi-jōng	西裝
westerner	sāi-yàhn, gwái-lóu	西人，鬼佬
wet	sāp	濕
whale	kìhng-yùh	鯨魚
wharf	máh-tàuh	碼頭

what	māt, māt-yéh	乜，乜嘢
what a coincidence!	Jàn-haih ngāam la!	真係啱嘞！
what a waste!	sāai-saai la!	嘥晒嘥！
wheel	chē-lūk, chē-lèuhn	車碌，車輪
when (at the time that)	...gó-jahn-sí	……嗰陣時
when?, at what time?	géi-sí, géi-sìh	幾時
where?	bīn-syu, bīn-douh	邊處，邊度
which?	bīn	邊
whisky	wāi-sih-géi	威士忌
whistle (n)*	ngàhn-gāi, saau-jí	銀雞，哨子
whistle (v)*	chèui háu-saau	吹口哨
white	baahk-sīk, baahk	白色，白
white wash	fùi-séui	灰水
who's?	bīn-go ge	邊個嘅
who?, whom?	bīn-go	邊個
whole	chyùhn-bouh	全部
whole day	sèhng-yaht	成日
wholeheartedly	jeuhn-sàm-jeuhn-lihk	盡心盡力
wholesale	pài-faat	批發
whose	bīn-go ge	邊個嘅
why?	dím-gáai	點解
why should...?	hòh-bīt..., sái-māt ...	何必……，駛乜……
wide, loose (dress)	fut	闊
widow	gwá-fúh	寡婦
wife	taai-táai, lóuh-pòh	太太，老婆
wig	gá-faat	假髮
wild	yéh-sāng	野生
wild animals, beast	yéh-sau	野獸
will (legal document)	wàih-jūk	遺囑
will, shall	wúih	會
will (mental power)	yi-ji	意志
will be in trouble	m̀-dāk-dihm	唔得掂

willing to	háng	肯
win	yèhng	贏
win a prize	dāk-jéung	得獎
wind, breeze	fùng	風
windbreaker	fùng-yì, fùng-làu	風衣，風褸
windmill	fùng-chè	風車
window	chēung, chēung-mún	窗，窗門
window curtain	chēung-lím	窗簾
windy	daaih-fùng	大風
wine	jáu	酒
wine bottle	jáu-jēun	酒樽
winepot	jáu-wùh	酒壺
wing	yihk	翼
wink, blink	jáam	貶
wink, in a wink	jáam-ngáahn	眨眼
winter	dūng-tìn, láahng-tìn	冬天，冷天
winter recess	hòhn-ga	寒假
wipe	maat	抹
wisdom	ji-wai	智慧
wise	chùng-mìhng	聰明
wish (well)	jūk	祝
wish or congratulate in advance	yuh-jūk	預祝
wish to, would like to	séung	想
wish, desire	yuhn-mohng	願望
with one's own hands	chàn-sáu	親手
with regard to	gwāan-yù	關於
with respect to, in regard to	deui (yù)	對（於）
without authorization	sì-jih	私自
witness	jing-yàhn, muhk-gīk-jé	證人，目擊者
wok (Chinese cooking pan)	wohk	鑊
woman, women	néuih-yán	女人
won't	m̀-wúih	唔會

wonder	gīng-kèih	驚奇
wood	muhk	木
woods	syuh-làhm	樹林
wool	yèuhng-mòuh	羊毛
woolen material	yúng	絨
Worcestershire sauce	gīp-jāp	喼汁
word, character (written word)	jih	字
work (v)*	jouh-sih	做事
work hard	nóu-lihk	努力
workshop	gùng-chèuhng, gùng-jok-fōng	工場，工作坊
world	sai-gaai	世界
world war	sai-gaai daaih-jin	世界大戰
worm, insects	chùhng	蟲
worried	bai-ngai	閉翳
worry about, worried	dāam-sàm	擔心
worship	baai	拜
worthwhile	jihk-dāk	值得
wound (n)*	sēung-háu	傷口
wrangle, strive	jāang	爭
wrap	bāau	包
wrist	sáu-wún	手腕
write	sé	寫
write (a letter)	sé-seun	寫信
write down	sé-dài	寫低
written examination	bāt-síh	筆試
wrong	cho	錯

X

X-ray	X-gwōng	X 光
xerox	yíng-yan	影印

yacht	yàuh-téhng	遊艇
Yangtze River	Chèuhng-gòng	長江
yard (3 feet)	máh	碼
yarn, wool	lāang	冷
yawn, yawning	dá haam-lòuh	打喊露
year	nìhn	年
year after next	hauh-nín, hauh-nìhn	後年
year before last	chìhn-nín, chìhn-nìhn	前年
yell	ngaai	嗌
yellow (color)	wòhng-sīk, wòhng	黃色，黃
Yellow River	Wòhng-hòh	黃河
yes	haih	係
yesterday	chàhm-yaht, kàhm-yaht	噚日，琴日
yet, but	daahn-haih	但係
you (pl.)*	néih-deih	你哋
you (sing.)*	néih	你
you're welcome	m̀-sái haak-hei	唔駛客氣
young	hauh-sāang	後生
young fellow	hauh-sāang-jái	後生仔
your, yours	néih ge, néih-deih ge	你嘅，你哋嘅
yourself	néih-jih-géi	你自己

zeal	yiht-sìhng, yiht-sàm	熱誠，熱心
zebra	bāan-máh	斑馬
zero	lìhng	零
zipper	lāai-lín	拉鍊
zodiac	sīng-joh	星座

| zoo | duhng-maht-yùhn | 動物園 |
| zoology | duhng-maht-hohk | 動物學 |

* n: noun
* v: verb
* pl.: plural
* sing.: singular

Part II

Specialized Glossaries,
with Special Reference
to Hong Kong

1. Where to go in Hong Kong

Names of Places	Deih-kèui-méng	地區名
Hong Kong	**Hèung-góng**	**香港**
Aberdeen	Hèung-góng-jái	香港仔
Causeway Bay	Tùhng-lòh-wàahn	銅鑼灣
Central District	Jùng-wàahn	中環
Chai Wan	Chàaih-wāan	柴灣
Happy Valley	Páau-máh-déi	跑馬地
Kennedy Town	Gīn-nèih-deih-sìhng	堅尼地城
Mid-Level	Bun-sāan-kèui	半山區
North Point	Bāk-gok	北角
Quarry Bay	Jāk-yùh-chùng	鰂魚涌
Sai Wan	Sāi-wàahn	西環
Sai Wan Ho	Sāi-wàan-hó	西灣河
Sai Ying Pun	Sāi-yìhng-pùhn	西營盤
Shau Kei Wan	Sāau-gèi-wàan	筲箕灣
Stanley	Chek-chyúh	赤柱
Tai Hang	Daaih-hāang	大坑
The Peak	Sāan-déng	山頂
Victoria Peak	Ché-kèih sāan-déng (sāan-déng)	扯旗山頂 （山頂）
Wanchai	Wāan-jái	灣仔
Wong Chuk Hang	Wòhng-jūk-hāang	黃竹坑
Kowloon	**Gáu-lùhng**	**九龍**
Cheung Sha Wan	Chèuhng-sā-wàahn	長沙灣
Choi Hung	Chói-hùhng	彩虹
East Tsim Sha Tsui	Jīm-dùng	尖東
Ho Man Tin	Hòh-màhn-tìhn	何文田

Hung Hom	Hùhng-ham	紅磡
Kowloon City	Gáu-lùhng-sìhng	九龍城
Kowloon Tong	Gáu-lùhng-tòhng	九龍塘
Kwun Tong	Gùn-tòhng	官塘
Lai Chi Kok	Laih-jì-gok	荔枝角
Lam Tin	Làahm-tìhn	藍田
Lei Yue Mun	Léih-yùh-mùhn	鯉魚門
Mong Kok	Wohng-gok	旺角
Ngau Tau Kok	Ngàuh-tàuh-gok	牛頭角
San Po Kong	Sàn-pòuh-gòng	新蒲崗
Sham Shui Po	Sàm-séui-bóu	深水埗
Shek Kip Mei	Sehk-gip-méih	石硤尾
Tai Kok Tsui	Daaih-gok-jéui	大角咀
To Kwa Wan	Tóu-gwà-wàahn	土瓜灣
Tse Wan Shan	Chìh-wàhn-sāan	慈雲山
Tseung Kwan O	Jēung-gwān-ngou	將軍澳
Tsim Sha Tsui	Jìm-sà-jéui	尖沙咀
Wang Tau Hom	Wàahng-tàuh-ham	橫頭磡
Wong Tai Sin	Wòhng-daaih-sìn	黃大仙
Yau Ma Tei	Yàuh-màh-déi	油麻地
Yau Tong	Yàuh-tòhng	油塘
Yau Yat Chuen	Yauh-yāt-chyùn	又一村

New Territories	Sàn-gaai	新界
Castle Peak	Chìng-sàan	青山
Fanling	Fán-léhng	粉嶺
Fo Tan	Fó-taan	火炭
Kwai Chung	Kwàih-chùng	葵涌
Lo Wu	Lòh-wùh	羅湖
Lok Ma Chau	Lohk-máh-jàu	落馬洲
Pearl Island	Lùhng-jyū-dóu	龍珠島
Sai Kung	Sài-gung	西貢

137

Sha Tin	Sā-tìhn	沙田
Sheung Shui	Sheuhng-séui	上水
Tai Po	Daaih-bou	大埔
Tai Po Market	Daaih-bou-hèui	大埔墟
Tai Wai	Daaih-wàih	大圍
Tin Shui Wai	Tīn-sēui-wàih	天水圍
Tsing Yi	Chìng-yì	青衣
Tsuen Wan	Chyùhn-wàan	荃灣
Tuen Mun	Tyùhn-mùhn	屯門
Yuen Long	Yùhn-lóhng	元朗

Beaches and Bays — Góng-wāan — 港灣

Big Wave Bay	Daaih-lohng-wāan	大浪灣
Chek Lap Kok	Chek-laahp-gok	赤鱲角
Clear Water Bay	Chìng-séui-wāan	清水灣
Deep Water Bay	Sàm-séui-wāan	深水灣
Discovery Bay	Yùh-gíng-wāan	愉景灣
Hau Hoi Wan (Deep Bay)	Hauh-hói-wāan	后海灣
Junk Bay	Jèung-gwàn-ngou	將軍澳
Kowloon Bay	Gáu-lùhng-wāan	九龍灣
Lei Yue Mun	Léih-yùh-mùhn	鯉魚門
Repulse Bay	Chín-séui-wāan	淺水灣
Silver Mine Bay	Ngàhn-kwong-wāan	銀礦灣
Tolo Harbour	Tou-louh-góng	吐露港
Victoria Harbour	Wàih-dò-leih-nga-góng	維多利亞港

Outlying Islands — Lèih-dóu — 離島

Ap Lei Chau	Ngaap-leih-jàu	鴨脷洲
Cheung Chau	Chèuhng-jàu	長洲

Hei Ling Chau	Héi-lìhng-jàu	喜靈洲
Lamma Island	Nàahm-ngā-dóu	南丫島
Lantau Island	Daaih-yùh-sàan	大嶼山
Peng Chau	Pìhng-jàu	坪洲
Po Toi Island	Pòuh-tòih-dóu	蒲台島
Stonecutters Island	Ngóhng-syùhn-jàu	昂船洲

Country Parks	Gāauyéh Gùngyún	郊野公園
Aberdeen	Hèung-góng-jái	香港仔
Cheung Sheung	Jèung-sheuhng	嶂上
Chi Ma Wan	Jì-màh-wāan	芝麻灣
Clear Water Bay	Chìng-séui-wāan	清水灣
Hoi Ha	Hói-hah	海下
Kei Ling Ha	Kéih-léhng-hah	企嶺下
Keung Shan	Gèung-sàan	羌山
Kowloon Hill	Gáu-lùhng-sāan	九龍山
Lion Rock	Sī-jí-sāan	獅子山
Pokfulam	Bok-fuh-làhm	薄扶林
Plover Cove	Syùhn-wāan	船灣
Quarry Bay	Jāk-yùh-chùng	鰂魚涌
Sai Kung	Sài-gung	西貢
Sham Tseng	Sàm-jéng	深井
Shek Pik	Sehk-bīk	石壁
Shing Mun	Shìhng-mùhn	城門
Tai Mei Tuk	Daaih-méih-dūk	大尾篤
Tai Po Kau	Daaih-bou-ngaau	大埔滘
Tai Lam Chung	Daaih-láahm-chùng	大欖涌
Tai Tam	Daaih-tàahm	大潭
Tung Chung Au	Dùng-chùng-ngaau	東涌坳
Twisk	Chyùhn-gám	荃錦

Reservoirs	Séui-fu	水庫
Aberdeen Reservoir	Hèung-góng-jái Séui-tòhng	香港仔水塘
High Island Reservior	Maahn-yìh Séui-fu	萬宜水庫
Jubilee (Shing Mun) Reservoir	Sìhng-mùhn Séui-tòhng	城門水塘
Plover Cove Reservoir	Syùhn-wāan Táahm-séui-wùh	船灣淡水湖
Pok Fu Lam Reservoir	Bok-fuh-làhm Séui-tòhng	薄扶林水塘
Shek Pik Reservoir	Sehk-bīk Séui-tòhng	石壁水塘
Tai Lam Chung Reservoir	Daaih-láahm-chùng Séui-tòhng	大欖涌水塘
Tai Tam Reservoir	Daaih-tàahm Séui-tòhng	大潭水塘

2. How to get there

Transportation	Gàau-tùng	交通
a chain collision	lìhn-wàahn johng chè	連環撞車
Aberdeen Tunnel (Happy Valley — Aberdeen)	Hèung-góng-jái seuih-douh	香港仔隧道
accelerator	yáu-mùhn, yàuh-mùhn	油門
adjustable mirror	dou-hauh-geng	倒後鏡
Airport Tunnel	Gèi-chèuhng seuih-douh	機場隧道
Blake Pier	Būk-gùng máh-tàuh	卜公碼頭
blow horn	gahm-hōn, héung-ōn	撳安，響安
bright, high light	gòu-dàng	高燈
bus	bā-sí	巴士
car fare	chè-fai	車費
car park	tìhng-chè-chèuhng	停車場

Central Harbour Services Pier	Jùng-wàahn Góng-noih-sin máh-tàuh	中環港內線碼頭
common stored value ticket	tùng-yuhng chyúh-jihk-piu	通用儲值票
convenient	fòng-bihn	方便
convertible	hòi-pùhng-chè	開蓬車
Cross-Harbour Tunnel (Wan Chai － Hung Hom)	Hói-dái seuih-douh	海底隧道
crowded	bīk	逼
dangerous driving	ngàih-hím ga-sái	危險駕駛
dim, low light	dài-dàng	低燈
don't have coins for the fare	móuh sáan-ngán	冇散銀
driving license	ga-sái jāp-jiu, ché-páaih	駕駛執照，車牌
driving test	háau-chè	考車
driving without license	mòuh-pàaih ga-sái	無牌駕駛
economic class	gìng-jai haak-wái	經濟客位
emergency stop	gán-gāp-saat-chè	緊急剎車
franchise public light bus	jyūn-sin síu-bā	專線小巴
garage	chè-fòhng	車房
gas station	dihn-yàuh-jaahm	電油站
get on the wrong bus	daap-cho chè	搭錯車
get stuck	pàau-màauh, pàau-làauh	拋錨
Hong Kong and Macau Ferry Terminal	Góng-Ngou máh-tàuh	港澳碼頭
Hong Kong and Yaumati Ferry	Yàuh-màh-déi síu-lèuhn	油麻地小輪
Hong Kong International Airport	Hèung-góng gwok-jai gèi-chèuhng	香港國際機場
Hunghom Ferry Pier	Hùhng-ham máh-tàuh	紅磡碼頭
Hunghom Railway Station	Hùhng-ham fó-chè júng-jaahm	紅磡火車總站
hydrofoil	séui-yihk-syùhn	水翼船
in a hurry	gón-sìh-gaan	趕時間

jalopy	lóuh-yèh-chè	老爺車
Lion Rock tunnel (Waterloo Rd 一 Shatin)	Sì-jí-sàan seuih-douh	獅子山隧道
meter	māi-bīu	咪錶
minibus (Public light bus)	síu-bā	小巴
MTR 一 Mass Transit Railway 一 subway system	deih-hah tit-louh, deih-tit	地下鐵路，地鐵
multi-storeyed garage	dò-chàhng tìhng-chè-chèuhng	多層停車場
no entry	bāt-jéun sái-yahp	不准駛入
no parking	bāt-jéun tìhng-ché	不准停車
no right (left) turn	bāt-jéun yauh (jó) jyun	不准右（左）轉
North Point Ferry Pier	Bāk-gok máh-tàuh	北角碼頭
number plate	chè-pàaih	車牌
Ocean Terminal	Hói-wahn daaih-hah	海運大廈
Octopus Card	Baat-daaht-tūng (kāat)	八達通（咭）
one way only	dāan-chìhng louh	單程路
Outlying Districts Services	Jùng-kèui Góng-ngoih-sin máh-tàuh	中區港外線碼頭
overtaking, passing	pàh-tàuh	爬頭
parking meter	hek gok-jí lóuh-fú-gèi, tìhng-chè sàu-fai-bīu	吃角子老虎機，停車收費錶
Peak Tram	Sàan-déng laahm-chè	山頂纜車
pier	máh-tàuh	碼頭
plane	fèi-gèi	飛機
plane ticket	gèi-piu	機票
please let me off (telling the minibus driver)	yáuh lohk	有落
public coach	hòuh-wàh bā-sí	豪華巴士
public transportation	gùng-guhng gàau-tùng	公共交通
refuel	yahp-yáu	入油
reverse	teui-hauh	退後

roll backward	làuh-hauh	溜後
safety first	ngòn-chyùhn daih-yāt	安全第一
safety island	ngòn-chyùhn-dóu	安全島
school bus (for children)	bóu-móuh-chè	保姆車
second-hand car	yih-sáu-chè	二手車
sport-car	páau-chè	跑車
Star Ferry	Tìn-sìng síu-lèuhn	天星小輪
Star Ferry Pier (HK side)	Tìn-sìng máh-tàuh	天星碼頭
Star Ferry Pier (Kowloon side)	Jìm-sà-jéui máh-tàuh	尖沙咀碼頭
student driver	hohk-sàhn	學神
subway station	deih-tit-jaahm	地鐵站
taxi	dīk-sí	的士
the car (engine) stops	séi-fó	死火
the tyre is leaking	lauh-hei	漏氣
through train (Kowloon-Canton)	jihk-tùng-chè	直通車
traffic control	gàau-tùng gún-jai	交通管制
traffic jam	sāk-chè	塞車
traffic light	gàau-tùng dàng, hùhng-luhk dàng	交通燈，紅綠燈
traffic signs	gàau-tùng bīu-ji	交通標誌
tram	dihn-chè	電車
tunnel bus	seuih-douh bā-sí	隧道巴士
turn indicator	jí-fài dàng	指揮燈
typhoon shelter	beih-fùng-tòhng	避風塘
use the turn indicator	da jí-fài-dàng	打指揮燈
wind-shield wiper	séui-buht	水撥
zebra crossing, zebra stripes	bāan-máh-sin	斑馬線

MTR SYSTEM Stations	Góng-tit chē-jaahm	港鐵車站
Mass Transit Railway (MTR)	Deih-tit	地鐵
MTR Stations	Deih-tit-jaahm	地鐵站

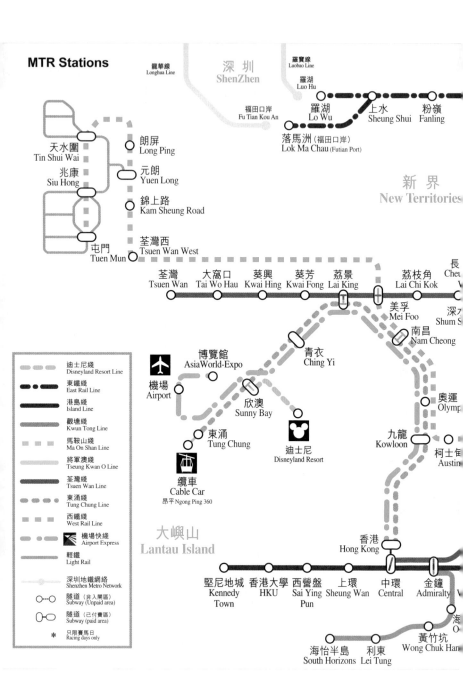

MTR Stations

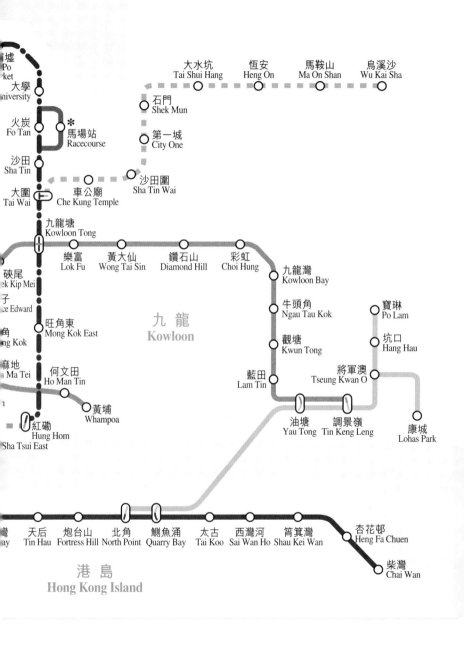

埔
Po
rket

大學
niversity

火炭
Fo Tan

*馬場站
Racecourse

沙田
Sha Tin

大水坑
Tai Shui Hang

恆安
Heng On

馬鞍山
Ma On Shan

烏溪沙
Wu Kai Sha

石門
Shek Mun

第一城
City One

沙田圍
Sha Tin Wai

大圍
Tai Wai

車公廟
Che Kung Temple

九龍塘
Kowloon Tong

硤尾
ek Kip Mei

子
ce Edward

樂富
Lok Fu

黃大仙
Wong Tai Sin

鑽石山
Diamond Hill

彩虹
Choi Hung

九龍灣
Kowloon Bay

牛頭角
Ngau Tau Kok

寶琳
Po Lam

角
ng Kok

旺角東
Mong Kok East

九 龍
Kowloon

觀塘
Kwun Tong

坑口
Hang Hau

麻地
Ma Tei

何文田
Ho Man Tin

藍田
Lam Tin

將軍澳
Tseung Kwan O

黃埔
Whampoa

紅磡
Hung Hom

油塘
Yau Tong

調景嶺
Tin Keng Leng

康城
Lohas Park

Sha Tsui East

灣
ay

天后
Tin Hau

炮台山
Fortress Hill

北角
North Point

鰂魚涌
Quarry Bay

太古
Tai Koo

西灣河
Sai Wan Ho

筲箕灣
Shau Kei Wan

杏花邨
Heng Fa Chuen

柴灣
Chai Wan

港 島
Hong Kong Island

Disneyland Resort Line	Dihk-sih-nèih-sin	迪士尼線
Sunny Bay	Yān-ngou	欣澳
Disneyland Resort	Dihk-sih-nèih	迪士尼

East Rail Line	Dūng-tit-sin	東鐵線
Train station	fó-chè-jaahm	火車站
Hung Hom	Hùhng-ham	紅磡
Mongkok East	Wohng-gok-dūng	旺角東
Kowloon Tong	Gáu-lùhng-tòhng	九龍塘
Tai Wai	Daaih-wàih	大圍
Sha Tin	Sà-tihn	沙田
Fo Tan	Fó-taan	火炭
Racecourse	Máh-chèuhng	馬場
University	Daaih-hohk	大學
Tai Po Market	Daaih-bou-hēui	大埔墟
Tai Wo	Taai-wòh	太和
Fanling	Fán-léhng	粉嶺
Sheung Shui	Seuhng-séui	上水
Lo Wu	Lòh-wùh	羅湖
Lok Ma Chau	Lohk-máh-jāu	落馬洲

Island Line	Góng-dóu-sin	港島線
Chai Wan	Chàaih-wāan	柴灣
Heng Fa Chuen	Hahng-fā-chyùn	杏花村
Shau kei wan	Sāau-gèi-wàan	筲箕灣
Sai Wan Ho	Sāi-wàan-hó	西灣河
Tai Koo	Taai-gú	太古
Quarry Bay	Jāk-yùh-chúng	鰂魚涌
North Point	Bāk-gok	北角
Fortress Hill	Paau-tòih-sàan	炮台山

Tin Hau	Tìn-hauh	天后
Causeway Bay	Tùhng-lòh-wàahn	銅鑼灣
Wan Chai	Wāan-jái	灣仔
Admiralty	Gàm-jùng	金鐘
Central	Jùng-wàahn	中環
interchange	jyun-sin-jaahm	轉線站
Sheung Wan	Seuhng-wàahn	上環
Kennedy Town	Gīn-nèih-deih-sìhng	堅尼地城
Hong Kong University (HKU)	Hèung-góng daaih-hohk	香港大學
Sai Ying Pun	Sāi-yìhng-pùhn	西營盤

Kwun Tong Line	Gùn-tòhng-sin	官塘線
Yaumati	Yàuh-màh-déi	油麻地
Mongkok	Wohng-gok	旺角
Prince Edward	Taai-jí	太子
Shek Kip Mei	Sehk-gip-méih	石硤尾
Kowloon Tong	Gáu-lùhng-tòhng	九龍塘
Lok Fu	Lohk-fu	樂富
Wong Tai Sin	Wòhng-daaih-sīn	黃大仙
Diamond Hill	Jyun-sehk-sàan	鑽石山
Choi Hung	Chói-hùhng	彩虹
Kowloon Bay	Gáu-lùhng-wāan	九龍灣
Ngau Tau Kok	Ngàuh-tàuh-gok	牛頭角
Kwun Tong	Gùn-tòhng	官塘
Lam Tin	Làahm-tìhn	藍田
Yau Tong	Yàuh-tòhng	油塘
Tiu Keng Leng	Tìuh-gíng-léhng	調景嶺
Hon Man Tin	Hòh-màhn-tìhn	何文田
Whampoa	Wòhng-bou	黃埔

South Island Line　Nàahm-Góng-dóu-sin　南港島線

Admiralty	Gàm-jùng	金鐘
Ocean Park	Hói-yèuhng gūng-yún	海洋公園
Wong Chuk Hang	Wòhng-jūk-hāang	黃竹坑
Lei Tung	Leih-dùng	利東
South Horizons	Hói-yìh bun-dóu	海怡半島

Ma On Shan Line　Máh-ngōn-sāan-sin　馬鞍山線

Tai Wai	Daaih-wàih	大圍
Che Kung Temple	Chē-gūng-míu	車公廟
Sha Tin Wai	Sā-tìhn-wàih	沙田圍
City One	Daih-yāt-sìhng	第一城
Shek Mun	Sehk-mùhn	石門
Tai Shui Hang	Daaih-séui-hāang	大水坑
Heng On	Hàhng-ngōn	恆安
Ma On Shan	Máh-ngōn-sāan	馬鞍山
Wu Kai Sha	Wū-kāi-sā	烏溪沙

Tseung Kwan O Line　Jēung-gwān-ngou-sin　將軍澳線

North Point	Bāk-gok	北角
Quarry Bay	Jāk-yùh-chūng	鰂魚涌
Yau Tong	Yàuh-tòhng	油塘
Tiu Keng Leng	Tìuh-gíng-léhng	調景嶺
Tseung Kwan O	Jēung-gwān-ngou	將軍澳
Hang Hau	Hāang-háu	坑口
Po Lam	Bóu-làhm	寶琳
Lohas Park	Hōng-sìhng	康城

Tsuen Wan Line	Chyùn-wāan-sin	荃灣線
Central	Jùng-wàahn	中環
Admiralty	Gàm-jùng	金鐘
Tsim Sha Tsui	Jìm-sà-jéui	尖沙咀
Jordon	Jó-dēun	佐敦
Yau ma ti	Yàuh-màh-déi	油麻地
Mong kok	Wohng-gok	旺角
Prince Edward	Taai-jí	太子
Sham Shui Po	Sàm-séui-bóu	深水埗
Cheung Sha Wan	Chèuhng-sā-wàahn	長沙灣
Lai Chi Kok	Laih-ji-gok	荔枝角
Mei Foo	Méih-fù	美孚
Lai King	Laih-gíng	荔景
Kwai Fong	Kwàih-fòng	葵芳
Kwai Hing	Kwàih-hing	葵興
Tai Wo Hau	Daaih-wō-háu	大窩口
Tsuen Wan	Chyùhn-wāan	荃灣

Tung Chung Line	Dūng-chūng-sin	東涌線
Hong Kong	Hèung-góng	香港
Kowloon	Gáu-lùhng	九龍
Olympic	Ngou-wahn	奧運
Nam Cheong	Nàahm-chēung	南昌
Lai King	Laih-gíng	荔景
Tsing Yi	Chīng-yī	青衣
Sunny Bay	Yān-ngou	欣澳
Tung Chung	Dūng-chūng	東涌

West Rail Line	Sāi-tit-sin	西鐵線
Hung Hom	Hùhng-ham	紅磡
East Tsim Sha Tsui	Jīm-dūng	尖東
Austin	Ngō-sih-dīn	柯士甸
Olympic	Ngou-wahn	奧運
Nam Cheong	Nàahm-chēung	南昌
Mei Foo	Méih-fū	美孚
Tsuen Wan West	Chyùhn-wāan-sāi	荃灣西
Kam Sheung Road	Gám-seuhng-louh	錦上路
Yuen Long	Yùhn-lóhng	元朗
Long Ping	Lóhng-pìhng	朗屏
Tin Shui Wai	Tīn-séui-wàih	天水圍
Siu Hong	Siuh-hōng	兆康
Tuen Mun	Tyùhn-mùhn	屯門

Light Rail	Hīng-tit	輕鐵
Yuen Long	Yùhn-lóhng	元朗
Tin Shui Wai	Tìn-séui-wàih	天水圍
Siu Hong	Siuh-hōng	兆康
Tuen Mun	Tyùhn-mùhn	屯門

Airport Experess	Gēi-chèuhng-faai-sin	機場快線
Hong Kong	Hèung-góng	香港
Kowloon	Gáu-lùhng	九龍
Tsing Yi	Chīng-yī	青衣
Airport	Gēi-chèuhng	機場
Asia World Expo	Bok-láahm-gún	博覽館

3. What major festivals people observe in Hong Kong

New year	Sān-nìhn	新年
Chinese New Year	Nùhng-lihk-Sān-nìhn, Chēun-jit	農曆新年，春節
Valentine's Day	Chìhng-yàhn-jit	情人節
Ching Ming Festival	Chīng-mìhng-jit	清明節
Easter	Fuhk-wuht-jit	復活節
The Buddha's Birthday	Faht-daan	佛誕
Tuen Ng Festival (Dragon Boat Festival)	Dyūn-Ńgh-jit	端午節
National Day	Gwok-hing	國慶
Mid-Autumn Festival	Jūng-chāu-jit	中秋節
Chung Yeung Festival	Chùhng-yèuhng-jit	重陽節
Christmas	Sing-daan-jit	聖誕節
Mother's Day	Móuh-chān-jit	母親節
Father's Day	Fuh-chān-jit	父親節
celebrate	hing-jūk	慶祝
Chinese New Year greeting	baai-nìhn	拜年
chocolate	jyū-gū-līk	朱古力
Christmas card	Sing-daan-kāat	聖誕咭
Dragon Boat race	pàh-lùhng-syùhn	扒龍船
display of fireworks	fong-yīn-fá	放煙花
festival	jit-yaht	節日
gift	láih-maht	禮物
give a gift	sung	送
Happy Chinese New Year! (Wish you prosperity)	Gūng-héi-faat-chòih	恭喜發財
Happy new year!	Sān-nìhn faai-lohk	新年快樂
lantern	dāng-lùhng	燈籠
lover	chìhng-yàhn	情人
Luck money	laih / leih-sih	利是
Merry Christmas!	Sing-daan faai-lohk	聖誕快樂

mooncake	yuht-béng	月餅
rose	múih-gwai-fā	玫瑰花
worship ancestors	baai jóu-sīn	拜祖先
worship the gods	baai sáhn	拜神

4. How to describe

A. Pleasant Feelings	yuh-faai-gám-gok	愉快感覺
anxious	hot-mohng	渴望
calm	jan-jìhng	鎮靜
certain	háng-dihng	肯定
comfortable	syū-fuhk	舒服
confident	yáuh seun-sām	有信心
considerate	tái-leuhng, tái-tip	體諒，體貼
content	múhn-jūk	滿足
curious	hou-kèih	好奇
determined	yáuh kyut-sām	有決心
enthusiastic	yiht-sām, gám hing-cheui	熱心，感興趣
excited	hīng-fáhn	興奮
fortunate	hahng-wahn	幸運
great	yuh-faai	愉快
happy	hōi-sām, faai-lohk	開心，快樂
hopeful	yáuh hēi-mohng	有希望
impulsive	chūng-duhng	衝動
kind	chān-chit	親切
lucky	hóu-chói, hóu-wahn	好彩，好運
optimistic	lohk-gūn	樂觀
pleased	múhn-yi, gōu-hing	滿意，高興
relaxed	hīng-sūng	輕鬆
satisfied	múhn-jūk	滿足

surprised	gīng-héi, gīng-kèih	驚喜，驚奇
thrilled	hīng-fáhn	興奮
warm	yiht-sìhng	熱誠

B. Unpleasant Feelings　　m̀-yuh-faai-gám-gok　唔愉快感覺

afraid	pa	怕
alone	gū-dāan	孤單
angry	nāu	嬲
anxious	dāam-yāu	擔憂
bored	muhn	悶
depressed	jéui-song	沮喪
disappointed	sāt-mohng	失望
embarrassed	gaam-gaai	尷尬
empty	hūng-hēui	空虛
fatigued	guih, pèih-leuih	攰，疲累
frightened	gēng	驚
frustrated	sāt-yi, tèuih-song	失意，頹喪
guilty	noih-gau	內咎
heartbroken	sām-seui	心碎
humiliated	beih sāu-yuhk	被羞辱
hurt	sēung-sām	傷心
indifferent	láahng-daahm, mohk-bāt-gwāan-sām	冷淡，漠不關心
lonely	jihk-mohk	寂寞
lost	sāt-lohk, kwan-waahk	失落，困惑
lousy	m̀-syū-fuhk	唔舒服
miserable	hó-lìhn, bāt-hahng	可憐，不幸
nervous	gán-jēung	緊張
pained	tung-fú	痛苦
panic	gīng-wòhng-sāt-chou	驚惶失措
pathetic	hó-lìhn	可憐
pessimistic	bēi-gūn	悲觀

sad	yāu-sàuh, yāu-sēung	憂愁，憂傷
shy	pa-cháu	怕醜
sorrowful	bēi-ngōi	悲哀
unhappy	m̀-hōi-sām	唔開心
upset	sām-fàahn	心煩
worried	dāam-sām	擔心

C. Weather	tīnhei	天氣
Autumn	chāu (tīn)	秋（天）
avalanche	syut-bāng	雪崩
Celsius (Centigrade)	Sip-sih	攝氏
clear and cool	chīng-sóng	清爽
cloudy	dō-wàhn	多雲
cold	dung, láahng	凍，冷
cool	(chīng) lèuhng	（清）涼
degree	douh	度
dry	gōn (chou)	乾（燥）
Fahrenheit	Wàh-sih	華氏
flooding	séui-jam	水浸
have a typhoon	dá-fūng	打風
hot	(yìhm) yiht	（炎）熱
humid	(chìuh) sāp	（潮）濕
landslide	sāan-nàih kīng-se	山泥傾瀉
observatory	tīn-màhn-tòih	天文台
overcast	tīn-yām, yām-tīn	天陰，陰天
rain	lohk-yúh	落雨
showers	jaauh-yúh	驟雨
snow	lohk-syut	落雪
Spring	chēun (tīn)	春（天）
Summer	hah (tīn)	夏（天）
sunlight	yaht-táu, yèuhng- gwōng	日頭，陽光

154

Sunny, fine	hóu-tīn	好天
temperature	wān-douh	溫度
thunder and lightning	hàahng-lèuih sím-dihn	行雷閃電
thunderstorms	leùih-bouh	雷暴
typhoon	tòih-fūng	颱風
typhoon signal	fūng-kàuh	風球
warm	nyúhn	暖
weather	tīn-hei	天氣
windy	daaih-fūng	大風
Winter	dūng (tīn)	冬 (天)

D. A person	**yàhn**	**人**
bald	gwōng-tàuh	光頭
beard, moustache	wùh-sōu	鬍鬚
big	daaih	大
big belly	daaih tóuh-láahm	大肚腩
contact lens	yán-yìhng ngáahn-géng	隱形眼鏡
cute	dāk-yi	得意
daughter	néui	女
elegant	sī-màhn	斯文
eye	ngáahn	眼
fat	fèih	肥
father	bàh-bā	爸爸
flat nose	bín-beih	扁鼻
freckle	jeuk-bāan	雀斑
graceful	daaih-fōng	大方
hair	tàuh-faat	頭髮
handsome	yīng-jeun	英俊
handsome boy	leng-jái	靚仔
look like	hóu-chíh	好似
mother	màh-mā	媽媽
nice figure	hóu sān-chòih	好身材

old	lóuh	老
pimple	ngam-chōng	暗瘡
poor	kùhng	窮
pretty	leng	靚
pretty girl	leng-néui	靚女
quite fat	fèih-féi-déi	肥肥哋
rich	yáuh-chín	有錢
rude	chōu-lóuh	粗魯
short & small	ngái-ngái-sai-sai	矮矮細細
small	sai	細
son	jái	仔
tall	gōu	高
tall and big	gōu-daaih	高大
thin, skinny	sau	瘦
wear glasses	daai ngáahn-géng	戴眼鏡
young	hauh-sāang	後生

5. What to do

Recreation and Sports	Yùh-lohk kahp wahn-duhng	娛樂及運動
academy awards	gàm-jeunhg-jéung	金像獎
admission ticket	yahp-chèuhng-gyun	入場券
adroit, agile	máhn-jiht	敏捷
adversary, counterpart	deui-sáu	對手
age limit	nìhn-lìhng hahn-jai	年齡限制
aggregate score	júng jìk-fàn	總績分
air bubble	chùng-hei jeung-mohk	充氣帳幕
all up betting	gwo-gwàan tàuh-jyu	過關投注
all-around sportsman	chyùhn-nàhng wahn-duhng-yùhn	全能運動員

all-events champion	chyùhn-nàhng gun-gwàn	全能冠軍
all-star team	mìhng-sìng-déui	明星隊
all-weather surface	chyùhn-tìn-hauh páau-douh	全天候跑道
Amah Rock	Mohng-fù-sàan	望夫山
amateur	yihp-yùh wahn-duhng-yùhn	業餘運動員
Amateur Sports Federation and Olympic Committee of HK	Hèung-góng Ngou-wái-wúi	香港奧委會
ambidextrous	jó-yauh-sáu dòu nàhng-yuhng-ge	左右手都能用嘅
announcement of results	sìhng-jìk gùng-bou	成績公佈
apparatus equipment	hei-haaih	器械
apparel, costume, attire	fuhk-jòng	服裝
appeal committee	juhng-chòih wái-yùhn-wúi	仲裁委員會
applause, cheer	hot-chói	喝采
apprentice	gin-jaahp kèh-sì	見習騎師
aquaplaner	waaht-séui wahn-duhng-yùhn	滑水運動員
archery	seh-jin	射箭
arena	jyú-chèuhng	主場
Art Festival	Ngaih-seuht-jit	藝術節
artificial turf	yàhn-jouh chóu-pèih	人造草皮
Asian Art Festival	Nga-jàu Ngaih-seuht-jit	亞洲藝術節
athlete, sportsman	wahn-duhng-yùhn	運動員
athletic meet	wahn-duhng-wúi	運動會
award	jéung-bán	獎品
away ground	haak-fòng choi-chèuhng	客方賽場
back stall	hauh-joh	後座
back stroke	bui-wihng	背泳

badminton	yúh-mòuh-kàuh	羽毛球
ball games	kàuh-leuih wahn-duhng	球類運動
ball talk	kàuh-gìng	球經
banish, foul out, chase out	faht chēut-chèuhng	罰出場
banker	máh-dáam	馬膽
bar	jáu-bà	酒巴
barbecue (B.B.Q)	sìu yéh-sihk, yéh-fó-wúi	燒嘢食，野火會
barred horses	tìhng-choi máh-pāt	停賽馬匹
baseball	páahng-kàuh	棒球
basketball	làahm-kàuh	籃球
beat, win	yèhng, sing	贏，勝
bench coach	làhm-chèuhng gaau-lihn	臨場教練
berth	yahp-wàih	入圍
best actor (movie king)	yíng-dai	影帝
best actress (movie queen)	yíng-hauh	影后
betting	bok-chói	博彩
betting centre	tàuh-jyu-jaahm	投注站
betting pool	(tàuh-jyu) chói-chìh	（投注）彩池
betting ticket	bok-chói chói-piu	博彩彩票
billiards	cheuk-kàuh	桌球
billiards parlour	cheuk-kàuh-sàt	桌球室
black and white picture	hāak-baahk pín	黑白片
bleachers	louh-tìn hon-tòih	露天看台
blinkers	ngáahn-jaau	眼罩
body building exercise	gihn-sàn-chòu	健身操
bonus	dahk-jéung	特獎
boo	hèu-sèng	噓聲
book in advance	dehng wái	訂位
booking office	piu-fòhng	票房
bowling	bóu-lìhng-kàuh	保齡球
boxing	kyùhn-gìk wahn-duhng	拳擊運動

break the record	po géi-luhk	破紀錄
break the world record	po sai-gaai géi-luhk	破世界紀錄
breast stroke	wà-sìk	蛙式
bridge	kìuh-páai	橋牌
bring down,defeat,out perform	dá-baaih	打敗
broad jump	tiu-yúhn	跳遠
broad jump pit	sà-chìh	沙池
bronze medal winner	gwai-gwàn	季軍
butterfly stroke	wùh-dihp-sìk, dihp-wihng	蝴蝶式，蝶泳
calisthenics	yàuh-yúhn tái-chòu	柔軟體操
call off	làhm-sìh chéui-sìu	臨時取消
call the score	bou-fàn	報分
call the toss	jaahk-ngán dihng syù-yèhng	擲銀定輸贏
canoe	duhk-muhk-jàu	獨木舟
canoe polo	duhk-muhk-jàu séui-kàuh	獨木舟水球
canoeing	duhk-muhk-jàu wahn-duhng	獨木舟運動
Cantonese film	yuht-yúh pín	粵語片
capacity crowd, full house, sold out	múhn-joh	滿座
captain	deuih-jéung	隊長
carry a game	sing yāt-guhk	勝一局
cartoon	kà-tùng pín	卡通片
catamaran vessel	sèung-tái-syùhn	雙體船
chalk up / create a record	chong géi-luhk	創紀錄
champion, gold medallist	gun-gwàn	冠軍
championship match	gám-bìu-choi	錦標賽
championship race (horse race)	gám-bìu-choi	錦標賽
change of courts / of ends / of goals	gàau-wuhn chèuhng-deih	交換場地

cheer-team, cheering-section	là-là-déui	啦啦隊
chess	gwok-jai jeuhng-kéi	國際象棋
Chinese chess	jeuhng-kéi	象棋
Chinese kung-fu	Jùng-gwok gùng-fù	中國功夫
choice of ends	syún-jaahk chèuhng-deih	選擇場地
chronograph	míuh-bìu	秒錶
clash, play, contend against	deui-jahn	對陣
closing ceremony	bai-mohk yìh-sìk	閉幕儀式
closing data for entries	jiht-jí bou-méng yaht-kèih	截止報名日期
coach	gaau-lihn	教練
coast home, walk-away, easy victory	hìng-yih chéui-sing	輕易取勝
combinations	gwo-gwàan jóu-hahp	過關組合
coming attraction	yuh-gou pín	預告片
coming soon	bāt-yaht-fong-yíng	不日放映
competition season	gihng-choi gwai-jit	競賽季節
competitor, contestant	chàam-choi-jé	參賽者
conduct of draw	chàu-chìm	抽籤
consolation	ngòn-wai-jéung	安慰獎
consolation tournament	ngòn-wai-choi	安慰賽
contest	béi-choi	比賽
country club	hèung-chyùn kèui-lohk-bouh	鄉村俱樂部
country park	gàau-yéh gùng-yún	郊野公園
covered playground	yáuh-goi chòu-chèuhng	有蓋操場
cowboy show	ngáuh-jái pín	牛仔片
cricket	báan-kàuh	板球
cross betting	sèung-bìn tàuh-jyu	雙邊投注
cycle racing	dàan-chè béi-choi	單車比賽
deadlock	gèung-guhk	僵局

default, withdraw	hei-kyùhn	棄權
defend one's title	waih-míhn	衛冕
defending team / side	fòhng-sáu-déui	防守隊
detective film	jìng-taam pín	偵探片
discus throw	jaahk tit-béng	擲鐵餅
dispute a title	jàng-dyuht gwun-gwàn	爭奪冠軍
disqualify	tòuh-taai	淘汰
disqualify, debar	chéui-sìu béi-choi jì-gaak	取消比賽資格
distrubution of awards	bàan-faat jéung-bán	頒發獎品
diver	chìhm-séui-yùhn	潛水員
dividend	chói-gàm	彩金
diving board	tiu-báan	跳板
division	(síu) jóu	(小) 組
documentary film	géi-luhk pín	紀錄片
dominate a game	jim ngaat-dóu-sing yàu-sai	佔壓倒性優勢
dope test	sái-yuhng hìng-fàhn-jài gìm-chàh	使用興奮劑檢查
double elimination	sèung-tòuh-taai-jai	雙淘汰制
doubles	séung-dá, sèung-yàhn choi	雙打，雙人賽
dragon-boat racing	lùhng-jàu gihng-choi, pàh lùhng-syùhn	龍舟競賽，扒龍船
draw	dá-sìhng pìhng-guhk	打成平局
dress circle	dahk-dáng	特等
dressing / changing room	gàng-yì-sàt	更衣室
drill, training, exercise	chòu-lihn	操練
drop out	jùng-tòuh teui-chēut béi-choi	中途退出比賽
edge, nose ahead	sáau-wàih líhng-sìn	稍為領先
elimination style contest	tòuh-taai-choi	淘汰賽
equalize a record	pìhng géi-luhk	平紀錄
event	béi-choi hohng-muhk	比賽項目

ex-champion	chìhn gwun-gwàn	前冠軍
exchange of pennants	gàau-wuhn déui-kèih	交換隊旗
exhibition match / competition	bíu-yín choi	表演賽
exotic bets	sàn-fún tàuh-jyu fòng-sìk	新款投注方式
fair play trophy	fùng-gaak-jéung	風格獎
fans	fēn-sí, yúng-dán, fán-sī	fan 屎，擁躉，粉絲
featherweight (boxing)	yúh-leuhng-kāp	羽量級
fencing	gim-gīk	劍擊
fiction film, literary film	màhn-ngaih pín	文藝片
field sports	yéh-ngoih wahn-duhng	野外運動
fighting film	dá-dau pín	打鬥片
figure skating	fā-sìk làuh-bìng	花式溜冰
final contest, finals, final round	kyut-choi	決賽
finish, finish line	jùng-dím	終點
first contest	chò-choi	初賽
first prize payout	tàuh-jéung jéung-gàm	頭獎獎金
first run theatre	sáu-lèuhn hei-yún	首輪戲院
fishing	diu-yú	釣魚
fitness test	sàn-tái-jāt-sou chàak-yihm	身體質素測驗
fitness trail	gihn-sàn-ging	健身徑
flash card	(chòih-pun-yuhng-ge) sih-fàn-páai	(裁判用嘅) 示分牌
fluke	hìu-hahng chéui-sing	僥倖取勝
foil fencing	sài-yèuhng gim-gīk	西洋劍擊
foreign film	sài-pín	西片
formula	tàuh-jyu fòng-sìk	投注方式
free / complementary ticket	jahng-gyuhn	贈券
free fight and kick boxing	jih-yàuh bok-gīk	自由搏擊
free style	jih-yàuh-sìk	自由式
friendly match	yàuh-yìh-choi	友誼賽

front stall	chìhn-joh	前座
full house	múhn-joh	滿座
gala premiere	yàu-sìn hin-yíng	優先獻映
game	béi-choi	比賽
game (M)	guhk	局
garrison finish, pull out of the fire	fáan-baaih-wàih-sing	反敗為勝
give a prize	bàan-jéung	頒獎
go, weichi	wàih-kéi	圍棋
goal net	lùhng-mùhn	龍門
goalless draw	lìhng-béi-lìhng, pìhng-guhk	零比零，平局
goggles	wuh-ngáahn-jaau	護眼罩
golf	gò-yíh-fù-kàuh	高爾夫球
golf course	gò-yíh-fù-kàuh-chèuhng	高爾夫球場
goose egg, horse-collar	lìhng-fàn	零分
grand slam, sweep	wohk chyùhn-sing	獲全勝
grandstand (covered)	(yáuh-goi) hon-tòih	（有蓋）看台
great!	hóu-yéh!	好嘢！
gymnasium	gihn-sàn-sàt	健身室
gymnastics	tái-chòu	體操
handball	sáu-kàuh	手球
have full power and discretion	chyùhn-kyùhn chyú-léih	全權處理
health club	gihn-hòng jùng-sàm	健康中心
heated swimming pool	lyúhn-séui wihng-chìh	暖水泳池
high jump	tiu-gòu	跳高
highest total pinfall (bowling)	jeui-gòu jīk-fàn	最高積分
hiring charge	jòu-yuhng-fai	租用費
hockey	kūk-gwan-kàuh	曲棍球
hold the record	bóu-chìh géi-luhk	保持紀錄
home team / side	jyú-déui	主隊

Hong Kong Football Association	Hèung-góng Jūk-kàuh Júng-wúi	香港足球總會
Hong Kong Coliseum	Hùhng-gún, (Hèung-góng) Hùhng-ham Tái-yuhk-gún	紅館，（香港）紅磡體育館
Hong Kong Stadium	(Jing-fú) Daaih-kàuh-chèuhng	（政府）大球場
horror film	húng-bou pín	恐怖片
horse racing	choi-máh, páau-máh	賽馬，跑馬
host country	jyú-baahn-gwok	主辦國
hurdle	tiu-làahn	跳欄
hurry up, faster	faai-dī, gà-yáu	快啲，加油
ice hockey	bìng-seuhng kūk-gwan-kàuh	冰上曲棍球
ice sports	bìng-seuhng wahn-duhng	冰上運動
in good form, in top shape	johng-taai-hóu	狀態好
in the saddle	chaak-kèh	策騎
individual competition	go-yàhn béi-choi	個人比賽
indoor competition	sāt-noih béi-choi	室內比賽
indoor games hall	sāt-noih tái-yuhk-gún	室內體育館
indoor sports	sāt-noih wahn-duhng	室內運動
interest club / group	hing-cheui síu-jóu	興趣小組
interschool competition	haauh-jai béi-choi	校際比賽
interval, intermission	yàu-sìk	休息
invitation tournament	yìu-chíng-choi	邀請賽
javelin throwing	bīu-chèung	標槍
jockey	kèh-sì	騎師
jogging	wùhn-bouh-páau, páau-bouh	緩步跑，跑步
Jubilee Sports Centre	Ngàhn-hèi Tái-yuhk Jùng-sàm	銀禧體育中心
judo	yàuh-douh	柔道
jump the gun	tàu-bouh	偷步

Kam Tin Walled Village	Gám-tìhn-wàih	錦田圍
karate	hùng-sáu-douh	空手道
keep fit	bóu-chìh sàn-tái gihn-hòng	保持身體健康
keeping time	gai-sìh	計時
kendo	gim-douh	劍道
knockout / qualifying match	tòuh-taai-choi	淘汰賽
lap	yāt hyùn	一圈
Lau Fau Shan	Làuh-fàuh-sàan	流浮山
lawn bowls	chóu-déi gwán-kàuh	草地滾球
league matches	lyùhn-choi	聯賽
life-guard	gau-sàang-yùhn	救生員
lightweight (boxing)	hìng-leuhng-kāp	輕量級
line-up	jahn-yùhng	陣容
linesman	sì-sin-yùhn	司線員
load	yahp-jaahp	入閘
locker room	yì-maht-gàan	衣物間
lodge seat	chìu-dáng	超等
Lok Ma Chau	Lohk-máh-jàu	落馬洲
lop-sided, one-sided	yāt-bìn-dóu	一邊倒
lose, bow, concede	syù	輸
manager, maestro	líhng-déui	領隊
Mandarin film	gwok-yúh pín	國語片
Marathon race	Máh-làai-chùhng-chèuhng-páau	馬拉松長跑
Mark Six	luhk-hahp-chói	六合彩
match	choi-sih	賽事
member's enclosure (Jockey Club)	wúi-yùhn-pàahng	會員棚
men's team	nàahm-jí jóu	男子組
meter	gùng-chek	公尺
mid-night show	ńgh-yeh-chèuhng	午夜場

midfield player	jùng-chèuhng kàuh-yùhn	中場球員
mini-soccer pitch	síu-yìhng jùk-kàuh-chèuhng	小型足球場
mixed team	nàahm-néuih wahn-hahp-déui	男女混合隊
morning show	jóu-chèuhng	早場
mountaineering	pàh-sàan wahn-duhng	爬山運動
movie	dihn-yíng	電影
movie star	(dihn-yíng) mìhng-sìng	(電影) 明星
music director	yàm-ngohk júng-gàam	音樂總監
neck and neck	bāt-sèung-seuhng-hah	不相上下
new record	sàn géi-luhk	新紀錄
next change	hah-kèih fong-yíng	下期放映
nick, nose out	hím-sing	險勝
novice, new-comer, beginner	sàn-sáu	新手
odds	pùih-léut	賠率
off course betting	ngoih-wàih tàuh-jyu	外圍投注
off form, out of shape	sàt-sèuhng	失常
old warhorse	lóuh-jeung	老將
Olympic Games	Ngou-wahn-wúi, Sai-wahn-wúi	奧運會，世運會
on course betting	yihng-chèuhng tàuh-jyu	現場投注
open competition / tournament	gùng-hòi-choi	公開賽
open playground	louh-tìn chòu-chèuhng	露天操場
open showers	louh-tìn fà-sá	露天花灑
open-air competition	louh-tìn béi-choi	露天比賽
Oscar	Ngou-sì-kà gàm-jeuhng-jéung	奧斯卡金像獎
owner of a horse	máh-jyú	馬主
panel of judges	pìhng-syún-tyùhn	評選團
parade ring (for horses)	sā-hyùn	沙圈
parallel bars	sèung-gong	雙槓

pari-mutuel	chói-chìh	彩池
pay out	paai-chói	派彩
pelota, jai alai	wùih-lihk-kàuh	回力球
performer	bíu-yín-jé	表演者
physique	tái-gaak	體格
ping-pong ball (table tennis)	bìng-bàm-bò	乒乓波
ping-pong paddle	bō-páak	波拍
ping-pong table	bìng-bàm-bò -tói	乒乓波枱
play rough	duhng-jok chòu-yéh	動作粗野
playing rules	béi-choi kwài-laih	比賽規例
pole vault jump	chìh gòn-tiu	持竿跳
polo	máh-kàuh	馬球
posture, pose, carriage, form	jì-sai	姿勢
preliminary round	yuh-choi	預賽
press box	gei-jé-jihk	記者席
preview	wá-tàuh	畫頭
prize-awarding, prize-giving ceremony	bàan-jéung dín-láih	頒獎典禮
professional, pro	jīk-yihp wahn-duhng-yùhn	職業運動員
public swimming pool	gùng-jung wihng-chìh	公眾泳池
pull up, catch up	yìhng-tàuh-gón-séuhng	迎頭趕上
punter	tàuh-jyu-jé	投注者
qualifying round	yàn-biht-choi	甄別賽
quantet	sei-chùhng-chói	四重彩
Queen Elizabeth Stadium	Yì-gún, Yì-leih-sà-baak Tái-yuhk-gún	伊館，伊利沙白體育館
quinella	lìhn-yèhng	連贏
race number (horse race)	chèuhng-chi	場次
racecourse	máh-chèuhng, choi-máh-chèuhng	馬場，賽馬場
raft	fàuh-tòih	浮台
receive a prize	líhng jéung	領獎

record breaking	po géi-luhk	破紀錄
recreational programme	hòng-lohk jit-muhk	康樂節目
referee, umpire	kàuh-jing	球證
registered retainer	sauh-ping kèh-sì	受聘騎師
regular show	jing-chèuhng	正場
reigning champion	bún-gaai gun-gwàn	本屆冠軍
relay	jip-lihk-choi	接力賽
relegation	gon-kàp	降級
repose, rest period	yàu-sìk sìh-gaan	休息時間
reverse, substitute	hauh-beih kàuh-yùhn	後備球員
roller skating	gwán-juhk làuh-bìng	滾軸溜冰
round robin, all play with all	chèuhn-wàahn-choi	循環賽
rowing, boating	pàh-téhng	扒艇
rubber game	kyut-sing-guhk	決勝局
rugby	láam-kàuh	欖球
runner-up, silver medallist	nga-gwàn	亞軍
rush seat	m̀-deui-houh ge gùng-jung-jihk	唔對號嘅公眾席
sailing	fùng-fàahn wahn-duhng	風帆運動
sauna	jìng-hei yuhk-sāt	蒸氣浴室
science fiction movie	fò-waahn pín	科幻片
score	dāk-fàn	得分
scoreboard	gei-fàn-páai	記分牌
scorekeeper	gei-fàn-yùhn	記分員
second run theatre	yih-lèuhn hei-yún	二輪影院
second-rated	yih-làuh ge	二流嘅
see-saw game	làai-geu-jin	拉鋸戰
seeded player	júng-jí syún-sáu	種子選手
select	syún-baht	選拔
semi-final	jéun-kyut-choi	準決賽
shooting	seh-gìk	射擊
shot putting	tèui yùhn-kàuh	推沿球

shower facilities	chùng-sàn chit-beih	沖身設備
side stroke	jāk-wihng	側泳
singles	dàan-dá, dàan-yàhn choi	單打，單人賽
Six Up	luhk-wàahn-chói	六環彩
skating	làuh-bìng	溜冰
skating rink	làuh-bìng-chèuhng	溜冰場
skiing	waaht-syut	滑雪
skittles	gwán-kàuh	滾球
snooker, billiards	tói-bò, cheuk-kàuh	枱波，桌球
soccer, football	jūk-kàuh	足球
softball	lèuih-kàuh	壘球
solar-heated changing room	taai-yèuhng-nàhng faat-yiht gàng-yi-sàt	太陽能發熱更衣室
spectator stand	gùn-jung hon-tòih	觀眾看台
spectators	gùn-jung	觀眾
sports gear, sporting goods	tái-yuhk yuhng-bán	體育用品
sports journalist, sports-writer	tái-yuhk gei-jé	體育記者
sports world / circles	tái-yuhk gaai	體育界
sportsmanship	tái-yuhk jìng-sàhn	體育精神
sprinter	dyún-páau-gà	短跑家
spy film	dahk-mouh pín	特務片
squash	bīk-kàuh	壁球
stage manage	móuh-tòih gìng-léih	舞台經理
standard pool	póu-tùng chói-chìh	普通彩池
starter	chēut-choi máh-pàt	出賽馬匹
starting pistol	seun-houh-chèung	信號槍
starting point	héi-dím	起點
storeroom	chyúh-maht-sāt	儲物室
substitution	tai-bou kàuh-yùhn	替補球員
surf ahead, take a large lead	yìuh-yìuh-líhng-sìn	遙遙領先
swim	yàuh-séui	游水
swimming gala	séui-wahn-wúi	水運會

swimming suit	wihng-yì, yàuh-wihng-fu	泳衣，游泳褲
swords-man fighting movie	móuh-hahp pín	武俠片
synchronized swimming	wáhn-leuht-wihng	韻律泳
synopsis	hei-kíu	戲橋
table tennis	bìng-bàm-bò	乒乓波
Taekwondo	Tòih-kyùhn-douh	跆拳道
Tai-chi (shadow Boxing)	Taai-gihk (kyùhn)	太極（拳）
teacher-training pool	fan-lihng-chìh	訓練池
team / squad	deuih-ńgh	隊伍
technicolor movie	chói-sìk pín	彩色片
telebet (telephone betting)	dihn-wá tàuh-jyu	電話投注
The Hong Kong Jockey Club	Máh-wúi , Hèung-góng choi-máh-wúi	馬會，香港賽馬會
third-string	sàam-làuh ge	三流嘅
ticket taker	sàu-piu-yùhn	收票員
tie score	jīk-fàn sèung-tùhng	積分相同
tierce	sàam-chùhng-chói	三重彩
time keeper	gai-sìh-yùhn	計時員
time out	jaahm-tìhng	暫停
time up, gun time, final whistle	yùhn-chèuhng	完場
to scalp	cháau-fèi	炒飛
top-class, top-flight, top-notch	yàt-làuh ge	一流嘅
toss, toss-up	jaahk-ngán kyut-dihng	擲銀決定
tournament schedule	béi-choi sìh-gaan-bíu	比賽時間表
track	páau-douh	跑道
trackwork, track gallop	sàhn-chòu	晨操
trainer	lihn-máh-sì	練馬師
trampoline	daahn-chòhng	彈牀
treble	sàam-bóu	三寶
tug-of-war	baht-hòh, ché daaih-laahm	拔河，扯大纜
turnstile	jyun-sàan	轉柵
TV film	dihn-sih pín	電視片

TV star	dihn-sih mìhng-sìng	電視明星
up-and-coming star	hauh-héi-jì-sau	後起之秀
usher	daai-wái	帶位
variety show	gò-móuh pín	歌舞片
velodrome	wún-yìhng dàan-chè-chèuhng	碗形單車場
versus	deui	對
vision display screen	yìhng-gwòng-mohk	熒光幕
visiting team	haak-déui	客隊
volleyball	pàaih-kàuh	排球
walkathon	bouh-hàhng wahn-duhng	步行運動
warming up / loosening up exercise	yiht-sàn wahn-duhng	熱身運動
water skiing	waaht-séui	滑水
water / aquatic sports, aquatics	séui-seuhng wahn-duhng	水上運動
waterpolo	séui-kàuh	水球
wave-surfing	waaht-lohng, chùng-lohng wahn-duhng	滑浪，衝浪運動
weightlifting	géui-chúhng	舉重
Western film	sài-bouh pín	西部片
win (horse race)	duhk-yèhng	獨贏
win favourite	duhk-yèhng daaih yiht-mún	獨贏大熱門
wind-surfing	waaht-lohng fùng-fàahn	滑浪風帆
withdrawal	teu-ichèut	退出
women's team	néuih-jí-jóu	女子組
wrestling	séut-gok	摔角
Yacht Club	Yàuh-téhng-wúi	遊艇會
Yoga	Yùh-gà	瑜珈

Museum	Bok-maht-gún	博物館
Flagstaff House Museum of Tea Ware	Chàh-geuih màhn-maht-gún	茶具文物館
Hong Kong Museum of Arts	Hēung-góng ngaailh-seuht-gún	香港藝術館
Hong Kong Museum of History	Hēung-góng lihk-sí bok-maht-gún	香港歷史博物館
Hong Kong Museum of Medical Sciences	Hēung-góng yī-hohk bok-maht-gún	香港醫學博物館
Hong Kong Racing Museum	Hēung-góng choi-máh bok-maht-gún	香港賽馬博物館
Hong Kong Railway Museum	Hēung-góng tit-louh bok-maht-gún	香港鐵路博物館
Hong Kong Science Museum	Hēung-góng fō-hohk-gún	香港科學館
Hong Kong Space Museum	Hēung-góng taai-hūng-gún	香港太空館
Law Uk Folk Museum	Lòh-ngūk màhn-juhk-gún	羅屋民俗館
Lei Cheng Uk Han Tomb Museum	Léih-jehng-ngūk Hon-mouh bok-maht-gún	李鄭屋漢墓博物館
Museum of Hong Kong Police	Gíng-déui bok-maht-gún	警隊博物館
Sam Tung Uk Museum	Sāam-duhng-ngūk bok-maht-gún	三棟屋博物館
The Culture and Heritage Museum of Hong Kong	Hēung-góng màhn-fa bok-maht-gún	香港文化博物館
Sheung Yiu Folk Museum	Seuhng-yìuh màhn-juhk mahn-maht-gún	上窰民俗文物館
Hong Kong Museum of Coastal Defence	Hēung-góng hói-fòhng bok-maht-gún	香港海防博物館

Public Amenities	Gùng-guhng-màhn-yùh-chit-sì	公共文娛設施
Academic Community Hall	Daaihi-jyùn wúi-tòhng	大專會堂
Arts Center	Ngaih-seuht jùng-sàm	藝術中心
City Hall	Daaih-wuih-tòhng	大會堂
City Hall Concert Hall	Daaih-wuih-tòhng yàm-ngohk-tèng	大會堂音樂廳
City Hall Theatre	Daaih-wuih-tòhng kehk-yún	大會堂劇院
Convention and Exhibition Center	Wuih-jín, Hèung-góng wuih-yih jín-láahm jūng-sām	會展，香港會議展覽中心
Cultural Centre	Màhn-fa jūng-sām	文化中心
Hong Kong Academy for Performing Arts	Hèung-góng yín-ngaih hohk-yún	香港演藝學院
Hongkong Coliseum	Hùhng-ham tái-yuhk-gún	紅磡體育館
Ko Shan Theatre	Gòu-sàan kehk-chèuhng	高山劇場
Queen Elizabeth Stadium	Yì-gún,Yì-leih-sà-baak tái-yuhk-gún	伊館，伊利沙白體育館
Tuen Wan Town Hall	Chyùhn-wàan daaih-wuih-tòhng	荃灣大會堂
Yuen Long Town Hall	Yùhn-lóhng daaih-wuih-tòhng	元朗大會堂

Fine Arts	Ngaih-seuht	藝術
City Contemporary Dance company	Sìhng-síh dòng-doih móuh-douh-tyùhn	城市當代舞蹈團
Hong Kong Children's Choir	Hēung-góng yìh-tùhng hahp-cheung-tyùhn	香港兒童合唱團
Hong Kong Chinese Orchestra	Hēung-góng jùng-ngohk-tyùhn	香港中樂團

173

Hong Kong Dance Company	Hēung-góng móuh-douh-tyùhn	香港舞蹈團
Hong Kong Philharmonic Orchestra	Hēung-góng gún-yìhn ngohk-tyùhn	香港管弦樂團
Hong Kong Repertory Theatre	Hēung-góng wá-kehk-tyùhn	香港話劇團
Hong Kong Youth Theatre Company	Hēung-góng chìng-nìhn kehk-tyùhn	香港青年劇團

Places of Interest	**Hóu-heui-chyu**	**好去處**
Hong Kong Island	Hēung-góng-dóu	香港島
Dr. Sun Yat-Sen Museum	Syūn-Jūng-Sāan géi-nihm-gún	孫中山紀念館
Golden Bauhinia Square	Gām-jí-gīng gwóng-chèuhng	金紫荊廣場
Happy Valley Racecourse	Faai-wuht-gūk máh-chèuhng	快活谷馬場
Hollywood Road	Hòh-léih-wuht douh	荷李活道
Hong Kong Park	Hēung-góng gūng-yún	香港公園
Lan Kwai Fong	Làahng-wai-fōng	蘭桂坊
Murray House	Méih-leih làuh	美利樓
Ocean Park	Hói-yéuhng gūng-yún	海洋公園
Repulse Bay	Chín-séui-wāan	淺水灣
Soho	Sōu-hòh	蘇豪
Stanley Market	Chek-chyúh (síh-jaahp)	赤柱（市集）
The Peak	(Taai-pìhng)-Sāan-déng	（太平）山頂
Western Market	Sāi-góng-sìhng	西港城
Kowloon	Gáu-lùhng (bun-dóu)	九龍（半島）
Ap Liu Street	Ngaap-lìuh gāai	鴨寮街
Avenue of Stars	Sīng-gwōng daaih-douh	星光大道

Bird Garden	Jeuk-níuh fā-yún	雀鳥花園
Flea Market	tiu-jóu síh-chèuhng	跳蚤市場
Flower Market	Fā-Hēui	花墟
Goldfish Market	Gām-yú gāai	金魚街
Jade Market	Yuhk-hei-síh-chèuhng	玉器市場
Kowloon Walled City Park	Gáu-lùhng sìhng-jaaih gūng-yún	九龍城寨公園
(Monkok) Ladies' Market	(Wohng-gok) Néuih-yán gāai	（旺角）女人街
Lei Yue Mun Seafood Bazzar	Léih-yùh-mùhn hói-sìn-méih-sihk-chyūn	鯉魚門海鮮美食村
Nan Lian Garden	Nàahm-lìhn-yùhn-chìh	南蓮園池
Street of Sneakers	Bō-hàaih gāai	波鞋街
Temple street Night market	míu-gāai yeh-síh	廟街夜市
Wong Tai Sin Temple	Wòhng-daaih-sīn (chìh)	黃大仙（祠）

New Territories	Sān-gaai	新界
Che Kung Temple	Chē-gūng míu	車公廟
Ching Chung Koon (Taoist Temple)	Chīng-chùhng gun	青松觀
Hong Kong Heritage Museum	Hēung-góng màhn-fa bok-maht-gún	香港文化博物館
Hong Kong Wetland Park	Hēung-góng sāp-deih gūng-yún	香港濕地公園
Lam Tsuen Wishing Trees	Làhm-chyūn héui-yuhn-syuh	林村許願樹
Ma Wan Park Noah's Ark	Máh-wāan gūng-yún nòih-nga fōng-jāu	馬灣公園挪亞方舟
Mai Po Wetlands	Máih-bou sāp-deih	米埔濕地
Sai Kung Town	Sāi-gung hēui	西貢墟
Sha Tin Racecourse	Sā-tìhn Máh-chèuhng	沙田馬場
Tsing Ma Bridge	Chīng-máh daaih-kìuh	青馬大橋

Outlying Islands	Lèih-dóu	離島
Cheung Chau	Chèuhng-jāu	長洲
Giant Buddha	Tīn-tàahn Daaih-faht	天壇大佛
Hong Kong Disneyland	Hēung-góng Dihk-sih-nèih lohk-yùhn	香港迪士尼樂園
Lamma Island	Nàahm-ngā-dóu	南丫島
Lantau Island	Daaih-yùh-sāan	大嶼山
Ngong Ping 360	Ngóhng-pìhng sāam-luhk-lihng	昂平 360
Po Lin Monastery	Bóu-Lìhn (Sìhm) jí	寶蓮 (禪) 寺
Tai O Fishing Village	Daaih-ngou (yùh-chyūn)	大澳 (漁村)
The Wisdom Path	Sām-gīng gáan-làhm	心經簡林

Chinese Musical Instruments	Jùng-gwok ngohk-hei	中國樂器
Bass gehu	dài-yàm gaak-wú	低音革胡
Daruan	daaih-yún	大阮
Di	dék	笛
Erhu	yih-wú	二胡
Gaohu	gòu-wú	高胡
Gehu	gaak-wú	革胡
Guan	gún	管
Guzheng	gú-jàng	古箏
Liuqin	láuh-yihp-kàhm	柳葉琴
Percussion	hàau-gìk ngohk-hei	敲擊樂器
Pipa	pèih-pá	琵琶
Sanxian	sàam-yìhn	三弦
Sheng	sāng	笙
Suona	sāau-nahp	嗩吶
Yangqin	yèuhng-kàhm	洋琴

| Zhonghu | jùng-wú | 中胡 |
| Zhongruan | jùng-yún | 中阮 |

6. *What to eat and drink*

Food	sihk-bán	食品
appetizer	tàuh-pún	頭盆
bacon	yìn-yuhk	煙肉
bean curd	dauh-fu	豆腐
beef	ngàuh-yuhk	牛肉
beverage	yám-bán	飲品
bird's nest	yin-wò	燕窩
bread	mihn-bàau	麵包
butter	ngàuh-yàuh	牛油
cake	daahn-gòu	蛋糕
candy	tóng	糖
catchup (ketchup)	ké-jāp	茄汁
cheese	jì-sí, chì-sí	芝士
chestnut	leuht-jí	栗子
Chinese sausage	laahp-chéung	臘腸
coldmeat platter	pìng-pún	拼盆
congee, rice gruel	jùk	粥
cookies	kūk-kèih-béng	曲奇餅
cornflakes	sūk-máih-pín	粟米片
cube sugar	fòng-tòhng	方糖
curry	ga-lēi	咖喱
date	jóu	棗
dessert	tìhm-bán	甜品
dimsum	dím-sàm	點心
egg (preserved)	pèih-dáan	皮蛋
eggwhite	dáan-báak	蛋白

fish	yú	魚
French fries	syùh-tíu	薯條
frog	tìhn-gài	田雞
ham	fó-téui	火腿
hamburger	hon-bóu bàau	漢堡包
hot dog	yiht-gáu	熱狗
ingredient	yuhng-líu	用料
instant noodle	gùng-jái mihn, jìk-sihk mihn	公仔麵，即食麵
jam	gwó-jìm	果占
lamb chop	yèuhng pá	羊扒
macaroni	tùng-sàm fán	通心粉
main course	jyú-choi	主菜
milk	ngàuh-náaih	牛奶
mungbean vermicelli	fán-sì	粉絲
noodle	mihn	麵
oatmeal	mahk-pèih	麥皮
Peking duck	Bāk-gìng ngáap	北京鴨
pie	pài	批
pigeon	yúh-gaap	乳鴿
pizza	pī-sàh, yi-daaih-leih bohk-béng	□□，意大利薄餅
popsicle	syut-tíu	雪條
pork chop	jyù pá	豬扒
pork rib	pàaih-gwàt	排骨
pudding	bou-dīn	布甸
rice (cooked)	faahn	飯
rice gruel	lāang-lóu-jùk, hèi-faahn	冷佬粥，稀飯
rice-noodle	máih-fán	米粉
roast duck	sìu-ngaap	燒鴨
roast suckling pig	yúh-jyù	乳豬
salad	sà-léut	沙律

178

salad dressing	sà-léut jeung	沙律醬
salt	yìhm	鹽
salty egg (preserved)	hàahm-dáan	鹹蛋
sandwich	sàam-màhn-jih	三文治
sausage	hèung-chéung	香腸
seafood	hói-sìn	海鮮
seasoning	tìuh-meih-bán	調味品
shark's fin soup	yùh-chi	魚翅
soup (thick)	gàng	羹
soup (thin)	tòng	湯
soy sauce	sih-yàuh	豉油
steak	ngàuh pá	牛扒
steamed chicken	baahk-chit-gài	白切雞
sugar	tòhng	糖
tomato sauce	fàan-ké jeung	番茄醬
veal cutlet	ngàuh-jái-yuhk	牛仔肉
vinegar	chou	醋
walnut	hahp-tòuh	合桃
won-ton noodle	wàhn-tàn mihn	雲吞麵
won-ton	wàhn-tàn	雲吞
yogurt	syùn ngàuh-náaih	酸牛奶

Basic Seasonings and Ingredients for Chinese Cooking	Jùng-choi tìuh-meih-bán kahp yuhng-líu	中菜調味品及用料

Chinese rose wine	mùih-gwai-louh	玫瑰露
chilli sauce	laaht-jìu jeung	辣椒醬
chilli oil	laaht-jìu yàuh	辣椒油
mustard paste	gaai-laaht	芥辣
curry powder	ga-lèi fán	咖喱粉
red vinegar	jit-chou	浙醋
scallops (dried)	gon-yìuh-chyúh	乾瑤柱

dried shrimp	hà-máih	蝦米
dried mushroom	dùng-gù	冬菇
straw mushroom	chóuh-gù	草菇
Jew's ear mushroom	wàhn-yíh	雲耳
sesame (black)	hàak jì-màh	黑芝麻
sesame (white)	baahk jì-màh	白芝麻
date (red)	hùhng-jóu	紅棗
date (preserved honey)	math-jóu	蜜棗
dried tangerine peel	gwó-pèih	果皮
pepper	wùh-jiu-fán	胡椒粉
soysauce (light color)	sàang-chàu	生抽
soysauce (dark color)	lóuh-chàu	老抽
ginger	gèung	薑
green onion	chùng	葱
sugar	tòhng	糖
salt	yìhm	鹽
oil	yàuh	油
oyster sauce	hòuh-yàuh	蠔油
sesame oil	màh-yàuh	麻油
sesame sauce	jì-màh jeung	芝麻醬
fermented black beans	dauh-sih	豆豉
fermented soybean paste	mihn-sí	麵豉
Chinese Wine (Shao Hsing)	siuh-hing jáu	紹興酒
triple distilled Chinese wine	sàam-jìng jáu	三蒸酒
corn starch	dauh-fán, yìng-sūk-fán	豆粉，鷹粟粉

Cantonese Dishes	Gwóng-dùng-choi / Yuht-choi	廣東菜／粵菜
Cold dish	Láahng-pún	冷盤
assorted barbecued meats	sìu-méi pìng-pún	燒味拼盆
barbecued pork	chà-sìu	叉燒

roasted goose	sìu-ngó	燒鵝
roasted pork	sìu-yuhk	燒肉
roasted spareribs	sìu pàaih-gwàt	燒排骨
soy sauce chicken	sih-yàuh gài	豉油雞

Soup	Tòng	湯
diced winter melon with mixed meats and seafood soup	jaahp-gám dùng-gwà-nāp tòng	雜錦冬瓜粒湯
doubled boiled whole winter melon soup	dùng-gwà jùng	冬瓜盅
minced beef and egg white soup	sài-wùh ngàuh-yuhk gàng	西湖牛肉羹
shark's fin soup with shredded chicken	gài-sì chi	雞絲翅
shredded duck meat with conpoy soup	gòn-yìuh-chyúh ngaap-sì gàng	乾瑤柱鴨絲羹
snake soup (in winter only)	sèh gàng	蛇羹
sweet corn with crab meat (or: minced chicken) soup	háaih-yuhk / gài-yùhng sùk-méih gàng	蟹肉／雞蓉粟米羹

Poultry	Gài-ngaap	雞鴨
deep-fried duckling with mashed taro	laih-yùhng hèung-sòu ngaap	荔蓉香酥鴨
diced chicken with walnuts / cashew nuts	hahp-tòuh / yìu-gwó gài-dìng	合桃／腰果雞丁
fried chicken	ja jí-gài	炸子雞
pan-fried lemon duck / chicken	nìhng-mùng ngaap / gài	檸檬鴨／雞
roasted pigeon	sìu yúh-gaap	燒乳鴿

Beef & Pork	yuhk	肉
deep-fried salt & pepper spareribs	jìu-yìhm pàaih-gwàt	椒鹽排骨
stir-fried sliced fillet of beef in oyster sauce	hòuh-yàuh ngàuh-yuhk	蠔油牛肉
sweet & sour pork	gù-lòu-yuhk	咕嚕肉
sweet & sour spare-ribs	sàang-cháau pàaih-gwàt	生炒排骨

Seafood	Hói-sìn	海鮮
baked (fried) crab in ginger & onion sauce	gēung-chùng guhk háaih	薑葱焗蟹
baked (fried) crab / lobster in black bean & chilli sauce	sih-jìu guhk háaih / lùhng-hà	豉椒焗蟹／龍蝦
deep-fried crab claws	ja yeuhng háaih-kìhm	炸釀蟹鉗
deep-fried salt & pepper squid	jìu-yìhm sìn-yáu	椒鹽鮮魷
fried prawns with garlic sauce	syun-yùhng hà	蒜蓉蝦
fried prawns with salt, pepper & chilli	jìu-yìhm hà	椒鹽蝦
poached shrimps (blanched shrimps)	baahk-cheuk hà	白灼蝦
sautéed broccoli with scallop	sài-làahn-fà cháau daai-jí	西蘭花炒帶子
steamed bean-curd stuffed with minced shrimp	baak-fā jìng-yeuhng dauh-fuh	百花蒸釀豆腐
steamed fish in salted-bean sauce	sih-jāp jìng yú	豉汁蒸魚
steamed garoupa	chìng-jìng sehk-bāan	清蒸石斑

Vegetable	Sō-choi	蔬菜
sautéed broccoli	cháau sài-làahn-fà	炒西蘭花

sautéed Chinese flowering vegetable	cháau choi-sàm	炒菜心
sautéed Chinese kale	cháau gaai-láan	炒芥蘭
sautéed fresh asparagus	cháau sìn louh-séun	炒鮮露筍
sautéed fresh mushroom with crabmeat	háaih-yuhk pàh sìn-gù	蟹肉扒鮮菇
sautéed pea-shoots with crabmeat	háaih-yuhk pàh dauh-miuh	蟹肉扒豆苗

Desserts	Tìhm-bán	甜品
almond soup	hahng-yàhn-wú	杏仁糊
honey dew melon sago soup with coconut juice	math-gwà sài-máih-louh	蜜瓜西米露
red bean soup	hùhng-dáu-sà	紅豆沙

Chinese Tea	Jùng-gwok chàh	中國茶
Chrysanthemum	Hòhng-gūk	杭菊
Jasmine Tea	Hèung-pín	香片
Lok-on	Luhk-ngòn	六安
Lung-Ching	Lùhng-jéng	龍井
Pu-erh	bóu-léi	普洱
Pu-erh + Chrysanthemum	Gūk-bóu	菊普
Shou-mei	Sauh-méi	壽眉
Shui-hsien	Séui-sìn	水仙
Tikuanyin	Tit-gùn-yàm	鐵觀音
Wu Long	Wù-lúng	烏龍

Cooking Methods	Pàang-yahm faat	烹調法
bake	guhk	焗
blanch	cheuk, luhk	焯，淥

boil	jyú, saahp	煮，燴
boil (water, soup)	bòu	煲
braise	hùhng-sìu	紅燒
Cantonese hot pot	dá bìn-lòuh	打邊爐
deep-fried	ja, jaau	炸
double boil	dahng	燉
grill	sìu-hàau	燒烤
Mongolian hot pot	fó-wò	火鍋
pan-fried	jìn	煎
roast	sìu	燒
simmer	maahn-fó jyú	慢火煮
smoke	fàn	燻
steam	jìng	蒸
stew	màn	炆
stir-fried	cháau	炒

Dim-Sum	Dím sàm	點心
steamed rice flour rolls with barbecued pork	chà-sìu chéung (fán)	叉燒腸（粉）
steamed barbecued pork bun	chà-sìu-bàau	叉燒包
deep fried spring rolls with pork, chicken and bamboo shoot	chēun-gyún	春卷
stuffed cake with egg-yolk	chìn-chàhng-gòu	千層糕
custard tart	daahn-tāat	蛋撻
mashed lotus seed bun with egg-yolk	daahn-wóng lìhn-yùhng-bāau	蛋黃蓮蓉包
mashed sesame seed bun with egg-yolk	daahn-wóng màh-yùhng-bāau	蛋黃麻蓉包
steamed sweet egg pudding	dahng gài-dáan	燉雞蛋
double boiled fresh milk	dahng sèung-péi náaih	燉雙皮奶
steamed shrimps and bamboo shoot dumpling	fán-gwó	粉果

steamed chicken feet with soyed bean and chilli	fuhng-jáau	鳳爪
steamed assorted meat and chicken rolls	gài-jaat	雞扎
steamed dumpling stuffed with pork and chicken soup	gun-tòng-gáau	灌湯餃
deep fried dumpling with pork, shrimp and bamboo shoot	hàahm-séui-gók	鹹水角
steamed shrimp dumpling	hà-gáau	蝦餃
steamed fried rice in lotus leaf wrapping	hòh-yihp faahn	荷葉飯
lotus seed in red bean soup	lìhn-jí hùhng-dáu-sà	蓮子紅豆沙
almond bean curd and fruit	jaahp-gwó-hahng-yàhn-dauh-fuh	雜果杏仁豆腐
sweet mashed black sesame rolls	jì-màh-gyún	芝蔴卷
glutinous rice dumpling wrapped in bamboo leaves	júng	粽
crisp and sticky sweet cake topped with walnut	máh-jái	馬仔
steamed sponge cake	máh-làai-gòu	馬拉糕
stuffed duck's web in oyster sauce	ngaap-geuk-jaat	鴨腳扎
steamed tripe in black beans and chilli sauce	ngàuh-paak-yihp	牛柏葉
mango pudding	mòng-gwó bou-dìn	芒果布甸
steamed beef ball	ngàuh-yuhk	牛肉
steamed dumpling filled with sweet coconut, peanuts & sesame	pàhn-yihp-gók	蘋葉角
steamed minced beef ball with bean curd skin	sàan-jùk ngàuh-yuhk	山竹牛肉
steamed pork chop with soyed bean sauce	sih-jàp pàaih-gwàt	豉汁排骨
steamed fresh cuttle fish	sìn-yáu	鮮魷

deep fried bean curd roll with pork, shrimp in oyster sauce	sìn-jùk-gyún	鮮竹卷
steamed pork dumpling	sìu-máai	燒賣
deep fried Taro dumplings	wuh-gók	芋角
steamed sweet coconut pudding	yèh-jàp-gòu	椰汁糕
sweet coconut glutinous cake	yèh-sì noh-máih-chìh	椰絲糯米糍
fried green pepper with pork or fish	yeuhng chèng-jìu	釀青椒
steamed dumpling filled with shark's fin, pork and bamboo shoots	yùh-chi-gáau	魚翅餃
mango pudding	mòng-gwó bou-dīn	芒果布甸

Drinks	yám-bán	飲品
black coffee	jàai-fē	齋啡
bubbling wine	hei-jáu	汽酒
champagne	hèung-bàn (jáu)	香檳（酒）
chocolate	jyù-gù-lìk	朱古力
cider	pìhng-gwó jáu	蘋果酒
cocktail	gài-méih jáu	雞尾酒
cocoa	gūk-gú	唂咕
coffee	ga-fē	咖啡
condensed milk	lihn-náaih	煉奶
draught	sàang-bè	生啤
distil water	jìng-lauh séui	蒸餾水
fresh lemon juice	sìn nìng-jàp	鮮檸汁
fresh milk	sìn náaih	鮮奶
fruit juice	gwó-jàp	果汁
fruit punch	jaahp-gwó bàn-jih	雜果賓治
gin	jìn-jáu	毡酒
Guinness Stout	Bō-dá jáu	波打酒
Horlicks	Hóu-lahp-hāak	好立克
lemon tea	nìhng-mùng chàh	檸檬茶
lemonade	nìhng-mùng jāp	檸檬汁

milk	ngàuh-náaih	牛奶
milk powder	náaih-fán	奶粉
mineral water	kwong-chyùhn séui	礦泉水
orange juice	cháang jāp	橙汁
Ovaltine	Ngò-wàh-tìhn	阿華田
red wine	hùhng jáu	紅酒
rum	làm jáu	冧酒
skimmed milk	tyut-jì náaih	脫脂奶
spirit, liquor	liht jáu	烈酒
tea	chàh	茶
vodka	fuhk-dahk-gā jáu	伏特加酒
whisky	wài-sih-géi	威士忌
white wine	baahk jáu	白酒
whole milk	chyùhn-jì náaih	全脂奶
wine	jáu	酒

Beer	**Bē-jáu**	**啤酒**
Blue Girl	Làahm-mùi	藍妹
Blue Ribbon	Làahm-dáai	藍帶
Budweiser	Baak-wāi	百威
Carlsberg	Gā-sih-baak	嘉士伯
Heineken	Héi-lihk	喜力
Kirin	Kèih-lèuhn	麒麟
Lowenbaru	Lòuh-wàhn-bóu	盧雲堡
San Miguel	Sàng-lihk	生力
Tsing Tao	Chìng-dóu	青島

Brandy	**baahk-làan-déi**	**白蘭地**
Bisquit V.S.O.P.	Baak-sih-gāt	百事吉
Courvoiser V.S.O.P.	Nàh-po-lèuhn	拿破崙
Hennesy X.O.	Hìn-nèih-sì	軒尼詩
Martell	Làahm-dáai	藍帶
Remy Martin	Yàhn-tàuh-máh	人頭馬

Chinese wine	Jùng-gwok-jáu	中國酒
Bamboo-leaf Green	Jūk-yihp-chèng	竹葉青
Da Chu	Daaih-kūk	大麯
Fen Jiu	Fàhn-jáu	汾酒
Maotai	Màauh-tòih	茅台
rice wine	máih-jáu, sèung-jìng	米酒，雙蒸
Wu Chia Pi	Ńgh-gà-pèih	五加皮

Soda	Hei-séui	汽水
Coca Cola	(Hó-háu) hó-lohk	（可口）可樂
Fanda	Fàn-daaht	芬達
Green Spot	Luhk-bóu	綠寶
Pepsi Cola	Baak-sih-hó-lohk	百事可樂
Schweppes	Yuhk-chyùhn	玉泉
Seven up	Chàt-héi	七喜
Sprite	Syut-bīk	雪碧
Sunkist	Sàn-kèih-sih	新奇士
Vita-soy	Wàih-tà-náaih	維他奶

Fruits	sāang-gwó	生果
apple	pìhng-gwó	蘋果
apricot	hahng	杏
Australian pear	bē-léi	啤梨
avocado	ngàuh-yàuh-gwó	牛油果
banana	hèung-jiu	香蕉
cantaloup	hèung-gwā	香瓜
cherry	chè-lèih-jí	車厘子
coconut	yèh-jí	椰子
dragon eye	lùhng-ngáan	龍眼
durian	làuh-lìhn	榴槤

fig	mòuh-fà-gwó	無花果
grape	(pòuh) tàih-jí	（葡）提子
grapefruit	sài-yáu	西柚
green apple	chèng pìhng-gwó	青蘋果
guava	fàan-sehk-láu	番石榴
honey dew melon	math-gwà	蜜瓜
Kiwi Fruit	kèih-yih-gwó	奇異果
lemon	nìhng-mùng	檸檬
lichee	laih-jì	荔枝
loquat	pèih-pàh-gwó	枇杷果
Mandarin orange	gàm	柑
mango	mòng-gwó	芒果
mangosteen	sāan-jùk	山竹
orange	cháang	橙
papaya	muhk-gwà	木瓜
peach	tóu	桃
pear	léi	李
persimmon	nàhm-chí	腍柿
pineapple	bò-lòh	菠蘿
plum	bou-lām, léi	布冧，李
pomelo	sà-tìhn-yáu, lūk-yáu	沙田柚，碌柚
star-fruit	yèuhng-tóu	洋桃
strawberry	sih-dò-bè-léi	士多啤梨
tangerine	gāt, gàm-jái	桔，柑仔
water melon	sài-gwà	西瓜

Kitchen Utensils	**chyùh-fóng yuhng-geuih**	**廚房用具**
bowl	wún	碗
can-opener	gun-táu dòu	罐頭刀
chopper	choi dòu	菜刀
chopping block	jàm-báan	砧板

chopsticks	faai-jí	筷子
coffee pot	ga-fē wú	咖啡壺
earthenware cooking pot	sā-bòu	沙煲
egg cup	dáan-bùi	蛋杯
egg-beater	dá-dáan gèi	打蛋機
electric rice cooker	dihn faahn-bōu	電飯煲
fork	chà	叉
frying-pan	pìhng-dái wohk	平底鑊
glass	bùi	杯
kettle	chàh-bòu	茶煲
knife	dòu	刀
microwave–oven	mèih-bò(guhk)lòuh	微波（焗）爐
mixer	gáau-buhn-gēi	攪拌機
napkin	chàan-gàn	餐巾
oil pitcher	yàuh-jèun	油樽
oven	guhk-lòuh	焗爐
plate	díp, dihp	碟
refrigerator	syut-gwaih	雪櫃
rice ladle	faahn-hok	飯殼
sauce plate	meih-díp	味碟
soup ladle	tòng-hok	湯殼
soup pot (Chinese style)	wàhn-díng-bòu	雲頂煲
spatula	wohk-cháan	鑊鏟
spoon	chìh-gàng	瓷羹
steaming rack	jing-long, sung-gá	蒸口，餸架
stove (L.P. gas)	sehk-yàuh-hei lòuh	石油汽爐
stove (electric)	dihn lòuh	電爐
stove (gas)	mùih-hei lòuh	煤氣爐
strainer (for drying)	sāau-gèi	筲箕
strainer (for frying)	jaau-lèi	罩籬
strainer (tea)	chàh-gaak	茶隔
table cloth	tói-bou	枱布
teapot	chàh-wú	茶壺

toaster	dò-sí lòuh	多士爐
tooth pick	ngàh-chìm	牙籤
toothpick-holder	ngàh-chìm túng	牙籤筒
wok (Chinese cooking pan)	wohk	鑊

Noodle and Rice — Faahn-mihn 飯麵

| noodle (Cantonese style) | mihn | 麵 |

Braised noodle (per dish) — Baahn-mihn 辦麵

with barbecued pork	chà-sìu baahn-mihn	叉燒辦麵
with brisket of beef	ngàuh-láahm baahn-mihn	牛腩辦麵
with ginger & green onion	gèung-chùng baahn-mihn	薑葱辦麵
with mixed vegetables	lòh-hon baahn-mihn	羅漢辦麵
with mushroom	bāk-gù baahn-mihn	北菇辦麵
with prawns	hà-kàuh baahn-mihn	蝦球辦麵
with shredded chicken	gài-sì-baahn-mihn	雞絲辦麵

E-Fu noodle (per dish) — Yì-mihn 伊麵

stewed	gòn-sìu yì-mihn	乾燒伊麵
with crab cream	háaih-wòhng yì-mihn	蟹黃伊麵
with crab meat	háaih-yuhk yì-mihn	蟹肉伊麵

Fried noodle (per dish) — Cháau-mihn 炒麵

with barbecued pork	chà-sìu cháau-mihn	叉燒炒麵
with brisket of beef	ngàuh-láahm cháau-mihn	牛腩炒麵
with chicken balls	gài-kàuh cháau-mihn	雞球炒麵

with garoupa balls	bàan-kàuh cháau-mihn	斑球炒麵
with pork ribs	pàaih-gwàt cháau-mihn	排骨炒麵
with prawn balls	hà-kàuh cháau-mihn	蝦球炒麵
with shredded pork	yuhk-sì cháau-mihn	肉絲炒麵
with sliced beef	ngàuh-yuhk cháau-mihn	牛肉炒麵

Noodles in soup (per bowl)	**Tòng-mihn**	**湯麵**
with barbecued pork	chà-sìu tòng-mihn	叉燒湯麵
with braised duck's leg	ngaap-téui tòng-mihn	鴨腿湯麵
with chicken balls	gài-kàuh tòng-mihn	雞球湯麵
with ham	fó-téui seuhng-tòng sàang-mihn	火腿上湯生麵
with pork ribs	pàaih-gwàt tòng-mihm	排骨湯麵
with roasted goose	sìu-ngòh laaih-fán	燒鵝瀨粉
with sliced beef	ngàuh-yuhk tòng-mihn	牛肉湯麵
with soyed chicken	yàuh-gài tòng-mihn	油雞湯麵

Noddle in soup (per tureen)	**Wò-mihn**	**窩麵**
with assorted meat	Yèuhng-jàu wò-mihn	揚州窩麵
with chicken balls	gài-kàuh wò-mihn	雞球窩麵
with crab meat & egg	hùhng-tòuh wò-mihn	鴻圖窩麵
with garoupa balls	bāan-kàuh wò-mihn	斑球窩麵
with shrimp balls	hà-kàuh wò-mihn	蝦球窩麵

Rice noodle (per dish)	**Hó / máih-fán**	**河／米粉**
stewed rice-noodle with beef	gòn-cháau ngàuh-hó	乾炒牛河
Vermicelli "singapore" style	Sìng-jàu cháau máih	星洲炒米
Vermicelli "Fook Chow" style	Hah-mùhn cháau máih	廈門炒米
with beef	ngàuh-yuhk cháau hó	牛肉炒河

with brisket of beef	ngàuh-náahm cháau hó	牛腩炒河
with sliced beef, soyed bean and chilli	sih-jìu ngàuh-hó	豉椒牛河

diced chicken noodles	lyuhn-gài wùi mihn	嫩雞煨麵
pekinese noodles with minced pork (without soup)	ja-jeung mihn	炸醬麵
pekinese noodles with mixed meat	daaih lóuh mihn	大滷麵
with mixed vegetables	sou jaahp-gám mihn	素什錦麵
with pork chop	pàaih-gwàt mihn	排骨麵
with shredded chicken & ham	gài-sì-fó-téui-mihn	雞絲火腿麵
with shredded pork and chinese pickles	ja-choi-yuhk-sì-mihn	榨菜肉絲麵
with shredded pork and sour vegetables	syut-choi-yuhk-sì-mihn	雪菜肉絲麵
with shrimps	hà-yàhn-mihn	蝦仁麵
with sour & chilli sauce	syùn-laaht-mihn	酸辣麵

Rice   Faahn   飯

fried rice with assorted meat	Yèuhng-jàu cháau faahn	揚州炒飯
with barbecued pork	chà-sìu faahn	叉燒飯
with barbecued pork & salty egg	hàahm-dáan chà-sìu faahn	鹹蛋叉燒飯
with chicken ball & vegetable	choi-yúhn gài-kàuh faahn	菜遠雞球飯
with curry brisket of beef	ga-lēi ngàuh-náahm faahn	咖喱牛腩飯
with curry chicken	ga-lēi gāi faahn	咖喱雞飯

with curry beef	ga-lēi ngàuh-yuhk faahn	咖喱牛肉飯
with diced meat & sweet corn	sūk-máih yuhk-nāp faahn	粟米肉粒飯
with diced pork and green peas	chèng-dáu yuhk-nāp faahn	青豆肉粒飯
with fresh tomato and beef	sìn-ké ngáu faahn	鮮茄牛飯
with garoupa ball and vegetable	choi-yúhn bàan-kàuh faahn	菜遠斑球飯
with ham & fried egg	fó-téui jìn dáan faahn	火腿煎蛋飯
with minced beef & raw egg	wò-dáan ngàuh-yuhk faahn	窩蛋牛肉飯
with pork chop	jyù pá faahn	豬扒飯
with pork rib & vegetable	choi-yúhn pàaih-gwàt faahn	菜遠排骨飯
with prawn ball & vegetable	choi-yúhn hà-kàuh faahn	菜遠蝦球飯
with scrambled egg & shrimps	waaht-dáan hà-yàhn faahn	滑蛋蝦仁飯
with soyed chicken	yàuh-gài faahn	油雞飯
with steamed chicken	chit-gài faahn	切雞飯
with sweet corn and garoupa	sùk-máih bàan-pín faahn	粟米斑片飯

Seafood	hói-sīn	海鮮
abalone	bàau-yùh	鮑魚
carp	léih-yú	鯉魚
clam	hín	蜆
crab	háaih	蟹
crabmeat	háaih-yuhk	蟹肉
cuttle fish	mahk-yùh	墨魚
eel	síhn	鱔
eel (cooked Japanese style)	maahn-yú	鰻魚

fish	yú	魚
garoupa	sehk-bàan-yú	石斑魚
jelly fish	hói-jit	海蜇
lobster	lùhng-hà	龍蝦
mussel	daahm-choi	淡菜
octopus	baat-jáau-yùh	八爪魚
oyster	hòuh	蠔
prawn	daaih hà	大蝦
red snapper	hùhng-sàam-yú	紅衫魚
salmon	sàam-màhn-yú	三文魚
scallop (dry)	gòn-yìuh-chyúh	乾瑤柱
scallop (fresh)	daai-jí	帶子
sea cucumber	hói-sàm	海參
shark's fin	yùh-chi	魚翅
shrimp	hà	蝦
sole	lùhng-leih	龍脷
squid	yàuh-yú	魷魚
tuna fish	tān-nàh-yú	吞拿魚
turtle	séui-yú	水魚

Vegetables	sò-choi	蔬菜
apple cucumber, fuzzy melon	jit-gwà, mòuh-gwà	節瓜，毛瓜
arrowhead	chìh-gù	茨菇
asparagus	louh-séun	露筍
bamboo shoots	dùng-séun	冬筍
bean sprouts	ngàh-choi	芽菜
bell pepper	dàng-lùhng-jìu	燈籠椒
bitter melon	fú-gwà	苦瓜
broccoli	sài-làahn-fà	西蘭花
button mushroom	mòh-gù	蘑菇
cabbage	yèh-choi	椰菜

carrot	gàm-séun, hùhng-lòh-baahk	甘筍，紅蘿蔔
cauliflower	yèh-choi-fà	椰菜花
celery	sài-kàhn	西芹
Ceylon spinach	sàahn-choi	潺菜
chayote	faht-sáu-gwà	佛手瓜
Chinese box thorn	gáu-géi	枸杞
Chinese broccoli	gaai-láan	芥蘭
Chinese celery	kàhn-choi	芹菜
Chinese flowering vegetable	choi-sàm	菜心
Chinese parsley	yùhn-sài	芫茜
Chinese spinach	yihn-choi	莧菜
chives	gáu-choi	韮菜
cucumber	chèng-gwà	青瓜
egg plant	ngái-gwà	矮瓜
garlic	syun-tàuh	蒜頭
ginger	gēung	薑
green pepper	chèng-jiu	青椒
green radish	chèng lòh-baahk	青蘿蔔
head lettuce	sài sàang-choi	西生菜
kudzu	fán-got	粉葛
leek	syun	蒜
lettuce	sàang-choi	生菜
lotus root	lìhn-ngáuh	蓮藕
mushroom	chóu-gù, sìn-gú	草菇，鮮菇
mustard green	gaai-choi	芥菜
onion	yèuhng-chùng	洋葱
pea shoots	dauh-mìuh	豆苗
peas	hòh-làan-dáu	荷蘭豆
potato	syùh-jái	薯仔
pumpkin	fàan-gwà, nàahm-gwà	番瓜，南瓜
radish	hùhng (pèih) lòh-baahk	紅（皮）蘿蔔
red chilli	hùhng laaht-jiu	紅辣椒

scallions	gáu-wòhng	韮黃
shallots	gòn chùng-tàuh	乾葱頭
silk melon, angled luffa	sì-gwà	絲瓜
soybean sprouts	daaih-dáu ngàh-choi	大豆芽菜
spinach	bò-choi	菠菜
spring onion	chùng	葱
stem ginger	jí-gèung	子薑
string bean	dauh-gok	豆角
sweet corn	sūk-máih	粟米
sweet potato	fàan-syú	番薯
taro	wuh-táu	芋頭
Tientsin cabbage	siuh-choi, wòhng-ngàh-baahk	紹菜，黃牙白
tomato	fàan-ké	番茄
turnip	lòh-baahk	蘿蔔
water chestnuts	máh-tái	馬蹄
water cress	sài-yèuhng-choi	西洋菜
water spinach	ngung-choi, tùng-choi	甕菜，通菜
white cabbage	baahk-choi	白菜
wild rice shoots	gàau-séun	膠筍
winter melon	dùng-gwà	冬瓜

7. Where to get help if you are sick

Medical Service and Health Terminology	Yì-lìuh waih-sàng fuhk-mouh seuht-yúh	醫療衛生服務術語
abnormal behaviour	yih-sèuhng hàhng-wàih	異常行為
accident and emergency section	gàp-gau jùng-sàm	急救中心
acupuncture treatment room	jàm-gau-sāt	針灸室
ambulance	gau-sèung-ché, sahp-jih-chè	救傷車，十字車

197

ambulance depot	gau-wuh-chè jaahm	救護車站
Auxiliary Medical Services	yì-lìuh fuh-joh-déui	醫療輔助隊
bed	behng-chòhng	病牀
blood bank	hyut-fu	血庫
blood gas analyzer	yihm-hyut-yìh	驗血儀
casualty ward	gàp-jing-sàt	急症室
Chai Wan Health Centre	Chàaih-wàan gihn-hòng-yún	柴灣健康院
child assessment	yìh-tùhng tái-náhng ji-lihk chàak-yihm	兒童體能智力測驗
chiropractor	jek-jèui jih-lìuh-sì	脊椎治療師
community physician	séh-kèui-yì-hohk yì-sàng	社區醫學醫生
community psychiatric nurse	jìng-sàhn-fò séh-hòng wuh-léih yàhn-yùhn	精神科社康護理人員
community medicine	séh-kèui yì-hohk	社區醫學
community nursing service centre	séh-hòng wuh-léih jùng-sàm	社康護理中心
consultant	jyú-yahm gu-mahn yi-sàng	主任顧問醫生
consulting room	chán-jing-sàt	診症室
convalescent home	lìuh-yéuhng-yún	療養院
custodial ward	gèi-làuh behng-fóng	羈留病房
dental clinic	ngàh-fò chán-só	牙科診所
dental hygienist	ngàh-chí waih-sàng-yùhn	牙齒衛生員
dental therapist	ngàh-fò jih-lìuh-yùhn	牙科治療員
director of medical and health services	yì-mouh waih-sàng-chyu chyu-jéung	醫務衛生處處長
dispensary	yeuhk-fòhng	藥房
enrolled nurse	dàng-gei wuh-sih	登記護士
evening clinic service	yeh-chán fuhk-mouh	夜診服務
externship	fèi jyu-yún saht-jaahp	非駐院實習
eye clinic	ngáahn-fò chán-lìuh-só	眼科診療所

Families Visiting Medical Office	gùng-mouh-yùhn gà-suhk chán-lìuh-só	公務員家屬診療所
Family Health Service Centre	móuh-yìng gihn-hóng-yún	母嬰健康院
fellowship examination	yún-sih háau-síh	院士考試
first aid service	gau-sèung fuhk-mouh	救傷服務
first class ward	tàuh-dáng behng-fóng	頭等病房
follow-up	fùk-chán	覆診
free medical treatment	míhn-fai yì-lìuh	免費醫療
general clinic (government)	póu-tùng-fò mùhn-chán	普通科門診
general hospital	póu-tùng-fò yì-yún	普通科醫院
general ward	póu-tùng behng-fóng, daaih-fóng	普通病房，大房
government hospital	jing-fú yì-yún	政府醫院
Government Community Nursing Service	Jing-fú séh-hòng wuh-léih fuhk-mouh	政府社康護理服務
government laboratory	jing-fú fa-yihm-só	政府化驗所
government chemist	jing-fú fa-yihm-sì	政府化驗師
government health warning	jing-fú gihn-hòng jùng-gou	政府健康忠告
half-way house	jùng-tòuh sūk-séh	中途宿舍
health and medical services	yì-lìuh waih-sàng fuhk-mouh	醫療衛生服務
health centre	gihn-hòng-yún	健康院
health education	gihn-hòng gaau-yuhk	健康教育
heart attack	sām-johng-behng faat	心臟病發
herbalist	jùng-yì	中醫
Hong Kong Psychiatric Centre	Hèung-góng jìng-sàhn-behng chán-lìuh-só	香港精神病診療所
Hong Kong Anticancer Society	Hèung-góng fòhng-ngàahm-wúi	香港防癌會
Hong Kong College of General Practitioners	Hèung-góng chyùhn-fò yì-hohk-yún	香港全科醫學院

Hong Kong Dental Association	Hèung-góng ngàh-yì hohk-wúi	香港牙醫學會
Hong Kong Medical Association	Hèung-góng yì-hohk-wúi	香港醫學會
Hong Kong Red Cross Blood Transfusion Service	Hèung-góng hùhng-sahp-jih-wúi syù-hyut fuhk-mouh jùng-sàm	香港紅十字會輸血服務中心
Hong Kong Red Cross Society	Hèung-góng hùhng-sahp-jih-wúi	香港紅十字會
hospital administrator	yún-mouh jyú-yahm	院務主任
hospital admission certificate	yahp-yún jí / jing-mìhng-syù	入院紙 / 證明書
hospital discharge certificate	chèut-yún-jí / jing-mìhng-syù	出院紙 / 證明書
hospitalization	làuh-yì, làuh-yún chán-jih	留醫，留院診治
infirmary	wuh-yéuhng-yún	護養院
inoculation centre	jyu-seh jaahm	注射站
intensive care unit	sàm-chit jih-lìuh-sàt/ behng-fóng	深切治療 / 病房
isolation ward	gaak-lèih behng-fóng	隔離病房
Kwai Chung Hospital	Kwàih-chùng yì-yún	葵涌醫院
leprosy clinic	màh-fùng chán-lìuh-só	痲瘋診療所
Maclehose Medical Rehablitation Centre	Mahk-léih-houh fuhk-hòng-yún	麥理浩復康院
Margaret Trench Medical Rehabilitation Centre	Daai-lèuhn-jí fù-yàhn fuhk-hòng-yún	戴麟趾夫人復康院
maternal unit	cháan-fò-bouh	產科部
maternity home	làuh-cháan-só	留產所
medicaid	yì-yeuhk wùhn-joh	醫藥援助
Medical and Health Department	Yì-mouh waih-sàng-chyu	醫務衛生處
medical care	yì-lìuh fuhk-mouh	醫療服務
medical certificate	yì-sàng jing-mìhng-syù	醫生證明書

medical congress	yì-hohk wuih-yíh	醫學會議
Medical Council	Yì-mouh wái-yùhn-wúi	醫務委員會
Medical Development Advisory Committee	yì-mouh faat-jín jì-sèun wái-yùhn-wúi	醫務發展諮詢委員會
medical ethics	yì-dàk	醫德
medical examination	tái-gaak gim-yihm	體格檢驗
medical laboratory technician	yì-lìuh saht-yihm-sàt geih-seuht-yùhn	醫療實驗室技術員
medical personnel	yì-mouh yàhn-yùhn	醫務人員
medical service	yì-lìuh fuhk-mouh	醫療服務
medical social work	yì-mouh séh-wúi gúng-jok	醫務社會工作
Methadone Detoxification Clinic	Méih-sà-tùhng gaai-duhk chán-só	美沙酮戒毒診所
motorcycle ambulance support system	gau-wuh dihn-dàan-chè jì-wùhn gai-waahk	救護電單車支援計劃
nurse training school	wuh-sih fan-lihn hohk-haauh	護士訓練學校
nursing officer	wuh-léih jyú-yahm	護理主任
nursing staff	wuh-léih yàhn-yùhn	護理人員
operation theatre	sáu-seuht-sàt	手術室
optometrical profession	sih-gwòng-hohk	視光學
oral health clinic	háu-hòng gihn-hòng chán-só	口腔健康診所
Orthopaedic and Traumatic Surgery Department	gíu-yìhng ngoih-fò kahp chong-séung hohk-haih	矯形外科及創傷學系
out-patient clinic / department	mùhn-chán-bouh	門診部
overseas medical qualifications	hói-ngoih yì-hohk jì-gaak	海外醫學資格
para-medical staff	fuh-joh yì-lìuh yàhn-yùhn	輔助醫療人員
personal hygiene	go-yàhn waih-sàng	個人衛生
physical medicine unit	yì-lìuh fuhk-hòng-yún	醫療復康院

polyclinic	fàn-fó-chán-só	分科診所
Port Health Office	góng-háu waih-sàng-chyu	港口衛生處
private hospital	sì-gà yì-yún	私家醫院
psychiatric centre	jìng-sàhn-behng jih-lìuh jùng-sàm	精神病治療中心
public hospital	gùng-lahp yì-yún	公立醫院
quarantine station	gím-yihk-jaahm	檢疫站
Radiation Board	fong-seh maht-jàt gún-léih gúk	放射物質管理局
radiodiagnostic department	fong-seh chán-dyun bouh	放射診斷部
regional hospital	fàn-kèui yì-yún	分區醫院
registered nurse	jyu-chaak wuh-sih	註冊護士
rehabaid centre	fuhk-hòng yuhng-geuih jùng-sàm	復康用具中心
scanner unit	dihn-nóuh sou-mìuh bouh	電腦掃描部
school children's dental clinic	hohk-tùhng ngàh-fò chán-só	學童牙科診所
school dental care service	hohk-tùhng ngàh-chí bóu-gihn gai-waahk	學童牙齒保健計劃
social hygiene clinic	séh-wúi waih-sàng-fò chán-só	社會衛生科診所
specialist clinic	jyùn-fò mùhn-chán	專科門診
St. John Ambulance Association and Brigade	Sing-yeuk-hohn gau-sèung-wúi kei gau-sèung-déui	聖約翰救傷會暨救傷隊
stroke	jung-fūng	中風
student nurse	wuh-sih hohk-sàang	護士學生
subvented hospital	bóu-joh yì-yún	補助醫院
surveillance system	gàam-chaat jóu-jìk	監察組織
teaching hospital	gaau-hohk yì-yún	教學醫院
tuberculosis and chest clinic	hùng-fai chán-lìuh-só	胸肺診療所

ward	behng-fóng	病房
wheel-chair	lèuhn-yí	輪椅

Hospitals	**Yi-yún**	**醫院**
Baptist Hospital	Jam-wúi yi-yún	浸會醫院
Canossa Hospital	Gà-nok-saat yi-yún	嘉諾撒醫院
Caritas Medical Center	Mìhng-ngoi yi-yún	明愛醫院
Castle Peak Hospital	Chìng-sàan-yi-yún	青山醫院
Christain United Hospital	Lyùhn-hahp yi-yún	聯合醫院
Duchess of Kent Childrens' Hospital	Gàn-dàk gùng-jeuk fù-yàhn yih-tùhng yi-yún	根德公爵夫人兒童醫院
Elizabeth Hospital	Yi-leih-sà-baak yi-yún	伊利沙伯醫院
Evangel Hospital	Bo-douh yi-yún	播道醫院
Gleneagles Hong Kong Hospital	Góng-yìh yi-yún	港怡醫院
Grantham Hospital	Got-leuhng-hùhng yi-yún	葛量洪醫院
Haven of Hope Hospital	Lìhng-saht yi-yún	靈實醫院
HK Adventist Hospital	Góng-ngòn yi-yún	港安醫院
HK Buddhist Hospital	Hèung-góng faht-gaau yi-yún	香港佛教醫院
HK Central Hospital	Góng-jùng yi-yún	港中醫院
Hong Kong Sanatorium and Hospital	Yéuhng-wòh yi-yún	養和醫院
Kowloon Hospital	Gáu-lùhng yi-yún	九龍醫院
Kwong Wah Hospital	Gwóng-wàh yi-yún	廣華醫院
Matilda and War Memorial Hospital	Mìhng-dàk yi-yún	明德醫院
Nam Long Hospital	Nàahm-lóhng yi-yún	南朗醫院
Nethersole Hospital	Nàh-dà-sou yi-yún	那打素醫院
Our Lady of Maryknoll Hospital	Sing-móuh yi-yún	聖母醫院
Pok Oi Hospital	Bok-ngoi yi-yún	博愛醫院

203

Precious Blood Hospital	Bóu-hyut yì-yún	寶血醫院
Prince of Wales Hospital	Wài-yíh-sì chàn-wòhng yì-yún	威爾斯親王醫院
Prince Philip Dental Hospital	Fèi-lihp chàn-wòhng ngàh-fò yì-yún	菲臘親王牙科醫院
Princess Margaret Hospital	Máh-gà-liht-yì-yún	瑪嘉烈醫院
Queen Mary Hospital	Máh-laih yì-yún	瑪麗醫院
Ruttonjee Hospital	Leuht-dēun-jih yì-yún	律敦治醫院
St. Paul's Hospital	Sing-bóu-luhk yì-yún, Faat-gwok yì-yún	聖保祿醫院，法國醫院
St. Teresa's Hospital	Sing-dāk-laahk-saat yì-yún	聖德肋撒醫院
Tang Shiu Kin Hospital	Dahng-siuh-gìn yì-yún	鄧肇堅醫院
Tsuen Wan Adventist Hospital	Chyùhn-wàan Góng-ngòn yì-yún	荃灣港安醫院
Tung Wah Eastern Hospital	Dùng-wàh Dùng-yún	東華東院
Tung Wah Hospital	Dùng-wàh yì-yún	東華醫院
Union Hospital	Yàhn-ngōn yì-yún	仁安醫院
Yan Chai Hospital	Yàhn-jai yì-yún	仁濟醫院

Parts of the Body　　Sàn-tái gok bouh-fahn　身體各部份

abdomen	tóuh, fūk	肚，腹
ankle	geuk-ngáahn	腳眼
appendix	làahn-méih	闌尾
arm	(sáu) bei	(手)臂
artery	duhng-mahk	動脈
anus	gòng-mùhn	肛門
brain	nóuh	腦
back	bui	背
bronchi	ji-hei-gún	支氣管
bladder	pòhng-gwòng	膀胱
bone	gwàt	骨
blood	hyut	血

blood vessel	hyut-gún	血管
breast	hùng, sàm-háu	胸，心口
cheek	mihn	面
chin	hah-pàh	下巴
chest	hùng	胸
calf	síu-téui	小腿
caecum	màahng-chéung	盲腸
cervix uteri	jí-gùng-géng	子宮頸
diaphram	wàahng-gaak-mók	橫隔膜
duoderum	sahp-yih jí-chèuhng	十二指腸
ear	yíh, yíh-jái	耳，耳仔
ear lobe	yíh-jyù, yíh-sèuih	耳珠，耳垂
eyes	ngáahn	眼
eyebrow	ngáahn-mèih	眼眉
eyelashes	ngáahn-jiht-mòuh	眼睫毛
elbow	sáu-jàang, jáau	手踭，肘
foot	geuk	腳
forearm	chìhn-bei	前臂
finger	sáu-jí	手指
fingernails	sáu-jí-gaap	手指甲
fallopian tube	syù-léun-gún	輸卵管
gum	ngàh-yuhk	牙肉
gland	sin	腺
gall bladder	dáam (nòhng)	膽（囊）
head	tàuh	頭
hair (fine)	mòuh	毛
hair (on the head)	tàuh-faat	頭髮
hard palate	seuhng-ngohk	上顎
heart	sàm	心
heart valves	sàm-fáan	心瓣
heel	geuk-jàang	腳踭
hand	sáu	手
instep	geuk-bui	腳背

intestine (large)	daaih chéung	大腸
intestine (small)	síu chéung	小腸
jaw	hah-pàh, hahp	下巴，頜
joint	gwàan-jit	關節
kidney	sáhn, yìu	腎，腰
knee	sàt (tàuh)	膝（頭）
lip	(háu) sèuhn	（口）唇
larynx	hàuh-lùhng, yìn	喉嚨，咽
lung	fai	肺
liver	gòn	肝
leg	téui, geuk	腿，腳
mouth	háu, jéui	口，嘴
muscle	gèi-yuhk	肌肉
mucous membrane	nìm-mók	黏膜
nose	beih (gō)	鼻（哥）
neck	géng	頸
nerve	sàhn-gìng	神經
nipple	náaih-tàuh	奶頭
oesophagus	sihk-douh	食道
ovary	léun-chàauh	卵巢
pleura	hùng-mók, lahk-mók	胸膜，肋膜
pancreas	yìh (sin)	胰（腺）
palm	sáu-jéung	手掌
prostate gland	chìhn-liht-sin, sip-wuh-sin	前列腺，攝護腺
penis	yàm-ging	陰莖
prepuce	bàau-pèih	包皮
rectum	jihk-chéung	直腸
rib	lahk-gwàt	肋骨
senses	jì-gok	知覺
hearing	ting-gok	聽覺
smell (n)	meih-gok	味覺
taste (v)	si-meih-douh	試味道

touch	jūk-gok	觸覺
vision	sih-gok	視覺
skull	tàuh (lòuh)-gwàt	頭（顱）骨
shoulder	bok-tàuh, gin	膊頭，肩
spleen	pèih	脾
stomach	waih	胃
scrotum	yàm-nòhng	陰囊
spine	jek-chyúh, jek-jèui	脊柱，脊椎
scalp	tàuh-pèih	頭皮
skin	pèih	皮
spinal cord	jek-seuih	脊髓
throat	hàuh-lùhng	喉嚨
thyroid gland	gaap-johng-sin	甲狀腺
tonsils	hàuh-wát, bín-tòuh-sin	喉核，扁桃腺
trachea	hei-gún	氣管
thumb	sáu-jí-gùng, móuh-jí	手指公，拇指
thigh	daaih-béi, daaih-téui	大脾，大腿
toes	geuk-jí	腳趾
toenails	geuk (jí)-gaap	腳（趾）甲
testis	gòu-yún	睪丸
tongue	leih, siht	脷，舌
upper arm	seuhng-bei	上臂
ureter	syù-niuh-gún	輸尿管
urethra	niuh-douh	尿道
uterus	jí-gùng	子宮
vein	jihng-mahk	靜脈
vagina	yàm-douh	陰道
vasdeferens	syù-jìng-gún	輸精管
wrist	sáu-wún	手腕
waist	yìu	腰
circulatory system	chèuhn-wàahn haih-túng	循環系統
digestive system	sìu-fa haih-túng	消化系統

endocrine system	noih-fàn-bei haih-túng	內分泌系統
muscular system	gèi-yuhk haih-túng	肌肉系統
nervous system	sàhn-gìng haih-túng	神經系統
reproductive system	sàng-jihk haih-túng	生殖系統
respiratory system	fù-kàp haih-túng	呼吸系統
skeletal system	gwàt-gaak haih-túng	骨骼系統
urinary system	pàaih-niuh haih-túng	排尿系統

8. How to plan for a trip

Air Lines Companies	Hòhng-hùng gūng-sì	航空公司
Air Canada	Gā-nàh-daaih hòhng-hùng gūng-sì	加拿大航空公司
Air China	Jūng-gwok gwok-jai hòhng-hùng gūng-sì	中國國際航空公司
Air France	Faat-gwok hòhng-hùng gūng-sì	法國航空公司
Air India	Yan-douh hòhng-hùng gūng-sì	印度航空公司
Air Lanka	Sì-léih-làahn-kà hòhng-hùng gūng-sì	斯里蘭卡航空公司
Air Nauru	Nàh-nóu hòhng-hùng gūng-sì	那魯航空公司
Air New Zealand	Náu-sài-làahn hòhng-hùng gūng-sì	紐西蘭航空公司
Air Niugini	Sàn-gèi-noih-nga hòhng-hùng gūng-sì	新畿內亞航空公司
Alitalia Airlines	Yi-daaih-leih hòhng-hùng gūng-sì	意大利航空公司
All Nippon Airways	Chyùhn-yaht-hùng hòhng-hùng gūng-sì	全日空航空公司
British Airways	Yìng-gwok hòhng-hùng gūng-sì	英國航空公司

British Caledonian Airways	Yìng-gwok Gàm-sì hòhng-hùng gūng-sì	英國金獅航空公司
Cathay Pacific Airways	Gwok-taai hòhng-hùng gūng-sì	國泰航空公司
China Airlines	Jùng-wàh hòhng-hùng gūng-sì	中華航空公司
Delta Airlines	Sàam-gok-jàu hòhng-hùng gūng-sì	三角洲航空公司
Dragon Air	Góng-lùhng hòhng-hùng gūng-sì	港龍航空公司
Emirates	Nga-lyùhn-yàuh hòhng-hùng gūng-sì	阿聯酋航空公司
Garuda Indonesian Airways	Gà-nóuh-daaht Yan-nèih hòhng-hùng gūng-sì	嘉魯達印尼航空公司
Gulf Air	Hói-wàan hòhng-hùng gūng-sì	海灣航空公司
Japan Air Lines	Yaht-bún hòhng-hùng gūng-sì	日本航空公司
KLM Royal Dutch Airlines	Hòh-lāan hòhng-hùng gūng-sì	荷蘭航空公司
Korean Air	Daaih-hòn hòhng-hùng gūng-sì	大韓航空公司
Lufthansa German Airlines	Dāk-gwok Hon-sā hòhng-hùng gūng-sì	德國漢莎航空公司
Malaysia Airlines	Máh-lòih-sài-nga hòhng-hùng gūng-sì	馬來西亞航空公司
Northwest Orient Airlines	Sài-bàk hòhng-hùng gūng-sì	西北航空公司
Philippine Airlines	Fèi-leuht-bàn hòhng-hùng gūng-sì	菲律賓航空公司
Qantas Airways	Ngou-jàu hòhng-hùng gūng-sì	澳洲航空公司
Royal Brunei Airlines	Wòhng-gà Màhn-lòih hòhng-hùng gūng-sì	皇家汶萊航空公司

Singapore Airlines	Sàn-ga-bō hòhng-hùng gūng-sì	新加坡航空公司
South Africa Airways	Nàahm-fèi hòhng-hùng gūng-sì	南非航空公司
Swissair	Seuih-sih hòhng-hùng gūng-sì	瑞士航空公司
Thai International Airways	Taai-gwok gwok-jai hòhng-hùng gūng-sì	泰國國際航空公司
United Airlines	Lyùhn-hahp hòhng-hùng gūng-sì	聯合航空公司
Western Airlines	Sài-fòng hòhng-hùng gūng-sì	西方航空公司

Banks	**Ngàhn-hòhng**	**銀行**
DBS Bank	Síng-jín ngàhn-hòhng	星展銀行
Bank of America	Méih-gwok ngàhn-hòhng	美國銀行
Bank of China	Jùng-gwok ngàhn-hòhng	中國銀行
Bank of Communication	Gàau-tùng ngàhn-hòhng	交通銀行
Bank of Tokyo	Dùng-gìng ngàhn-hòhng	東京銀行
Banque Nationale De Paris	Faat-gwok gwok-gà Bā-làih ngàhn-hòhng	法國國家巴黎銀行
Barclays Bank	Paak-hāak-lòih ngàhn-hòhng	柏克萊銀行
Belgian Bank	Wàh-béi ngàhn-hòhng	華比銀行
Fuji Bank	Fu-sih ngàhn-hòhng	富士銀行
Hang Seng Bank	Hàhng-sàng ngàhn-hòhng	恒生銀行
Hong Kong & Shanghai Banking Corporation	Wuih-fùng ngàhn-hòhng	滙豐銀行
Standard Chartered Bank	Jàdá ngàhn-hòhng	渣打銀行

Citibank	Fā-kèih ngàhn-hòhng	花旗銀行
China Construction Bank	Júng-gwok gin-chit ngàhn-hòhng	中國建設銀行

Hotels and Guest Houses	Jáu-dim, Bàn-gún	酒店，賓館

Hong Kong Island

Conrad	Góng-laih Jáu-dim	港麗酒店
Cosmopolitan	Laih-dōu Jáu-dim	麗都酒店
Excelsior	Yìh-dūng Jáu-dim	怡東酒店
Four Seasons	Sei-gwai Jáu-dim	四季酒店
Grand Hyatt	Gwān-yuht Jáu-dim	君悅酒店
Harbour Plaza	Hói-yaht Jáu-dim	海逸酒店
Harbour View	Hói-gíng Jáu-dim	海景酒店
Harbour View International House	Wāan-gíng gwok-jai bān-gún	灣景國際賓館
Island Shangri-La	Góng-dóu Hēung-gaak-léih-lāai daaih Jáu-dim	港島香格里拉大酒店
JW Marriot	JW Maahn-hòuh Jáu-dim	JW 萬豪酒店
Le Meridien Cyberport	Sou-máh-góng Ngaaih-méih jáu-dim	數碼港艾美酒店
Mandarin Oriental	Màhn-wàh Dūng-fōng Jáu-dim	文華東方酒店
Metropark	Wàih-gíng Jáu-dim	維景酒店
Newton	Laih-dūng Jáu-dim	麗東酒店
Newton Inn	Laih-dūng-hīn	麗東軒
Park Lane	Paak-lìhng Jáu-dim	柏寧酒店
Regal Hong Kong	Fu-hòuh Hēung-góng Jáu-dim	富豪香港酒店
Renaissance Harbour View	Maahn-laih hói-gíng Jáu-dim	萬麗海景酒店

Rosedale on the Park	Paak-laih Jáu-dim	珀麗酒店
Y.W.C.A.	Néuih Chìng-nìhn-wúi	女青年會

B.P. International House	Lùhng-bóu gwok-jai bān-gún	龍堡國際賓館
Dorsett Olympic	Dai-hòuh Ngou-wahn Jáu-dim	帝豪奧運酒店
Dorsett Seaview	Dai-hòuh Hói-gíng Jáu-dim	帝豪海景酒店
Eaton	Yaht-dūng Jáu-dim	逸東酒店
Gateway	Góng-wāi Jáu-dim	港威酒店
Gold Coast	Wòhng-gām Hói-ngohn Jáu-dim	黃金海岸酒店
Harbour Plaza	Hói-yaht Jáu-dim	海逸酒店
Harbour Plaza Metropolis	Dōu-wuih Hói-yaht Jáu-dim	都會海逸酒店
Harbour Plaza Resort City	Gā-wùh Hói-yaht Jáu-dim	嘉湖海逸酒店
Holiday Inn Golden Mile	Gām-wihk Ga-yaht Jáu-dim	金域假日酒店
Imperial	Daih-gwok Jáu-dim	帝國酒店
Intercontinental	Jāu-jai Jáu-dim	洲際酒店
Kimberley	Gwān-yìh Jáu-dim	君怡酒店
Kowloon Shangri-La	Gáu-lùhng Hēung-gaak-léih-lāai Daaih Jáu-dim	九龍香格里拉大酒店
Lanham place	Lóhng-hòuh Jáu-dim	朗豪酒店
Marco Polo	Màh-hó-buht-lòh Jáu-dim	馬可孛羅酒店
Miramar	Méih-laih-wàh Jáu-dim	美麗華酒店
Nikko	Yaht-hòhng Jáu-dim	日航酒店
Penisula	Bun-dóu Jáu-dim	半島酒店
Prince	Taai-jí Jáu-dim	太子酒店

Regal Kowloon	Fu-hòuh Gáu-lùhng Jáu-dim	富豪九龍酒店
Renaissance Kowloon	Gáu-lùhng Maahn-laih Jáu-dim	九龍萬麗酒店
Royal Garden	Daih-yún Jáu-dim	帝苑酒店
Royal Pacific	Wòhng-gā Taai-pìhng-yèuhng Jáu-dim	皇家太平洋酒店
Royal Park	Daih-dōu Jáu-dim	帝都酒店
Royal Plaza	Daih-gīng Jáu-dim	帝京酒店
Royal View	Daih-gíng Jáu-dim	帝景酒店
Sheraton	Héi-lòih-dāng Jáu-dim	喜來登酒店
Y.M.C.A.	Chīng-nìhn-wúi	青年會

Outlying Islands

Disney's Hollywood	Dihk-sih-nèih Hóu-loih-wū jáu-dim	迪士尼好萊塢酒店
Disneyland	Dihk-sih-nèih Lohk-yùhn jáu-dim	迪士尼樂園酒店
Novotel Citygate	Nok-fu-dahk Dūng-wuih-sìhng jáu-dim	諾富特東薈城酒店
Regal Airport	Fu-hòuh gēi-chèuhng jáu-dim	富豪機場酒店

Major Cities in China	Jùng-gowk jyú-yiu sìhng-síh	中國主要城市
Beijing	Bāk-gìng	北京
Chengdu	Sìhng-dōu	成都
Chongqing	Chùhng-hing	重慶
Guangzhou	Gwóng-jàu	廣州
Guilin	Gwai-làhm	桂林
Hangzhou	Hòhng-jàu	杭州
Harbin	Hā-yíh-bàn	哈爾濱

Huhhot	Fù-wòh-houh-dahk	呼和浩特
Jinan	Jai-nàahm	濟南
Kunming	Kwàn-mìhng	昆明
Nanjing	Nàahm-gìng	南京
Sanya	Sāam-nga	三亞
Shanghai	Seuhng-hói	上海
Shenyang	Sám-yèuhng	瀋陽
Shenzhen	Sàm-jan	深圳
Taipei	Tòih-bāk	台北
Tienjing	Tìn-jèun	天津
Urumqi	Wù-lóuh-muhk-chàih	烏魯木齊
Wuhan	Móuh-hon	武漢
Xiamen	Hah-mùhn	廈門
Xian	Sài-ngòn	西安

Major Cities in the World	**Sai-gaai jyú-yiu sìhng-síh**	**世界主要城市**
Aden	Nga-dìng	亞丁
Amsterdam	A-móuh-sì-dahk-dāan	亞姆斯特丹
Athens	Ngáh-dín	雅典
Bangkok	Maahn-gūk	曼谷
Beijing	Bāk-gìng	北京
Belfast	Bui-yíh-faat-sì-dahk	貝爾法斯特
Belgrade	Bui-yíh-gaak-lòih-dāk	貝爾格萊德
Berlin	Paak-làhm	柏林
Bermuda	Baak-mouh-daaht	百慕達
Bogota	Bò-gò-daaih	波哥大
Bohn	Bò-yàn	波恩
Boston	Bō-sih-déun	波士頓
Brasilia	Bà-sài-leih-nga	巴西利亞
Brussels	Bou-lóuh-choi-yíh	布魯塞爾
Budapest	Bou-daaht-pui-sì	布達佩斯

Buenos Aires	Bou-yìh-nok-sì-ngaaih-leih-sì	布宜諾斯艾利斯
Cairo	Hòi-lòh	開羅
Capetown	Hòi-póu-dèun	開普敦
Caracas	Gā-làai-gā-sì	加拉加斯
Chicago	Jì-gā-gò	芝加哥
Colombo	Gò-lèuhn-bò	哥倫波
Copenhagen	Gò-bún-hā-gàn	哥本哈根
Dakar	Daaht-kaak-yíh	達喀爾
Damascus	Daaih-máh-sih-gaak	大馬士革
Darwin	Daaht-yíh-màhn	達爾文
Delhi	Dāk-léih	德里
Detroit	Dái-dahk-leuht	底特律
Dublin	Dōu-paak-làhm	都柏林
Frankfurt	Faat-làahn-hāak-fùk	法蘭克福
Geneva	Yaht-noih-ngáh	日內瓦
Glasgow	Gaak-làai-sì-gò	格拉斯哥
Guadalajara	Gwà-daaht-làai-hā-làai	瓜達拉哈拉
Guam	Gwàan-dóu	關島
Guatemala	Ngàih-deih-máh-làai	危地馬拉
Havana	Hah-wāan-nàh	夏灣拿
Helsinki	Hāak-yíh-sàn-gèi	赫爾辛基
Hong Kong	Hèung-góng	香港
Honolulu	Tàahn-hèung-sàan	檀香山
Houston	Hàuh-sì-déun	侯斯頓
Islamabad	Yī-sì-làahn-bóu	伊斯蘭堡
Jakarta	Yèh-gà-daaht	耶加達
Jerusalem	Yèh-louh-saat-láahng	耶路撒冷
Johannesburg	Yeuk-hohn-nèih-sì-bóu	約翰尼斯堡
Kabul	Kaak-bou-yíh	喀布爾
Kaula Lumpur	Gāt-lùhng-bò	吉隆坡
Kiev	Gèi-fuh	基輔
Kobe	Sàhn-wuh	神戶

Kolkata	Gā-yíh-gok-daap	加爾各答
Kuwait	Fō-wài-dahk	科威特
La Paz	Làai-bā-sì	拉巴斯
Las Vegas	Làai-sī-wàih-gā-sì, dóu-sìhng	拉斯維加斯，賭城
Lima	Leih-máh	利馬
Lisbon	Léih-sì-bún	里斯本
Liverpool	Leih-maht-póu	利物浦
London	Lèuhn-dèun	倫敦
Los Angeles	Lok-chaam-gèi , Lòh-sáang	洛杉磯，羅省
Lyons	Léih-ngòhng	里昂
Madrid	Máh-dāk-léih	馬德里
Manila	Máh-nèih-lāai	馬尼拉
Marseille	Máh-choi	馬賽
Melbourne	Mahk-yíh-bún	墨爾本
Mexico City	Mahk-sài-gō-sìhng	墨西哥城
Miami	Maaih-nga-máih/méih	邁亞米／美
Milan	Máih-làahn	米蘭
Montreal	Múhn-deih-hó	滿地可
Moscow	Mohk-sì-fò	莫斯科
Mumbai	Maahng-máaih	孟買
Munich	Mouh-nèih-hāak	慕尼克
New York	Náu-yeuk	紐約
Osaka	Daaih-báan	大坂
Oslo	Ngou-sì-luhk	奧斯陸
Panama	Bà-nàh-máh sìhng	巴拿馬城
Paris	Bà-làih	巴黎
Penang	Bàn-sìhng	檳城
Perth	Paak-sì	柏思
Philadelphia	Fai-sìhng	費城
Pnom Penh	Gàm-bin	金邊
Prague	Bou-lāai-gaak	布拉格

Quito	Gēi-dò	基多
Rangoon	Yéuhng-gwòng	仰光
Rio de Janeiro	Léih-yeuk-yiht-noih-lòuh	里約熱內盧
Rome	Lòh-máh	羅馬
Saigon	Sài-gung	西貢
San Francisco	Sàam-fàahn-síh, Gauh-gàm-sàan	三藩市，舊金山
Santiago	Sing-deih-ngàh-gò	聖地牙哥
Seattle	Sài-ngáh-tòuh	西雅圖
Seoul	Sáu-yíh	首爾
Shanghai	Seuhng-hói	上海
Singapore	Sàn-ga-bò	新加坡
St. Petersburg	Sing-béi-dak-bóu	聖彼得堡
Stockholm	Sì-dāk-gò-yíh-mò	斯德哥爾摩
Sydney	Sīk-nèih, Syut-nèih	悉尼，雪尼
Tehran, Teheran	Dāk-hàak-làahn	德黑蘭
Tel Aviv	Tòih-lāai-wàih-fù	台拉維夫
Tokyo	Dùng-gìng	東京
Toronto	Dò-lèuhn-dò	多倫多
Vancouver	Wān-gò-wàh	溫哥華
Venice	Wāi-nèih-sī	威尼斯
Vienna	Wàih-yáh-naahp	維也納
Warsaw	Wàh-sà	華沙
Washington D.C.	Wàh-sihng-deuhn , Wàh-fú	華盛頓，華府
Wellington	Wài-nìhng-deuhn	威靈頓
Zurich	Sòu-làih-sai	蘇黎世

9. How to find out what's happening

Mass Media	Daaih-jung Mùih-gaai	大眾媒介
advertising control	gwóng-gou gún-jai	廣告管制
advertising agent	gwóng-gou gùng-sì	廣告公司
air (v)	bo-fong	播放
air photograph	hùng-jùng sip-yíng jiu-pin	空中攝影照片
airport conference room	gèi-chèuhng gei-jé sāt	機場記者室
anti-piracy committee	fáan douh-yan síu-jóu	反盜印小組
approved for exhibition	pài-jéun gùng yíng	批准公映
ban	gam-yíng	禁映
broadcast by satellite	(yàhn-jouh) waih-sìng jyún-bo	（人造）衛星轉播
broadcast live	yihn-chèuhng jihk-bo	現場直播
broadcast picture	dihn-sih wá-mín	電視畫面
Broadcasting Review Board	Gwóng-bo sih-yihp gím-tóu wái-yùhn-wúi	廣播事業檢討委員會
cable systems	yáuh-sin chyùhn-bo haih-túng	有線傳播系統
cable television	yáuh-sin dihn-sih	有線電視
censorship	sàn-màhn gím-chàh	新聞檢查
children's programme	yìh-tùhng jit-muhk	兒童節目
Chinese language typesetting	Jùng-màhn pàaih-jih	中文排字
circulation	sìu-louh	銷路
commercial advertising	sèung-yihp gwóng-gou	商業廣告
commercials	gwóng-gou pín	廣告片
compact / digital audio disc system	lùih-seh sou-máh cheung-pín haih-túng	鐳射數碼唱片系統
compere	jit-muhk jyú-chìh-yàhn	節目主持人
copyright infringement	chàm-faahn báan-kyùhn	侵犯版權
copyright	báan-kyuhn	版權

copywriter	jaan-góu-yàhn	撰稿人
current affairs programme	sìh-sih jit-muhk	時事節目
data transmission	sou-geui chyùhn-sung	數據傳送
deadline	jiht-góu sìh-gaan	截稿時間
direct satellite transmissions	yàhn-jouh waih-sìng jihk-jip jyún-bo	人造衛星直接轉播
Director of Information Services	Sàn-màhn-chyu Chyu-jéung	新聞處處長
Director of Boardcasting	Gwóng-bo-chyu Chyu-jéung	廣播處處長
disc jockey	cheung-pín kèh-sì	唱片騎師
drama series	kehk-jaahp	劇集
editing	pìn-chàp gùng-jok	編輯工作
electronic media	dihn-jí mùih-gaai	電子媒介
enfranchised commercial broadcast television station	dahk-héui sèung-yihp dihn-sih-tòih	特許商業電視台
enrichment programme	yìk-ji jit-muhk	益智節目
exposure	bouh-gwòng chìhng-douh	曝光程度
facsimile machine	chyùhn-jàn-gèi	傳真機
family viewing hours (TV)	hahp-gà-fùn sìh-gaan	合家歡時間
feature article	dahk-góu	特稿
film censorship regulations	dihn-yíng gím-chàh kwài-laih	電影檢查規例
film editing	dihn-yíng jín-chàp	電影剪輯
FM broadcasting	tìuh-pàhn gwóng-bo	調頻廣播
foreign news agency	ngoih-gwok sàn-màhn-séh	外國新聞社
free air time	mìhn-fai bo-yíng sìh-gaan	免費播影時間
freelance writer	jih-yàuh jok-gà	自由作家
front page headline	tàuh-tìuh sàn-mán	頭條新聞
government programme	jing-fú sip-jai jit-muhk	政府攝製節目
home viewer	gà-tìhng gùn-jung	家庭觀眾

Hong Kong Journalists' Association	Hèung-góng gei-jé hip-wúi	香港記者協會
interference	gòn-yíu	干擾
location filming	paak-sip ngoih-gíng	拍攝外景
mass communication	daaih-jung chyùhn-bo	大眾傳播
mass media	daaih-jung mùih-gaai	大眾媒介
media photographer	sip-yíng gei-jé	攝影記者
mobile radio	làuh-duhng deui-góng-gèi	流動對講機
morning post	jóu-bou	早報
multiplex sound system	dò-sìng-douh buhn-yàm haih-túng	多聲道伴音系統
multiplex sound-casting	dò-sìng-douh gwóng-bo	多聲道廣播
news headlines	sàn-màhn tàih-yiu	新聞提要
news report	sàn-màhn bou-gou	新聞報告
no comment	mòuh-hó-fuhng-gou	無可奉告
not recommended for young children	yìh-tùhng bāt-yìh	兒童不宜
overhead projector	gòu-yíng-gèi	高映機
Panal of Film Censors	Dihn-yíng gím-chàh-chyu	電影檢查處
photostated / xeroxed copy	yíng-yan-bún	影印本
pirate	douh-yan-yàhn	盜印人
poor reception	jip-sàu haauh-gwó chà	接收效果差
poster	hói-bou	海報
press and publicity manager	sàn-màhn kahp syùn-chyùhn jyú-yahm	新聞及宣傳主任
press briefing	sàn-màhn gáan-bou-wúi	新聞簡報會
press conference	gei-jé jìu-doih-wúi	記者招待會
prime time	wòhng-gàm sìh-gaan	黃金時間
programme promos	jit-muhk syùn-chyùhn pin	節目宣傳片

public affairs programme	gùng-guhng sih-mouh jit-muhk	公共事務節目
Publicity Division (GIS)	syùn-chyùhn jóu	宣傳組
radio license	gwóng-bo dihn-tòih jàp-jiu	廣播電台執照
radio pager	mòuh-sin-dihn chyùhn-fù-gèi	無線電傳呼機
radio with VHF / FM reception	chīu-dyún-bō tìuh-pàhn sàu-yàm-gèi	超短波調頻收音機
radio-paging	mòuh-sin-dihn chyùhn-fù	無線電傳呼
re-boardcast	chùhng-bo	重播
re-run programme	chùhng-bo jit-muhk	重播節目
relay station	jyún-bo-jaahm	轉播站
revocation of license	chit-sìu pàaih-jiu	撤消牌照
royalties	báan-kyùhn seui	版權稅
serial drama	lìhn-juhk kehk-jaahp	連續劇集
simulcast	tùhng-sìh bo-fong	同時播放
sound broadcasting	dihn-tòih gwóng-bo	電台廣播
stop press	jeui-sàn sìu-sìk	最新消息
switch stations	jyun tòih	轉台
tele-communication	yúhn-chìhng tùng-seun	遠程通訊
telecommunications system	mòuh-sin-dihn tùng-seun haih-túng	無線電通訊系統
teletext	dihn-sih chyùhn-jàn	電視傳真
Television Advisory Board	Dihn-sih jì sèun wái yùhn-wúi	電視諮詢委員會
television critic	dihn-sih pìhng-leuhn-yùhn	電視評論員
television drama	dihn-sih kehk	電視劇
television viewer	dihn-sih gùn-jung	電視觀眾
telex	jyùn-yuhng dihn-bou, yuhng-wuh dihn-bou	專用電報，用戶電報
the press	sàn-màhn gaai	新聞界

time slot	jit-muhk bo-fong sìh-gaan	節目播放時間
trailer	yuh-gou pín	預告片
transmission / viewing time	bo-fong sìh-gaan	播放時間
up-to-the-minute	jeui-sàn	最新
video recording centre	luhk-yíng jùng-sàm	錄影中心
walkie-talkie	mòuh-sin-dihn tùng-wah-gèi	無線電通話機
weather report	tìn-hei bou-gou	天氣報告

Magazines	**Jaahp-ji**	**雜誌**
National Geographic	Gwok-gà deih-léih yuht-hón	國家地理月刊
Newsweek	Sàn-màhn jàu-hón	新聞週刊
Playboy	Fā-fā-gùng-jí yuht-hón	花花公子月刊
Reader's Digest	Duhk-jé màhn-jaahk	讀者文摘
Time	Sìh-doih jàu-hón	時代週刊

News Agency	**Tùng-seun-séh**	**通訊社**
AFP (Agency France-Presse)	Faat-sàn-séh	法新社
AP (Associated Press)	Méih-lyùhn-séh	美聯社
China News Agency	Jùng-gwok sàn-màhn-séh	中國新聞社
Reuter (Reuter's News Agency)	Louh-tau-séh	路透社
TASS (Telegrafnoie Agentstvo Sovietskovo Soyuza)	Taap-sì-séh	塔斯社
UPI (United Press International)	Hahp-jung gwok-jai-séh	合眾國際社
Xinhua News Agency	Sàn-wàh-séh	新華社
CNA (HK China News Agency)	Jūng-tūng-séh	中通社

| Bloomberg News | Pàahng-bok sān-màhn-séh | 彭博新聞社 |

Apple Daily	Pìhng-gwó Yaht-bou	蘋果日報
China Daily	Jùng-gwok Yaht-bou	中國日報
Hong Kong Economic Journal	Seun-Bou	信報
Hong Kong Economic Times	Gīng-jai Yaht-bou	經濟日報
Kung Kao Po	Gūng-gaau Bou	公教報
Ming Pao	Mìhng Bou	明報
New York Times	Náu-yeuk Sìh-bou	紐約時報
Oriental Daily News	Dùng-fòng Yaht-bou	東方日報
Sing Tao Jih Pao	Sìng-dóu Yaht-bou	星島日報
South China Morning Post	Nàahm-wàh Jóu-bou	南華早報
Sun Daily	Taai-yèuhng bou	太陽報
Ta Kung Pao	Daaih-gùng bou	大公報
The Standard	Ngajāu Wàh-yíh-gāai Yaht-bou	亞洲華爾街日報
Wall Street Journal	Wàh-yíh-gàai Yaht-bou	華爾街日報
Washington Post	Wàh-sìhng-deuhn yàuh-bou	華盛頓郵報
Wen Wei Po	Màhn-wuih bou	文匯報

Cable TV	Yáuh-sin dihn-sih	有線電視
Chinese channel	Jùng-màhn tòih	中文台
Commercial Radio	Sèung-yihp dihn-tòih	商業電台
English channel	Yìng-màhn tòih	英文台
HD Jade	Gōu-chīng Féi-cheui tòih	高清翡翠台
Jade-TVB Chinese Channel	Féi-cheui tòih	翡翠台

Metro Broadcast Ltd.	Sān-sìhng dihn-toìh	新城電台
Pearl-TVB English Channel	Mìhng-jyù tòih	明珠台
Phoenix Satellite Television	Fuhng-wòhng-waih-sih	鳳凰衛視
RTHK (Radio Television Hong Kong)	Hèung-góng dihn-tòih	香港電台
TVB (H.K. Television Broadcasts Ltd.)	Mòuh-sin, Hèung-góng dihn-sih-gwóng-bo yáuh-haahn-gùng-sì	無線，香港電視廣播有限公司

10. How Hong Kong is run

Government Departments	Jing-fú bouh-mùhn	政府部門
Hong Kong Special Administrative Region of The People's Republic of China	Jùng-wàh yàhn-màhn guhng-wòh-gwok Hēung-góng dahk-biht hàhng-jing kèui	中華人民共和國香港特別行政區
Chief Executive of H.K. Special Administrative Region	Hēung-góng dahk-biht hàhng-jing-kèui sáu-jéung, Dahk-sáu	香港特別行政區首長，特首
Department of Administration	Jing-mouh sī	政務司
Department of Finance	Chòih-jing sī	財政司
Department of Justice	Leuht-jing sī	律政司
Chief Secretary for Administration's Office	Jing-mouh-sī sī-jéung	政務司司長
Financial Secretary	Chòih-jing-sī sī-jéung	財政司司長
Secretary for Justice	Leuht-jing-sī sī-jéung	律政司司長
Civil Service Bureau	Gùng-mouh-yùhn sih-mouh gúk	公務員事務局
Commerce, Industry and Technolgy Bureau	Gūng-sēung kahp fō-geih gúk	工商及科技局
Constitutional Affairs Bureau	Jing-jai sih-mouh gúk	政制事務局
Economic Development and Labour Bureau	Ging-jai faat-jin kahp lòuh-gūng gúk	經濟發展及勞工局

Education Bureau	Gaau-yuhk gúk	教育局
Environment, Transport and Works Bureau	Wàahn-ging wahn-syū kahp gūng-mouh gúk	環境運輸及工務局
Financial Services and the Treasury Bureau	Chòih-gìng sih-mouh kahp fu-mouh gúk	財經事務及庫務局
Health, Welfare and Food Bureau	Waih-sàng fūk-leih kahp sihk-maht gúk	衛生福利及食物局
Home Affairs Bureau	Màhn-jing sih-mouh gúk	民政事務局
Housing, Planning and Lands Bureau	Fòhng-ngūk kahp kwāi-waahk deih-jing gúk	房屋及規劃地政局
Security Bureau	Bóu-ngòn gúk	保安局
Administration Wing	Hàhng-jing chyúh	行政署
Airport Authority, Hong Kong	Hēung-góng gèi-chèuhng gún-léih gúk	香港機場管理局
Architectural Services Department	Gin-jūk chyúh	建築署
Audit Commission	Sám-gai chyúh	審計署
Births and Deaths Registries	Sāng-séi jyu-chaak-chyu	生死註冊處
Broadcasting Authority	Gwóngbo sih-mouh gún-léih gúk	廣播事務管理局
Buildings Department	Ngūk-yúh chyúh	屋宇署
Census and Statistics Department	Jing-fú túng-gai chyúh	政府統計署
Central Policy Unit	Jùng-yèung jing-chaak-jóu	中央政策組
Civil Aviation Department	Màhn-hòhng-chyu	民航處
Consumer Council	Siu-fai-jé wái-yùhn-wúi	消費者委員會
Correctional Services Department	Chihng-gaau-chyúh	懲教署
Customs and Excise Department	Hēung-góng hói-gwāan	香港海關

Electoral Affairs Commission	Syún-géui gún-léih wái-yùhn-wúi	選舉管理委員會
Executive Council	Hàhng-jing wuih-yíh	行政會議
Executive Council Member	Hàhng-jing wuih-yíh sìhng-yùhn	行政會議成員
Environmental Protection Department	Wàahn-gíng bóu-wuh-chyúh	環境保護署
Equal Opportunities Commission	Pìhng-dáng gèi-wuih wái-yùhn-wúi	平等機會委員會
Fire Services Department	Siu-fòhng-chyu	消防處
Home Affairs Department	Màhn-jing sih-mouh júng-chyúh	民政事務總署
Hong Kong Examinations and Assessment Authority	Hēung-góng háau-síh kahp pìhng-haht-gúk	香港考試及評核局
Hong Kong Housing Society	Hēung-góng fòhng-ngūk hip-wúi	香港房屋協會
Hong Kong Monetary Authority	Hēung-góng gàm-yùhng gún-léih-gúk	香港金融管理局
Hong Kong Observatory	Hēung-góng tìn-màhn-tòih	香港天文台
Hong Kong Police Force	Hēung-góng gíng-mouh-chyu	香港警務處
Hong Kong Post Office	Hēung-góng yàuh-jing-chyúh	香港郵政署
Hong Kong Tourist Association	Hēung-góng léuih-yàuh hip-wúi	香港旅遊協會
Hong Kong Trade Development Council	Hēung-góng mauh-yihk faat-jin-gúk	香港貿易發展局
Hospital Authority	Yi-yún gún-léih-gúk	醫院管理局
Housing Authority and Housing Department	Fóhng-ngūk wái-yùhn-wúi kahp fòhng-ngūk-chyúh	房屋委員會及房屋署
Immigration Department	Yahp-gíng sih-mouh-chyu	入境事務處

Independent Commission Against Corruption	Lìhm-jing gùng-chyúh	廉政公署
Industry Department	Gùng-yihp chyúh	工業署
Information Services Department	Jing-fú sàn-màhn-chyu	政府新聞處
Inland Revenue Department	Seui-mouh-gúk	稅務局
Labour Department	Lòuh-gùng-chyu	勞工處
Lands Department	Deih-jing júng-chyúh	地政總署
Legal Aid Department	Faat-leuht wùhn-joh-chyúh	法律援助署
Legislative Council	Lahp-faat-wúi	立法會
Legislative Council Members	Lahp-faai-wúi yíh-yùhn	立法會議員
Leisure and Cultural Services Department	Hōng-lohk kahp màhn-fa sih-mouh-chyúh	康樂及文化事務署
Marine Department	Hói-sih-chyu	海事處
Marriage Registries	Fàn-yān jyu-chaak-chyu	婚姻註冊處
Narcotics Division, Security Bureau	Gam-duhk-chyu	禁毒處
Office of the Ombudsman	Sàn-sou jyùn-yùhn gùng-chyúh	申訴專員公署
Office of the Telecommunications Authority	Dihn-seun gún-léih-gúk	電訊管理局
Registration and Electoral Office	Syún-géui sih-mouh-chyu	選舉事務處
Social Welfare Department	Séh-wúi fūk-leih-chyúh	社會福利署
Television and Entertainment Licensing Authority	Yíng-sih kahp yùh-lohk sih-mouh-chyu	影視及娛樂事務處
Territory Development Department	Tok-jín-chyúh	拓展署
The Court of Appeal of the High Court	Gòu-dáng faat-yún seuhng-sou faat-tìhng	高等法院上訴法庭
The Court of Final Appeal	Jùng-sām faat-yún	終審法院

The Court of First Instance of the High Court	Gòu-dáng faat-yún yùhn-juhng faat-tìhng	高等法院原訟法庭
The High Court	Gòu-dáng faat-yún	高等法院
The Magistracy	Chòih-pun faat-yún	裁判法院
Tourism Commission	Léuih-yàuh sih-mouh-chyúh	旅遊事務署
Treasury	Fu-mouh-chyúh	庫務署
University Grants Committee (U.G.C.)	Daaih-hohk gaau-yuhk jī-joh Wáih-yùhn-wúi	大學教育資助委員會
Water Supplies Department	Séui-mouh-chyúh	水務署

11. Where to worship in Hong Kong

Churches and Temples	Gaau-tòhng kahp Míu-yúh	教堂及廟宇
Che Kung Temple	Chè-gùng-míu	車公廟
Chinese Baptist Church	Jam-seun-wúi-tòhng	浸信會堂
Chinese Methodist Church (on H.K. side)	Jùng-wàh Chèuhn-douh gùng-wúi	中華循道公會
Chinese Methodist Church (on Kowloon side)	Jùng-wàh Chèuhn-douh-wúi	中華循道會
Ching Chung Koon Temple	Chìng-chùhng-gun	青松觀
Ching Leung Fat Yuen Temple	Chìng-lèuhng faat-yún	清涼法苑
Chuk Lam Sim Yuen Temple	Jūk-làhm sìhm-yún	竹林禪院
Confucius Hall	Húng-sing-tòhng	孔聖堂
Fung Ying Sin Koon Temple	Fùhng-yìhng sìn-gún	蓬瀛仙館
Hau Wong Temple	Hàuh-wòhng-míu	侯皇廟
Hop Yat Church	Hahp-yāt-tòhng	合一堂
Immaculate Heart of Mary's Church	Daaih-bou tìn-jyú-tòhng	大埔天主堂
Kowloon Mosque	Gáu-lùhng wùih-gaau-míu	九龍回教廟

Kun Yum Temple	Gùn-yàm-míu	觀音廟
Kung Lee Church	Gùng-léih-tòhng	公理堂
Living Spirit Lutheran Church	Seun-yih-wúi Wuht-lìhng-tòhng	信義會活靈堂
Man Mo Temple	Màhn-móuh-míu	文武廟
Moslem Mosque	Wùih-gaau láih-baai-tòhng	回教禮拜堂
Pentecostal Church	Ńgh-chèuhn-jit-tòhng	五旬節堂
Roman Catholic Cathedral	Tìn-jyú-gaau júng-tòhng	天主教總堂
Rosary Church	Mùih-gwai-tòhng	玫瑰堂
Sam Shing Temple	Sàam-sing-míu	三聖廟
Sikh Temple	Yan-douh-míu	印度廟
St. Andrew's Church	Sing-ngòn-dāk-liht-tòhng	聖安德烈堂
St. Francis of Assisi's Church	Sing-fòng-jai-gok-tòhng	聖方濟各堂
St. John's Cathedral	Sing-yeuk-hohn daaih gaau-tòhng	聖約翰大教堂
St. Joseph's Church	Sing-yeuk-sāt-tòhng	聖約瑟堂
St. Mary's Church	Sing-máh-leih-nga-tòhng	聖瑪利亞堂
St. Paul's Church	Sing-bóu-lòh-tòhng	聖保羅堂
St. Teresa's Church	Sing-dāk-laahk-saat-tòhng	聖德肋撒堂
Temple of 10,000 Buddhas	Maahn-faht-jí	萬佛寺
Tin Hau Temple	Tìn-hauh-míu	天后廟
Truth Lutheran Church	Jàn-léih-tòhng	真理堂
Tsing Shan Tsz Temple	Chìng-sàan-jí	青山寺
Tung Po To Temple	Dùng-póu-tòh	東普陀
Union Church	Yauh-lìhng-tòhng	祐寧堂
Wong Tai Sin Temple	Wòhng-daaih-sìn-míu	黃大仙廟
Yuen Yuen Hok Yuen Temple	Yùhn-yùhn hohk-yún	圓玄學院

12. How education is conducted

Higher Education Institutions	Gōu-dáng gaau-yuhk gēi-kau	高等教育機構
The University of Hong Kong	Hēung-góng Daaih-hohk	香港大學
Chinese University of Hong Kong	Hēung-góng Jūng-màhn Daaih-hohk	香港中文大學
Hong Kong University of Science and Technology	Hēung-góng Fō-geih Daaih-hohk	香港科技大學
The Hong Kong Polytechnic University	Hēung-góng Léih-gūng Daaih-hohk	香港理工大學
Hong Kong Baptist University	Hēung-góng Jam-wúi Daaih-hohk	香港浸會大學
City University of Hong Kong	Hēung-góng Sìhng-síh Daaih-hohk	香港城市大學
Lingnan University	Líhng-nàahm Daaih-hohk	嶺南大學
The Education University of Hong Kong	Hēung-góng Gaau-yuhk Daaih-hohk	香港教育大學
The Open University of Hong Kong	Hēung-góng Gūng-hōi Daaih-hohk	香港公開大學
Hong Kong Shue Yan University	Hēung-góng Syuh-yàhn Daaih-hohk	香港樹仁大學
Chu Hai College of Higher Education	Jyū-hói Hohk-yún	珠海學院
The Hong Kong Academy for Performing Arts	Hēung-góng Yín-ngáih Hohk-yún	香港演藝學院

A

academic / educational qualifications	hohk-lihk	學歷
academic achievement	hohk-yihp sìhng-jìk	學業成績

Academic Aptitude Test (A.A.T.)	hohk-yihp nàhng-lihk chāak-yihm	學業能力測驗
academic board	haauh-mouh wái-yùhn-wúi	校務委員會
academic secretary / registrar	gaau-mouh-jéung	教務長
academic year	hohk-nìhn	學年
accomplishment test	geih-nàhng chàak-yihm	技能測驗
achievement test	sìhng-jìk chàak-yihm	成績測驗
activity approach	wuht-duhng gaau-hohk-faat	活動教學法
admission of pupils	chéui-luhk hohk-sàang	取錄學生
Adult Education and Recreation Centre	sìhng-yàhn gaau-yuhk hòng-lohk jùng-sàm	成人教育康樂中心
adult education	sìhng-yàhn gaau-yuhk	成人教育
aided school	jì-joh hohk-haauh	資助學校
Alliance Francaise	Faat-gwok màhn-fa hip-wúi	法國文化協會
allocation slip	paai-wái-jing	派位證
alumni	haauh-yáuh	校友
application form	sàn-chíng-bíu	申請表
appointment service	jìk-yihp fuh-douh-chyu	職業輔導處
apprenticeship	hohk-tòuh-jai	學徒制
aptitude test	hohk-nàhng chāak-yihm	學能測驗
Area inspectorate	fàn-kèui sih-hohk-chyu	分區視學處
art and craft teacher	méih-lòuh gaau-sì	美勞教師
arts	màhn-fò	文科
associate degree	fu hohk-sih hohk-wái	副學士學位
attendance register	dím-méng-bóu	點名簿
Audio-visual Education Section	sih-ting gaau-yuhk-jóu	視聽教育組
audio-visual aid	sih-ting gaau-geuih	視聽教具

B

bazaar	maaih-maht-wúi	賣物會
behavioural psychology	hàhng-wàih sàm-léih-hohk	行為心理學
bi-sessional school	bun-yaht-jai hohk-haauh	半日制學校
block subsidy	dihng-ngáak jèun-tip	定額津貼
Board of Education	gaau-yuhk wái-yùhn-wúi	教育委員會
Bookstock	tòuh-syù chòhng-leuhng	圖書藏量
British Council	Yìng-gwok Màhn-fa Hip-wúi	英國文化協會
Business Studies	sèung-yihp-hohk	商業學

C

cafeteria	chàan-tèng	餐廳
canteen	faahn-tòhng	飯堂
capital / building grant	gin-haauh jèun-tip	建校津貼
Certificate in Education (Cert. Ed.)	gaau-yuhk jing-syù	教育證書
Certificated Master / Mistress (C.M.)	màhn-pàhng gaau-sì	文憑教師
Chancellor (H.K.U. and C.U.)	haauh-gàam	校監
Child Care Centre	Yau-yìh jùng-sàm	幼兒中心
Chung Chi College	Sùhng-gèi hohk-yún	崇基學院
civic education	gùng-màhn gaau-yuhk	公民教育
commercial and secretarial program	sèung-fò kahp bei-syù fo-chìhng	商科及秘書課程
communite college	séh-kēui hohk-yún, séh-kēui syū-yún	社區學院，社區書院
complementary education	fuh-joh gaau-yuhk	輔助教育
compulsory education	kèuhng-bìk gaau-yuhk	強迫教育

compulsory school attendance	kèuhng-bìk yahp-hohk	強迫入學
compuler program	dihn-nóuh fo-chìhng	電腦課程
cooking class	pàang-yahm bàan	烹飪班
correspondence program	hàahm-sauh fo-chìhng	函授課程
course	hohk-fò	學科
course number	fo-chìhng pìn-houh	課程編號
crash course	chūk-sìhng fo-chìhng	速成課程
credit	hohk-fàn	學分
curricular activity	fo-sāt wuht-duhng	課室活動
curriculum guides	fo-chíhng jí-nàahm	課程指南

D

day nursery	yaht-gàan yau-yìh jùng-sàm	日間幼兒中心
degree	hohk-wái	學位
Degree of Doctor of Laws, honoris causa	wìhng-yuh faat-hohk bok-sih hohk-wái	榮譽法學博士學位
demonstration room	sih-faahn sāt	示範室
Department of Extramural Studies	haauh-ngoih jeun-sàu bouh	校外進修部
Diploma in Education	gaau-yuhk màhn-pàhng	教育文憑
direct investment private school	jihk-jī hohk-haauh	直資學校
Discipline master	fan-douh jyú-yahm	訓導主任
Dismissal of pupils	hòi-chèuih hohk-sàang	開除學生
drop a course	teui-sàu	退修
drop-out	jùng-tòuh teui-hohk hohk-sàang	中途退學學生
duration of course	sàu-yihp kèih-haahn	修業期限

E

EAS (Early Admission Scheme for Secondary six students)	baht-jīm gai-waahk	拔尖計劃
education counselling	gaau-yuhk fuh-douh	教育輔導
Educaion Commission	gaau-yuhk túng-chàuh wái-yùhn-wúi	教育統籌委員會
Education Scholarships Fund Committee	gaau-yuhk jéung-hohk-gàm wái-yùhn-wúi	教育獎學金委員會
education officer	gaau-yuhk-gùn	教育官
education institution	gaau-yuhk gèi-kau	教育機構
Education Ordinance	gaau-yuhk tìuh-laih	教育條例
Education Television (E.T.V.)	gaau-yuhk dihn-sih	教育電視
educational psychology	gaau-yuhk sàm-léih-hohk	教育心理學
educational value	gaau-yuhk ga-jihk	教育價值
elite education	jìng-yìng gaau-yuhk	精英教育
enroll	yahp-duhk	入讀
entry qualification / requirement	yahp-hohk jì-gaak	入學資格
evening courses	máahn-gàan fo-chìhng	晚間課程
evening school	yeh-haauh	夜校
examination	háauh-síh / si	考試
examination system	háau-síh jai-douh	考試制度
Examination Division	Háau-síh jóu	考試組
exchange student	gàau-wuhn-sàng	交換生
external degree	haauh-ngoih hohk-wái	校外學位
external examinations	hói-ngoih háau-síh	校外考試
extra-curricular activity	fo-ngoih wuht-duhng	課外活動

F

faculty	hohk-yún	學院
floatation / floating class	fàuh-duhng-bāan	浮動班

free education	mı́hn-fai gaau-yuhk	免費教育
full-time course	chyùhn-yaht-jai fo-chìhng	全日制課程
full-time teacher	jyùn-yahm gaau-sì	專任教師
further education	sàm-chou	深造

G

games day	yàuh-hei yaht	遊戲日
general education	tūng-sı̀k gaau-yuhk, tùng-chòih gaau-yuhk	通識教育，通才教育
good honours degree	daaih-hohk gòu-kàp wìhng-yuh hohk-wái	大學高級榮譽學位
government secondary school	gūn-lahp jūng-hohk	官立中學
government school	gūn-lahp hohk-haauh, gūn-haauh	官立學校，官校
grade point average (G.P.A.)	pìhng-gwàn jı̀k-dı́m	平均積點
grade report	sìhng-jik-bı́u	成績表
grant school	bóu-joh jùng-hohk	補助中學

H

handicapped children	yeuhk-náhng yı̀h-tùhng	弱能兒童
health center	bóu-gihn-chyu	保健處
higher education	gòu-dáng gaau-yuhk	高等教育
Hong Kong Association for Continuing Education	Hēung-góng sìhng-yàhn gaau-yuhk hip-wúi	香港成人教育協會
Hong Kong Diploma of Secondary Education	Hēung-góng jūng-hohk màhn-pàhng háau-sı́h	香港中學文憑考試
Hong Kong Examinations Authority	Hēung-góng háau-sìh-gúk	香港考試局
Hong Kong Teacher's Association	Hēung-góng gaau-si-wúi	香港教師會

Hong Kong Training Council	Hēung-góng fan-lihn-gúk	香港訓練局
Hong Kong Children's Choir	Hēung-góng yìh-tùhng hahp-cheung-tyùhn	香港兒童合唱團
Hong Kong Federation of Education Workers	Hēung-góng gaau-yuhk gùng-jok-jé lyùhn-wúi	香港教育工作者聯會
Hong Kong International School	Hēung-góng gwok-jai hohk-haauh	香港國際學校
Hong Kong Schools Music Festival	Hēung-góng haauh-jai yàm-ngohk-jit	香港校際音樂節
honors degree	wìhng-yuh hohk-wái	榮譽學位

I

in-service retraining	joih-jìk gaau-sì fuk-sàu fan-lihn	在職教師復修訓練
Inspector	dùk-hohk	督學
Institute of International Education	gwok-jai gaau-yuhk hip-wúi	國際教育協會
intelligence quotient (IQ)	ji-sèung	智商
internship	saht-jaahp	實習
interview	mihn-síh	面試
invigilation	gàam-háau	監考

J

JUPAS (Joint University Programmes Admissions System)	lyùhn-jīu, daaih-hohk lyùhn-hahp jīu-sāng gai-waahk	聯招，大學聯合招生計劃
junior English school	Yìng-tùhng síu-hohk	英童小學

K

kindergarten	yau-jih-yún	幼稚園

L

laboratory technician	saht-yihm-sāt geih-seuht-yùhn	實驗室技術員
laboratory	saht-yihm-sāt	實驗室
language laboratory	yúh-yìhn saht-jaahp-sāt	語言實習室
language program	yúh-yìhn fo-chìhng	語言課程
language skill	yúh-yìhn geih-háau	語言技巧
liberal arts	daaih-hohk màhn-fò	大學文科
listening comprehension	ting-lihk léih-gáai	聽力理解

M

major subjects	jyú-sàu fō-muhk	主修科目
maladjusted and socially deprived children	chìhng-séuih mahn-tàih hohk-sàang	情緒問題學生
master / mistress (of the class)	bàan-jyú-yahm	班主任
mature student	chìu-lìhng hohk-sàang	超齡學生
medium of instruction	gaau-hohk yúh-yìhn	教學語言
minor staff	haauh-gùng	校工

N

New Asia College	Sàn-nga syù-yún	新亞書院
nine years of general education for all	gáu-nìhn póu-kahp gaau-yuhk	九年普及教育
nine-year subsidized primary and secondary education	gáu-nìhn jùng-síu-hohk jì-joh gaau-yuhk	九年中小學資助教育
non-graduate teacher	fèi hohk-wái gaau-sì	非學位教師
non-profit-making private secondary school	fèi màuh-leih sì-lahp jùng-hohk	非牟利私立中學

O

open day	hòi-fong yaht	開放日
oral examination	háu-síh	口試

orientation course	sìn-douh fo-chìhng	先導課程
outdoor education camp	wuh-ngoih gaau-yuhk yìhng	戶外教育營
outward bound courses	ngoih-jín fan-lihn fo-chihng	外展訓練課程

P

parent-teacher association	gaau-sì gà-jéung wúi	教師家長會
parents day	gà-jéung yaht	家長日
part-time degree program	gìm-duhk hohk-wái fo-chìhng	兼讀學位課程
part-time teacher	gìm-yahm gaau-sì	兼任教師
post-secondary college	daaih-jyùn, jyùn-seuhng hohk-yún	大專，專上學院
pre-school education	hohk-chìhn gaau-yuhk	學前教育
pre-vocational school	jìk-yihp sìn-sàu hohk-haauh	職業先修學校
presenter (E.T.V.)	dihn-sih gaau-sì	電視教師
primary school	síu-hohk	小學
principal	haauh-jéung	校長
private postsecondary colleges	daaih-jyùn hohk-yún	大專學院
private school	sì-lahp hohk-haauh, sì-haauh	私立學校，私校
private tutorial school	bóu-jaahp hohk-haauh	補習學校
Professional Teachers' Union	Gaau-hip,Hèung-góng gaau-yuhk yàhn-yùhn jyùn-yihp hip-wúi	教協，香港教育人員專業協會
professional education	jyùn-yihp gaau-yuhk	專業教育
programme	fo-chìhng	課程
public examination	gùng-hòi háau-síh	公開考試
pupil-teacher ratio	hohk-sàang yuh gaau-sì béi-léut	學生與教師比率

Q

quiz competition	mahn-daap béi-choi	問答比賽

R

Recreation and Sport Service (R.S.S.)	Hòng-tái-chyu, Hòng-lohk tái-yuhk sih-mouh-chyu	康體處，康樂體育事務處
refresher training	fùk-sàu-bàan	複修班
registered teacher	gím-dihng gaau-sì	檢定教師
registrar of the university	daaih-hohk jyu-chaak jyú-yahm	大學註冊主任
religious institution	jùng-gaau gèi-kau	宗教機構
residential course	jyuh-sùk fo-chìhng	住宿課程

S

sandwich course / programme	gàau-tai-jai fo-chìhng	交替制課程
scholarship	jéung-hohk-gàm	獎學金
School Dance Festival	hohk-haauh móuh-douh-jit	學校舞蹈節
school fee, tuition	hohk-fai	學費
School Medical Service Scheme	hohk-sàang bóu-gihn gai-waahk	學生保健計劃
School of Education	gaau-yuhk hohk-yún	教育學院
school road safety patrol	hohk-haauh gàau-tùng ngòn-chyùhn-déui	學校交通安全隊
school social worker	hohk-haauh séh-gùng	學校社工
School Social Work Scheme	hohk-haauh séh-wúi-gùng-jok gai-waahk	學校社會工作計劃
school uniform	haauh-fuhk	校服
seaman training centre	hói-yùhn fan-lihn jùng-sàm	海員訓練中心
seminar	yìhn-tóu-wúi	研討會
Senate (H.K.U. and C.U.H.K.)	daaih-hohk gaau-mouh-wúi	大學教務會

serving teacher	joih-jìk gaau-yùhn	在職教員
sex education	sing gaau-yuhk	性教育
special education	dahk-syùh gaau-yuhk	特殊教育
speech day	bàan-jéung yaht	頒獎日
speech therapy	yìhn-yúh jih-lìuh	言語治療
split classes	fàn-fò séuhng-fo bàan-kàp	分科上課班級
sports center	tái-yuhk jùng-sàm	體育中心
staff	gaau-jìk-yùhn	教職員
student assembly	hohk-sàang jaahp-wúi	學生集會
student guidance scheme	hohk-sàang fuh-douh gai-waahk	學生輔導計劃
student intake	jìu-sàu hohk-sàng yàhn-sou	招收學生人數
student subculture	hohk-sàang hyùn-noih màhn-fa	學生圈內文化
subject officer	fò(-muhk) jyú-yahm	科（目）主任
subject-oriented teaching	hohk-fō-wàih-bún gaau-hohk	學科為本教學
subsidized school	jèun-tip hohk-haauh	津貼學校
substitute / supply teacher	doih-fo gaau-sì	代課教師
summer recreation programme	syú-kèih hòng-lohk wuht-duhng	暑期康樂活動
summer vacation	syú-ga	暑假
supervisor	haauh-gàam	校監
swimming gala, aquatic meet	séui-wahn-wúi	水運會
syllabus	fo-chìhng gòng-yiu	課程綱要
symposium	jyùn-tàih yìhn-tóu-wúi	專題研討會

T

take school bus	daap haauh-bā	搭校巴
taped programme	luhk-yàm gaau-chòih	錄音教材
teachers' centre	gaau-sì jùng-sàm	教師中心

teaching aids	gaau-yuhk hei-chòih	教育器材
teaching block	haauh-se	校舍
team teaching	kwàhn-tái gaau-hohk	群體教學
technical institute	gùng-yihp hohk-haauh	工業學校
technical teacher	gùng-yihp gaau-sì	工業教師
test	chāak-yihm	測驗
terms of reference	jìk-kyùhn faahn-wàih	職權範圍
tertiary education	jyùn-seuhng gaau-yuhk	專上教育
training course	fan-lihn fo-chìhng	訓練課程
truancy	tòuh-hohk	逃學
tutorial class	douh-sàu-bàan	導修班

U

U.G.C. (University grants Committee)	daaih-hohk gaau-yuhk buht-fún wái-yùhn-wúi	大學教育撥款委員會
unitary system	túng-yàt-jai	統一制
United College	Lyùhn-hahp syù-yún	聯合書院
unruly behaviour	faahn-kwài hàhng-wàih	犯規行為

V

Vice-Chancellor (H.K.U. and C.U.)	haauh-jéung	校長
visual arts education	sih-gok ngaih-seuht gaau-yuhk	視覺藝術教育
vocational training	jìk-yihp fan-lihn	職業訓練
vocational guidance	jìk-yihp fuh-douh	職業輔導

W

what is (your) major?	duhk māt-yéh haih	讀乜嘢系
winter vacation	hòhn-ga	寒假
work camp	gùng-jok yìhng	工作營

workshop	yìhn-jaahp-bàan, gūng-jok-fōng	研習班，工作坊
written examination	bāt-síh	筆試

Y

Yale-in-China Chinese Language Center	Ngáh-láih Jūng-gwok yúh-màhn yìhn-jaahp-só	雅禮中國語文研習所

Appendices

1. Family relations	Chàn suhk Chìng waih	親屬稱謂
aunt	baak-leùhng (wife of father's elder brothers)	伯娘
aunt	gū-mà (father's elder sister)	姑媽
aunt	gū-jè (father's younger sister)	姑姐
aunt	yìh-mā (mother's elder sister)	姨媽
aunt	káuh-móuh, káhm-móuh (wife of mother's brother)	舅母，妗母
aunt	a sám (wife of father's younger brother)	阿嬸
aunty	a yì (mother's younger sister)	阿姨
aunty	a yì, yī-yī (general term)	阿姨，姨姨
brothers	hìng-daih	兄弟
brother-in-law	jé-fù (husband of one's elder sister)	姐夫
brother-in-law	muih-fù (husband of one's younger sister)	妹夫
brother-in-law	daaih-káuh (elder brother of one's wife)	大舅
brother-in-law	káuh-jái (younger brother of one's wife)	舅仔
brother-in-law	daaih-baak (elder brother of one's husband)	大伯
brother-in-law	sūk-jái (younger brother of one's husband)	叔仔

cousin	tòhng a-gō (elder male on father's side)	堂阿哥
cousin	tòhng sai-lóu (younger male on father's side)	堂細佬
cousin	tòhng gā-jè (elder female on father's side)	堂家姐
cousin	tòhng sai-múi (younger female on father's side)	堂細妹
cousin	bíu-jé (elder female on mother's side)	表姐
cousin	bíu-múi (younger female on mother's side)	表妹
cousin	bíu-gò (elder male on mother's side)	表哥
cousin	bíu-dái (younger male on mother's side)	表弟
daughter	néui	女
daughter-in-law	sàn / sàm-póuh	新抱
elder brother	gòh-gō, daaih-lóu, a gō	哥哥，大佬，阿哥
elder sister	ga-jē, jèh-jè	家姐，姐姐
father	bàh-bā, a bàh, fuh-chàn	爸爸，阿爸，父親
father-in-law	ngoih-fú, ngohk-fú (father of one's wife)	外父，岳父
father-in-law	lóuh-yèh (father of one's husband)	老爺
grand-daughter	syùn-néui (daughter of one's son)	孫女

grand-daughter	ngoih syùn-néui (daughter of one's daughter)	外孫女
grandfather	yèh-yé, a-yèh (on father's side)	爺爺，阿爺
grandfather	gùhng-gùng, ngoih-gùng, a-gùng (on mother's side)	公公，外公，阿公
grandmother	màh-màh, a-màh (on father's side)	嫲嫲，阿嫲
grandmother	pòh-pó, ngoih-pòh, a pòh (on mother's side)	婆婆，外婆，阿婆
grandson	syùn (son of one's son)	孫
grandson	ngoih syùn (son of one's daughter)	外孫
husband	sìn-sàang, lóuh-gùng, jeuhng-fū	先生，老公，丈夫
mother	màh-mà, a mā, móuh-chàn	媽媽，阿媽，母親
mother-in-law	nàaih-náai, gā-pó (mother of one's husband)	奶奶，家婆
mother-in-law	ngoih-móu, ngohk-móu (mother of one's wife)	外母，岳母
nephew	ját (son of one's brother)	姪
nephew	ngoih-sàng (son of one's sister)	外甥
niece	jaht-néui (daughter of one's brother)	姪女
niece	ngoih sàng-néui (daughter of one's sister)	外甥女

sister-in-law	a-sóu (wife of one's elder brother)	阿嫂
sister-in-law	daih-fúh (wife of one's younger brother)	弟婦
sister-in-law	daaih-yìh (elder sister of one's wife)	大姨
sister-in-law	yì-jái (younger sister of one's wife)	姨仔
sister-in-law	gù-nāai (eleder sister of one's husband)	姑奶
sister-in-law	gù-jái (younger sister of one's husband)	姑仔
sisters	jí-muih / múi	姊妹
son	jái	仔
son-in-law	néuih-sai	女婿
uncle	a-baak, baak-fuh (elder brother of one's father)	阿伯，伯父
uncle	a-sūk, sūk-fuh (younger brother of one's father)	阿叔，叔父
uncle	gù-jéung (husband of a sister of one's father)	姑丈
uncle	yìh-jéung (husband of a sister of one's mother)	姨丈
uncle	káuh-fú, káauh-fú (brother of one's mother)	舅父
uncle	sūk-sùk (general term)	叔叔
wife	taai-táai, lóuh-pòh, chàai-jí	太太、老婆、妻子
younger brother	dàih-dái, sai-lóu	弟弟、細佬
younger sister	mùih-múi, sai-múi	妹妹、細妹

2. "Loanwords" in Cantonese

Ngoih-lòih Yúh

外來語

Amen	a-mùhn, a-maahng	阿門，阿孟
baby	bìh-bì	啤啤
ball	bō	波
ballet	bà-lèuih-móuh	芭蕾舞
band	bēng	□
beer	bē-jáu	啤酒
boss	bō-sí	波士
bowling	bóu-lìhng-kàuh	保齡球
boxing	bōk-síng	□□
boycott	bùi-got	杯葛
brandy	baht-lāan-déi	白蘭地
bus	bā-sí	巴士
bye bye	bāai-baai	拜拜
cancer	kèn-sá	□□
card	kāat	卡
cartoon	kà-tùng	卡通
cash	kè-syùh	□□
cashmere	kè-sih-mē	茄士咩
catsup	ké-jāp	茄汁
certificate	sà-jí	沙紙
Charlie(Chaplin)	chā-léi	差利
check	chēk	□
cheese	jì / chī-sí	芝士
cheque	chēk	仄
cherry	chè-nèih-jí	車厘子
chocolate	jyù-gū-lìk	朱古力
cigar	syut-gā	雪茄
club	kèui-lohk-bouh	俱樂部
cocktail	gài-méih-jáu	雞尾酒
cocoa	gūk-gú	呼咕

248

coffee	ga-fē	咖啡
cookie	kùk-kèih	曲奇
coolie	gù-lēi	□□
cream soda	geih-lìm sō-dá	忌廉梳打
curry	ga-lēi	咖喱
daddy	dè-dìh	爹哋
darling	dā-líng	打令
dozen	dā	打
duce	dìu-sìh	刁時
fail	fèih-lóu	肥佬
fans	fan-sí	fan 屎
file, holder	fàai-lóu	快勞
film	fèi-lám	菲林
gallon	gā-léun	加侖
Gin	jìn-jáu	毡酒
golf	gò/gòu-yíh-fù kàuh	哥／高爾夫球
guitar	git-tà	結他
hot dog	yiht-gáu	熱狗
humor	yàu-mahk	幽默
jam	gwó-jīm	果占
James Bond	Jìm-sih-bòng	占士邦
Jazz	Jeuk-sih yàm-ngohk	爵士音樂
jelly	jē-léi	啫喱
karaoke	kā-lāai-ōu-kēi	卡拉 OK
lemon	nìhng-mùng	檸檬
lift	līp	軚
mammy	mā-mìh	媽咪
mango	mòng-gwó	芒果
microphone	māi	咪
mile	māi	咪
milk shake	náaih-sīk	奶昔
mince	míhn-jih	免治
mini	màih-néih	迷你

Miss	mīt-sìh	□□
model	mòuh-dahk-yìh	模特兒
modern	mō-dàng	摩登
motor	mō-dá	摩打
nylon	nàih / nèih-lùhng	尼龍
ounce	ōn-sí	安士
Ovaltine	Ō / ngō-wàh-tìhn	阿華田
pair	pē	□
pan cake	bāan-kīk	班戟
partner	pāat-nàh	□□
pass (examination)	pā-sìh	□□
passport	pā-sih-pòt	□□□
pear	bē-léi	啤梨
pie	pài	派
ping pong	bīng-bām-bò	乒乓波
port (wine)	būt-jáu	砵酒
postcard	pòu-sìh-kāat	甫士咭
potassium cyanide	sàan-(ng)àai	山埃
pound	bohng	磅
pudding	bou-dīn	布甸
quarter	gwāt	骨
radar	lèuih-daaht	雷達
salad	sà-léut	沙律
salmon	sàam-màhn-yú	三文魚
shirt	sèut-sàam	恤衫
sir	a sèuh	阿蛇
size	sāai-sí	晒士
sofa	sò-fá	梳化
solo	sōu-lòuh	□□
spare	sih-bē	士啤
stamp	sih-dāam	士擔
store	sih-dò	士多
strawberry	sih-dō-bē-léi	士多啤梨

Sunkist	Sàn-kèih-sih	新奇士
tank	táan-hāak	坦克
tart	daahn-tāat	蛋撻
taxi	dīk-sí	的士
Terylene	dahk-leih-lìhng	特麗令
tie	tāai	呔
tips	tìp-sí	貼士
toast	dò-sí	多士
toffee	tò-féi-tóng	拖肥糖
ton	dèun	噸
tyre	tāai	呔
vitamin	wàih-tà-mihng	維他命
waffle	wāi-fa-béng	威化餅
waltz	wàh-yíh-jì	華爾滋
whisky	wāi-shih-géi	威士忌
X-ray	īk-sìh-gwòng	X 光

3. Twelve animal signs of the Chinese Zodiac — Sahp-yih Sāng-chiu 十二生肖

Rat	Syú	鼠
Ox	Ngàuh	牛
Tiger	Fú	虎
Rabbit	Tou	兔
Dragon	Lùhng	龍
Snake	Sèh	蛇
Horse	Máh	馬
Sheep	Yèuhng	羊
Monkey	Hàuh	猴
Rooster	Gài	雞
Dog	Gáu	狗
Boar	Jyù	豬

Exercises

Exercise 1

Similar finals: o, oi, ou

-o	**-oi**	**-ou**
1. cho: wrong 錯	choi: vegetable 菜	chou: vinegar 醋
2. dò: many 多	dói: pocket 袋	dóu: to pour 倒
3. gō: elder brother 哥	gói: to correct 改	gòu: tall 高
4. hó: can / may 可	hói: sea 海	hóu: good 好
5. jó: left 左	joi: again 再	jóu: early 早

Exercise 2

Similar finals: eui, oi

-eui	**-oi**
1. kéuih: she / he 佢	koi: to cover 蓋
2. lèuih: the thunder 雷	lòih: to come 來
3. néuih: woman 女	noih: a long time 耐
4. séui: water 水	sòi: gill 腮
5. tèui: to push 推	tói: a table 枱

Exercise 3

Similar finals: ek, ik

-ek	**-ik**
1. chek: ruler 尺	chīk: scold 斥
2. hek: to eat 吃	nīk: to take 搦
3. lēk: smart 叻	lihk: strength 力
4. sehk: stone 石	sihk: to eat 食
5. tek: to kick 踢	tīk: to tick 剔

Exercise 4

Similar finals: ong, ung

-ong	**-ung**
1. chòhng: bed 牀	chùhng: worm 蟲

2. fóng: **room** 房   fùng: **wind** 風
3. góng: **to speak** 講   gùng: **job** 工
4. jòng: **to install** 裝   jùng: **clock** 鐘
5. mohng: **to look** 望   muhng: **dream** 夢

Exercise 5

Finals with p, t, k ending

-p	**-t**	**-k**
1. hip-joh: **to help** 協助	git-gwó: **result** 結果	dihk-yàhn: **enemy** 敵人
2. kāp: **inhale** 吸	kāt: **cough** 咳	hāk: **black** 黑
3. ngaap: **duck** 鴨	baat: **eight** 八	baak: **hundred** 百
4. sāp: **wet** 濕	sāt: **lose** 失	sāk: **congest** 塞
5. yihp: **tree leave** 葉	yiht: **hot** 熱	yihk: **wing** 翼

Exercise 6

Finals with n, ng ending

-n	**-ng**
1. cháan: **spade** 鏟	cháang: **orange** 橙
2. gán: **tight** 緊	gáng: **certainly** 梗
3. géng-gān: **scarf** 頸巾	chìh-gāng: **spoon** 匙羹
4. hàan: **thrifty** 慳	hàahng: **walk** 行
5. hàhn: **itch** 痕	háng: **willing to** 肯

Exercise 7

Similar initial n, ng

n-	**ng-**
1. nàahm: **south** 南	ngàahm: **cancer** 癌
2. nàahn: **difficult** 難	ngáahn: **eye** 眼
3. nàih: **mud** 泥	ngáih: **ant** 蟻
4. náu: **button** 鈕	ngáu: **vomit** 嘔
5. noih: **inside** 內	ngoih: **outside** 外

Exercise 8

Unaspirated and aspirated initials

unaspirated
1. bā: father 爸
2. dung: cold 凍
3. gá: false 假
4. gwok-gā: country 國家
5. jē: umbrella 遮

aspirated
pa: afraid 怕
tung: painful 痛
kā: karat 卡
kwok-daaih: to extend 擴大
chè: car 車

Exercise 9

Expressions with one syllable in different tones

1. chēung: window 窗
2. daai: to lead 帶
3. gà: to add 加
4. gáu: nine, dog 九，狗
5. géi: machine 機
6. gwái: ghost 鬼
7. jóu: early 早
8. juei: the most 最
9. lóuh: old 老
10. máaih: to buy 買
11. máahn: night 晚
12. mùhn: door 門
13. sài: west 西
14. sau: skinny 瘦
15. séi: die 死
16. seun: to believe 信
17. syù: book 書
18. tàu: to steal 偷
19. tói: table 枱
20. yāt: one 一

cheung: to sing 唱
daaih: large, big 大
gá: false 假
gau: enough 夠
gei: to send 寄
gwai: expensive 貴
jouh: to do 做
jeuih: sin 罪
louh: road 路
maaih: to sell 賣
maahn: slow 慢
múhn: full 滿
sai: small 細
sáu: hand 手
sei: four 四
sèuhn: lips 唇
syú: mouse 鼠
tàuh: head 頭
tòih: to carry 抬
yaht: a day 日

256

Exercise 10

Expressions with more than one syllables in different tones

1. chī-sin: **crazy** 黐線
   chìh-sihn: **charity** 慈善
2. dá-jih-gèi: **typewriter** 打字機
   dá-jih-géi: **hit oneself** 打自己
3. fèih gèi-dūk-tòuh: **non-Christian** 非基督徒
   fèi gèi-dūk-tòuh: **fat Christian** 肥基督徒
4. hóu dài: **very low** 好低
   hóu dái: **a good buy** 好抵
5. gài-jūk: **chicken porridge** 雞粥
   gai-juhk: **continue** 繼續
6. gwái-ngūk: **haunted house** 鬼屋
   gwai ngūk: **expensive house** 貴屋
7. lóuh-yàhn: **old people** 老人
   louh-yàhn: **pedestrian** 路人
8. màhn fā: **to smell flowers** 聞花
   màhn-fa: **culture** 文化
9. máaih hàaih: **to buy shoes** 買鞋
   máaih háaih: **to buy crabs** 買蟹
10. máahn-máahn: **every night** 晚晚
    maahn-máan: **slowly** 慢慢
11. ngoi-yàhn: **lover** 愛人
    ngoih-yàhn: **outsider** 外人
12. sai-lóu: **younger brother** 細佬
    sai-louh: **children** 細路
13. sài-yàhn: **westerner** 西人
    sai-yàhn: **all the people on the earth** 世人
14. sàn-fú: **taxing, exhausting** 辛苦
    sàhn-fuh: **Catholic priest** 神父
15. sīk kéuih: **to know him** 識佢
    sihk kéuih: **to eat him** 食佢
16. syù-gá: **bookshelf** 書架
    syú-ga: **summer vacation** 暑假
17. syù-jái: **booklet** 書仔
    syùh-jái: **potato** 薯仔
18. tàu yāt-go: **to steal one** 偷一個
    tàuh yāt-go: **the very first one** 頭一個
19. tóuh-ngò: **diarrhea** 肚痾
    tóuh-ngoh: **hungry** 肚餓
20. yāt bun: **one half** 一半
    Yaht-bún: **Japan** 日本

Exercise 11

"Loanwords" in Cantonese

1. **baby**   bìh-bì   啤啤
2. **ball**   bō   波
3. **beer**   bē-jáu   啤酒
4. **boss**   bō-sí   波士
5. **bowling**   bóu-lìhng-kàuh   保齡球
6. **brandy**   baht-lāan-déi   拔蘭地
7. **bus**   bá-sí   巴士

8.	card	kāat	咭
9.	cartoon	kà-tùng	卡通
10.	catsup / ketchup	ké-jāp	茄汁
11.	cheese	jì-sí	芝士
12.	chocolate	jyù-gū-līk	朱古力
13.	coffee	ga-fē	咖啡
14.	cookie	kùk-kèih	曲奇
15.	curry	ga-lēi	咖喱
16.	daddy	dè-dìh	爹哋
17.	golf	gò-yíh-fù-kàuh	哥爾夫球
18.	hot dog	yiht-gáu	熱狗
19.	lemon	nìhng-mùng	檸檬
20.	mammy	mā-mìh	媽咪
21.	mango	mòng-gwó	芒果
22.	mini	màih-néih	迷你
23.	model	mòuh-dahk-yìh	模特兒
24.	name card	kāat-pín	咭片
25.	pear	bē-léi	啤梨
26.	ping pong	bìng-bām-bō	乒乓波
27.	pound	bohng	磅
28.	pudding	bou-dīn	布甸
29.	salad	sà-léut	沙律
30.	salmon	sàam-màhn-yú	三文魚
31.	shirt	sēut-sàam	恤衫
32.	size	sāai-sí	晒士
33.	sofa	sò-fá	梳化
34.	store	sih-dò	士多
35.	strawberry	sih-dō-bē-léi	士多啤梨
36.	taxi	dìk-sí	的士
37.	tip	tìp-sí	貼士
38.	toast	dò-sí	多士
39.	vitamin	wàih-tà-mihng	維他命
40.	whisky	wāi-sih-géi	威士忌

Exercise 12

Useful expressions

1. **How are you?**
Néih hóu ma?
你好嗎？

   I'm fine, how are you?
Hóu, néih nē?
好，你呢？

2. **Good morning.**
Jóu-sàhn.
早晨。

3. **Have you eaten yet?**
Sihk-jó faahn meih a?
食咗飯未呀？

   Yes, thanks. How about you?
Sihk-jó la, m̀-gòi, néih nē?
食咗啦，唔該，你呢？

   Not yet.
Meih sihk.
未食。

4. **Goodbye.**
Joi-gin, bāai-baai.
再見，拜拜。

5. **Good night.**
Jóu-táu.
早抖。

6. **Thank you (for a gift); thanks for everything.**
Dò-jeh, dò-jeh-saai.
多謝，多謝晒。

7. **Don't mention it; don't stand on ceremony.**
M̀-sái haak-hei.
唔使客氣。

8. Thank you (for a favor); excuse me.
   M̀-gòi.
   唔該。

9. Don't mention it; you are welcome.
   M̀-sái m̀-gòi.
   唔使唔該。

10. Excuse me, please let me through , step aside.
    M̀-gòi je-mé , m̀-gòi je-je.
    唔該借歪，唔該借借。

11. Welcome!
    Fùn-yìhng, fùn-yìhng!
    歡迎、歡迎！

12. Take a seat, please!
    Chèuih-bín chóh lā!
    隨便坐啦！

13. Thank you for coming.
    Dò-jeh séung-mín.
    多謝賞面。

14. (PN) I, me   ngóh   我
    You (singular)   néih   你
    He, she, him, her   kéuih   佢
    We, us   ngóh-deih   我哋
    You (plural)   néih-deih   你哋
    They, them   kéuih-deih   佢哋

15. Who are you?
    Néih haih bìn-go a?
    你係邊個呀？

    I'm Mr. Wong.
    Ngóh haih Wòhng sìn-sàang.
    我係王先生。

16. Mr.   sìn-sàang   先生
    Miss   síujé   小姐
    Mrs.   taai-táai   太太

| Catholic priest | sàhn-fuh | 神父 |
| Catholic sister | sàu-néui | 修女 |

17. **What is your surname?**
(Néih) gwai sing a?
(你) 貴姓呀？

   My surname is Chan.
   Ngóh sing Chàhn.
   我姓陳。

18. **Chinese surname:**

Lee	Léih	李
Wong	Wòhng	王 / 黃
Cheung	Jèung	張
Ma	Máh	馬

19. **Which country do you come from? / What is your nationality?**
Néih haih bīn-gwok yàhn a?
你係邊國人呀？

I am
- Chinese.
- Amercian.
- Japanese.
- British.

Ngóh haih
- Jùng-gwok
- Méih-gwok
- Yaht-bún
- Yīng-gwok

yàhn.

我係
- 中國
- 美國
- 日本
- 英國

人。

20. Do you speak
- Cantonese?
- English?
- Japanese?
- French?
- German?
- Spanish?

I speak / don't speak Cantonese.
Ngóh wúih / m̀-wúih góng Gwóng-dùng-wá.
我會／唔會講廣東話。

21. **How did you come to* Hong Kong / pw?**
Néih dím-yéung làih Hèung-góng / pw ga?
你點樣嚟香港㗎？

I came by— plane.
├ train.
└ boat.

Ngóh chóh— fèi-gèi
├ fó-chè — làih ge.
└ syùhn

我坐— 飛機
├ 火車 — 嚟嘅。
└ 船

22. **Excuse me, where is the Cultural Centre / _pw_*?**
Chéng-mahn Màhn-fa Jùng-sàm / pw* hái bīn-douh a?
請問文化中心喺邊度呀？

23. **What can I take to get there?**
Ngóh hó-yíh chóh māt-yéh heui a?
我可以坐乜嘢去呀？

You can take a { taxi / bus / minibus / MTR } to go.

Néih hó-yíh chóh { dīk-sí / bā-sí / síu-bā / deih-tit } heui.

你可以坐 { 的士 / 巴士 / 小巴 / 地鐵 } 去。

24. **Is Tsim Sha Tsui far from here?**
Jìm-sà-jéui lèih nī-douh yúhn m̀-yúhn a?
尖沙咀離呢度遠唔遠呀？

Not very far from here.
M̀-haih géi yúhn jē.
唔係幾遠啫。

25. **Excuse me, where is the washroom?**
Chéng-mahn sái-sáu-gāan / chi-só hái bīn-douh a?
請問洗手間／廁所喺邊度呀？

It is in the front / on the left / on the right.
Hái chìhn-bihn / jó-bihn / yauh-bihn.
喺前便／左便／右便。

26. **What is this?**
Nī dī haih māt-yéh a?
呢啲係乜嘢呀？

27. **How much is it?**
Géi-dò chín a?
幾多錢呀？

28. **So expensive!**
Gam gwai àh!
咁貴呀！

29. **Cheaper, please!**
   Pèhng dī lā!
   平啲啦！

30. **I'm very hungry.**
   Ngóh hóu tóuh-ngoh.
   我好肚餓。

31. **I like (to eat) Chinese food.**
   Ngóh jùng-yi sihk tòhng-chāan.
   我鍾意食唐餐。

32. **This is (very) delicious / not delicious.**
   Nī dī yéh hóu hóu-sihk / m̀-hóu-sihk.
   呢啲嘢好好食／唔好食。

33.

I would like to drink⎰ coke.
               ⎱ coffee.
                 tea.
                 beer.

Ngóh séung yám⎰ hó-lohk.
               ⎱ ga-fē.
                 chàh.
                 bē-jáu.

我想飲⎰ 可樂。
       ⎱ 咖啡。
         茶。
         啤酒。

34. **Waiter, please give me a cup of tea.**
   Fó-gei, m̀-gòi béi yāt-būi-chàh ngóh.
   伙計，唔該俾一杯茶我。

35. **Please eat some more!**
   Sihk dò dī lā!
   食多啲啦！

36. **I have enough / I'm full.**
   (Ngóh) gau la / báau la.
   （我）夠啦／飽啦。

37. **Waiter, bill please.**
Fó-gei, m̀-gòi màaih-dāan.
伙計，唔該埋單。

38. **Who's going to pay?**
Bīn-go béi-chín a?
邊個俾錢呀？

I'll treat everybody.
Ngóh chéng lā!
我請啦！

39. **Do you accept credit card?**
Sàu m̀-sàu kāat a?
收唔收咭呀？

40. **Everyone pays for himself / go Dutch.**
Jih-géi béi jih-géi gó fahn / ei eī jai.
自己俾自己嗰份／ **AA** 制。

41. **Is 10% service charge added?**
Yáuh móuh gā-yāt a?
有冇加一呀？

42. **How much tips shall I leave?**
Béi géi-dò chín tīp-sí a?
俾幾多錢貼士呀？

43. **Keep the change.**
M̀-sái jáau la!
唔使找啦！

44. **What is the date today?**
Gàm-yaht haih géi yuht géi houh a?
今日係幾月幾號呀？

Today is March 10th.
Gàm-yaht haih sàam (No.*1-12) yuht sahp (No.*1-31) houh.
今日係 3 月 10 號。

45. What day of the week is it today?

Gàm-yaht haih láih-baai géi a?

今日係禮拜幾呀？

Today is ⎰ Monday.
Tuesday.
Wednesday.
Thursday.
Friday.
Saturday.
Sunday.

Gàm-yaht haih láih-baai ⎰ yāt.
yih.
sàam.
sei.
ńgh.
luhk.
yaht.

今日係禮拜 ⎰ 一。
二。
三。
四。
五。
六。
日。

46. What time is it now?

Yìh-gā géi-dím a?

而家幾點呀？

It is 9 **a.m. / p.m. now.**

Yìh-gā haih seuhng-jau / hahjau gáu dím (No.*1-12).

而家係上晝／下晝 9 點。

47. We are late.

Ngóh-deih chìh-dou la!

我哋遲到啦！

48. **Today's weather is very good.**
Gàm-yaht tìn-hei hóu hóu.
今日天氣好好。

49. **It's raining now. I don't have an umbrella, what can I do?**
Yìh-gā lohk-yúh, ngóh móuh jē, dím syun nē?
而家落雨，我有遮，點算呢？

50. **Today, typhoon signal No.8 is hoisted. We don't have to go to work / school.**
Gàm-yaht baat-houh fùng-kàuh, m̀-sái fàan-gùng / fàan-hohk.
今日八號風球，唔使返工／返學。

51. **There is sunshine today.**
Gàm-yaht yáuh yaht-táu.
今日有日頭。

52. **It is very cold / hot today.**
Gàm-yaht hóu dung / yiht.
今日好凍／熱。

53. **Where do you like to go to have fun during the weekend / holiday?**
Jàu-muht / fong-ga heui bīn-douh wáan a?
週末／放假去邊度玩呀？

I like to go to the Ocean Park / pw*.
Ngóh jùng-yi heui Hói-yèuhng gùng-yún / pw* waán.
我鍾意去海洋公園玩。

54. **What do you like to do when you're free?**
Dāk-hàahn néih jùng-yi jouh māt-yéh a?
得閒你鍾意做乜嘢呀？

I like to go to { see a movie. / concert. / visit friends.

Ngóh jùng-yi heui { tái-hei. / tèng yàm-ngohk. / taam pàhng-yáuh.

我鍾意去 { 睇戲。/ 聽音樂。/ 探朋友。

55. **Hello, may I speak to Miss Chan please?**
   Wái, m̀-gòi néih chéng Chàhn Síu-jé tèng dihn-wá.
   喂，唔咳你請陳小姐聽電話。

   Yes, speaking.
   Ngóh haih la.
   我係啦。

56. **Sorry, she / he is not here.**
   Deui-m̀-jyuh, keúih m̀-hái douh.
   對唔住，佢唔喺度。

57. **Please repeat; say it once more.**
   Chéng néih joi góng yāt chi.
   請你再講一次。

58. **Hong Kong / *pw** is very enjoyable.**
   Hèung-góng / *pw** hóu hóu waán.
   香港好好玩。

59. **You are very clever.**
   Néih hóu chùng-mìhng.
   你好聰明。

60. **You are flattering me.**
   Gwo-jéung / m̀-gám-dòng.
   過獎／唔敢當。

61. **That lady is very pretty.**
   Gó wái siu-jé hóu leng.
   嗰位小姐好靚。

62. **This student is very diligent.**
   Nì go hohk-sàang hóu kàhn-lihk.
   呢個學生好勤力。

63. **Congratulations!**
   Gùng-héi, gùng-héi!
   恭喜，恭喜！

64. **Happy Birthday!**
   Sàang-yaht faai-lohk!
   生日快樂！

65. **Merry Christmas!**
Sing-daan faai-lohk!
聖誕快樂！

66. **Happy New Year!**
Sàn-nìhn faai-lohk!
新年快樂！

67. **Happy Chinese New Year!**
Gùng-héi faat-chòih!
恭喜發財！

68. **I love you.**
Ngóh ngoi néih.
我愛你。

69. **Oh, god!**
Baih la! / séi lo!
弊啦！／死囉！

70. **Help!**
Gau-mehng a!
救命呀！

pw: place word

*No.: number

QR Codes

1. The 19 Initials in Cantonese (2:09)

2. The 51 Finals in Cantonese (3:40)

3. The 7 Tones in Cantonese (1:15)

4. Exercise 1 (1:16)

5. Exercise 2 (0:50)

6. Exercise 3 (0:48)

7. Exercise 4 (0:58)

8. Exercise 5 (1:36)

9. Exercise 6 (1:17)

10. Exercise 7 (1:01)

11. Exercise 8 (1:11)

12. Exercise 9 (4:10)

13. Exercise 10 (5:58)

14. Exercise 11 (7:13)

15. Exercise 12 (39:32)